"Elwood is today's supreme auth[o...]
She plunges you in and doesn't [...]
Stephen Volk, writer of BB[C...]
author of The Dark [...]

"Delicately disturbing, elegantly unc[...]
us in a school where even the ghostly can be a release and leads to
a conclusion that's as poignant as it is disquieting. A real treat for
connoisseurs of the classic supernatural tale."
Ramsey Campbell, "Britain's most respected living horror writer,"
Oxford Companion to English Literature

"*The Other Lives of Miss Emily White* is a gothic treat: class, femininity and the
hothouse atmosphere of a Victorian boarding school make the perfect backdrop
for a story of obsession and hysteria. Elwood's way with words is absolutely
enchanting, and I didn't want this book to end, but when it did… !"
Ally Wilkes, author of *All the White Spaces*

"Darkly enthralling, with a deftly woven and sinuous plot, secrets abound in this
beguilingly gothic tale of teenaged obsessions and sinister manifestations."
Lucie McKnight Hardy, author of *Water Shall Refuse Them*

"A hugely atmospheric tale set in the repressed atmosphere of
a young ladies' Victorian boarding school, that will have you
looking over your shoulder at every sound."
Marie O'Regan, author of *The Last Ghost and Other Stories*,
editor of *Phantoms*, *Cursed* and *Wonderland*

"Readers beware! The mystery at the heart of A. J. Elwood's latest eerie
and elegant novel is so irresistibly tantalising that everyday commitments
will fall by the wayside as you feel compelled to read 'just a few more
pages', and then 'just a few more', in your bid to uncover the truth."
Mark Morris, author of the *Obsidian Heart* trilogy

"Enough to make you scared of your own shadow."
Priya Sharma, author of *Ormeshadow*

"A. J. Elwood has carved a solid reputation with her spooky and
hauntingly beautiful historical fiction. This novel is no exception,
and its brilliance surely cements her place as one of the finest
British writers working today in any genre."
Tim Lebbon, author of *Eden* and *The Last Storm*

"A. J. Elwood draws us into an intricate, clastrophobic world
brimming with menace. The strange after-image of Emily
White will linger with readers long after the final page."
Verity M. Holloway, author of *The Others of Edenwell*

Also by A. J. Elwood and available from Titan Books

THE COTTINGLEY CUCKOO

THE OTHER LIVES OF MISS EMILY WHITE

A.J. ELWOOD

TITAN BOOKS

The Other Lives of Miss Emily White
Print edition ISBN: 9781803363707
E-book edition ISBN: 9781803363714

Published by Titan Books
A division of Titan Publishing Group Ltd
144 Southwark Street, London SE1 0UP.
www.titanbooks.com

First edition: April 2023
10 9 8 7 6 5 4 3 2 1

Printed and bound by
CPI Group (UK) Ltd, Croydon, CR0 4YY

THE OTHER LIVES OF MISS EMILY WHITE

LONDON 1922

It is one of those brilliant winter days, the sky as fragile as innocent youth and just as distant, although the air has a chill in it that touches my bones. Through the window the plane trees grasp at the brightness, their claws blacker by the contrast, unless it is only that they are darkened by all the pollution of this London street. They are said to be the only kind of tree that will grow here, able to withstand the soot that must have accumulated in layers since I was young; but still another plant twines around them, its leaves unnoticed and dusty, yet alive, even thriving.

Soon I shall be alone in these rooms and may consider those times. Inwardly I must have done so for upward of fifty years, for the days of my girlhood remain as clear to me as the one passing by outside; perhaps more so, since they have never left me, though this one, like so many others, shall.

There is a footfall on the stairs.

My dearest does not come in. A soft-spoken farewell reaches only my own ears and I hear the opening and closing of a door. We have a maid who comes in and helps clean and wash, but it is not her day and I expect no one; the house is empty.

This is what I have been waiting for, a little space of time alone, though I am still uncertain whether I can face making such a deliberate recollection. But I am old, and do not know when the chance will be taken from me; the days left for me to think of matters of the soul may be growing few. Of course, Society would have it that I am damned already. It may be that I was always bound for hell and there is no changing anything, but why then should anything remain to make me afraid? For I am afraid, though I keep it so well hidden I am no longer sure how to recognise it.

I stir from my place at the dressing table. That too belongs to another time, with its boar-bristle hairbrush, selection of hat pins, stoppered scent-bottles and cold cream in a ceramic pot, a design of daisies dancing around the rim. There is also the mirror. For many years I have disliked looking at my own reflection, even a glimpse as I pass along a hallway – perhaps especially that. I must sit there and arrange my hair and dress each day, but still I try not to see the figure in front of me. I prefer it to remain so hazy and unfocused it might be anyone. Originally this particular mirror was a tri-fold, but that I couldn't abide and had the side panels removed. I didn't like, when I leaned over the table to select a brooch or a pin, to see from the tail of the eye my image multiplied, receding away all about me; every one the same.

I walk into the drawing room, which is high-ceilinged and respectable and a little cold. It has all that pertains to such a room: the dignity of mahogany, the solidity of table and chairs, the showiness of gilt candelabra, the femininity of *objets de vertu*, the industry of needle-worked fire-screens and stools. These too belong to the past – they were here when I took the house – but I have little interest in such things and never troubled to dispose of them. There is also an embroidered motto in a frame: SEE NO EVIL. It makes no mention of hearing or speaking, and I often wonder why. Perhaps it was originally one of a set and its sisters have long since been lost.

And here is that item which Society decrees must belong in every drawing room, proper in every respect: a mirror set over the fireplace, taller than it is wide – of course, since the opposite would suggest low ceilings, compromise, even poverty. This has a carved design that might have been chosen for my name: Ivy. The clinging leaves are frozen in silver gilt, though they still possess the semblance of life: something that could grow, twine; cling.

'Faithfulness,' I whisper. And a shadow appears in the glass as I approach, though I don't immediately raise my head.

When I look, my appearance surprises me. It always does. Am I really this pale, crape-skinned creature? I've always been full of thoughts, feelings, colours. I once raced across a farmyard bellowing for Scampers, the old dog, to chase after me. I twined my fingers in a horse's mane so tightly my skin wore its imprint for hours. I had scabbed knees, a smeared pinafore, dirty shoes. My hair was lit with red and flying loose and I didn't know there was anything wrong in any of it, not then.

Now my countenance is blank and mild, nothing to offend, the image of what an old lady should be. My gown is neat and respectable. My hair, once so resistant to the brush and carrying

A . J . E L W O O D

that hint of rebellious red, has been tamed at last and turned entirely grey. I might have stepped out of the last century, though we are over twenty years into the next and there are more motor cars than carriages passing by outside. Skirts and hair are shorter, necklines lower, heels higher. There is new music and new freedom – something I once craved. Does it come to everyone, this being left behind? Or is it only that I never really moved on, and a part of me remains in Fulford, despite all I have done with my life?

It is ironic that I should be the one to appear so traditional. But mine isn't the face I am thinking of: the one that has troubled me, followed me, haunting my dreams and my waking hours alike for so many years, always so close I half expect her to appear in the mirror at my side, peeking over my shoulder.

Miss White. Mademoiselle Blanc. Emily.

I steal a glance behind me as if she really might be standing there. As if she might at any second touch my shoulder.

The eyes reflected in the mirror meet my own and a prickle of electricity jolts me to my fingertips.

I was a child. I had no conception of what would happen. I couldn't peer into the future as I do now into the past. I can change none of it, though I see it still; I recall, quite clearly, my thoughts when I first saw her. My feelings, however, remain jumbled; the emotions I had first and those that came after are like a dimly seen reflection, partly illuminated but much remaining dark.

I am still not certain I can unravel everything that happened, or begin to understand. I only know that she was my teacher, and I loved her.

I close my eyes and she rushes towards me.

2

YORKSHIRE 1864

The female character should possess the mild and retiring virtues rather than the bold and dazzling ones; great eminence in almost anything is sometimes injurious to a young lady; whose temper and disposition should appear to be pliant rather than robust; to be ready to take impressions rather than to be decidedly mark'd; as great apparent strength of character, however excellent, is liable to alarm both her own and the other sex; and to create admiration rather than affection.

Erasmus Darwin,
A Plan for the Conduct of Female Education in Boarding Schools

ADVERTISEMENT:
Young ladies' boarding school at
Miss Dawson's Seminary, Snaithby Dun.

For the daughters of independent gentlemen and professional men. Plain and ornamental needle work, music, dancing, painting. Also languages, grammar, history, geography, &c. &c. Twenty guineas p.a., no entrance

11

money, no vacation. The situation is commodious and delightful with extensive gardens and good air. The strictest attention is paid to health, morals and improvement, and to the duties of piety.

❦

It began one dull afternoon, the sky grey, the room likewise, when the eyes of twenty-six well-bred young ladies – and mine – turned to the rain-smeared windows to await the arrival of our new schoolmistress.

The weather was a disappointment, and not only because it was summer. We'd been hoping for it to brighten ever since the carriage left, though its veneer still shone with polish. Our headmistress would have insisted on that; it was going to town, after all, where common eyes might see and judge. As such, she preferred a flashy Clarence to a more practical wagonette, along with a pair of chestnut horses: perfectly matched, perfectly gleaming, perfectly in stride. Bard gave a little kick as he trotted away, likely shaking stones from his hooves. The turning circle by the front entrance, where guests alighted, was surfaced in neatly raked gravel. The lane itself, less closely examined, had fallen into disrepair, the gravel thinned until there was little but unmade earth. Every departure was announced by the rattle of iron-rimmed wheels on stones, followed by a softer hum before silence took its place.

Now we listened for those sounds in reverse, twenty-seven faces turning periodically to the window like sunflowers seeking new light. We all wanted the steady, persistent, railed-against rain to cease, so that when it returned, the carriage windows would be clear enough to glimpse its occupant. She was the source of much speculation and not a little hope.

All our established mistresses were as much a part of the seminary as the wainscoting and parquet and smell of ancient mothballs; as much as the dust or silence or air of impending disapproval. They were old and therefore dull, and we longed for the pure fresh breeze of springtime even if true spring was behind us, leaving only this dreary semblance of summer.

'Do you think she'll be elegant?' That was Grace's whisper.

Matilda turned to her and rolled her eyes, as if to say, *Of course she will. She is to teach* us, *after all.*

I sighed. I hoped for kindness rather than elegance – but then, I wasn't born to this like the rest of them. It was another sign, I supposed, that I wasn't all I should be, and I said nothing – as I so often did. A memory of my mother's voice came to me: *Such a funny, secret child you are, Ivy.* She had said that to me often, though I didn't quite think she'd meant that I made her laugh.

Twenty-seven sighs hung before our faces, clouding the glass, since the windows were closed. The school promised good air, but not here, not now; for one thing the day was too damp, which, heaven forbid, might strain our delicate feminine lungs. For another, we were in the eyrie.

This was Fulford's highest and largest room. It would be dangerous to open a window; they stretched up to the ceiling and down to the floor, as impressive as the space around us. The building had been part grand residence, part folly, and the eyrie took up most of the fourth storey, reduced only by little slices for the staircases. It must have once been used for balls and fancy gatherings. Now delicate yellow paper peeled from the plaster just as waltzes had faded from the air. The floorboards were whitened from scrubbing with liquid carbolic, rather than polished. A roughly constructed dais accommodated our assemblies and there was a piano, though its keys were silent and covered. There were a few cupboards of dulled wood, a coat-stand or two, some unremarkable paintings of better times and a portrait of the gentleman who had conceived the whole affair. None of us knew his name.

Still, the views were magnificent. To each side the landscape swept away, all the ploughing and planting and reaping and gleaning of the countryside reduced to stillness and ease by the distance.

I twisted to see better and was rewarded by a dig from my corset. When I came here, I'd stood on this windowsill and pressed my nose to the glass. It wasn't forbidden, but it was the first time the others scorned me; that had been enough.

'Back to your sewing, girls.' Sophia's voice carried easily; her clap, for emphasis, snapped around the room's empty corners. At sixteen, Sophia McKenzie Bideford was almost ready to leave, and liked to think we were already far behind her; or perhaps below. She was the daughter of a banker, one who'd managed to marry old money, and kept six servants – which I believed, though servant-keeping was a competitive pursuit and I often wondered if half of those spoken of by the girls were anything more than imaginary. We had been placed in her tender care, to practise our fancy-work in the eyrie's generous light, while the teachers – well, perhaps they awaited our new arrival as keenly as we did.

We returned to our samplers and silk threads and silver needles. I'd have preferred to hook a rag rug for my bedside to warm my first step into the day – I could have done it in a trice – but that was too practical. We were to be ladies, and I should be grateful, though it was all so tedious. I hid my expression as I bent over my embroidery frame, 'Thou Shalt . . .' already in place, and resumed my stitching. I still couldn't resist stealing glances at the window, which remained as dreary and rain-speckled as ever. The patter of droplets striking the glass sounded like spite.

Shhhhhhhhh . . .

The rumbling was as faint as a hush, but we all heard it. I pictured the horses trotting along the earthen track, throwing out their matching legs, tossing their matching heads, snorting foam from matching lips. Surely our new teacher would be peeking out? She must long to see her new home as much as we longed to see her. I pictured a gentle, oval face, and told myself she *would* be kind. She'd be sweet and pretty and sympathetic to girls torn from their homes and brought to this starched, stifling place. She'd have a comforting smile, a low voice, soft eyes with long silken lashes.

Another face rose before me for a moment, quite different to the image I painted, and laughing at me a little – a face so dear to me yet so very distant, and I pushed the vision away.

The rattle of wheels amplified. Through the window, in the grey afternoon, appeared a peculiar sight.

At first I didn't notice what was wrong. The carriage was there, just as we'd expected. Light sparkled from the raindrops clinging to its roof, though it wasn't raining any longer, certainly not, and twenty-seven breaths were held in twenty-seven throats.

The carriage approached, not at its usual pace but steadily, and as it grew closer I saw that it was no longer symmetrical. The picture was ruined, for the horse was no longer half of a pair. Only one remained, pulling with visible effort, straining his neck, hesitating slightly before placing his hooves.

Which is it?

I hoped, suddenly and deeply, that it was Captain who'd come back and not Bard. Of course, I shouldn't have a preference; none of the others would dream of learning the horses' names. I hadn't meant to myself. I'd once thought I might find friends among the girls, that we'd walk arm in arm and laugh, even forget our corsets and crinolines sometimes and run as if we were free. They'd never be like my sister of course, not like Daisy, but no one could ever be that. And in those first sweet days, it seemed I had found such a one – but I lost her again, or rather she was taken from me. And so I'd made a friend of a horse.

I strained to make out Captain's features but the angle was too steep and everything was darkened with rain. Gadling, coachman and groom, flicked his whip and adjusted his course; with a horse missing, the carriage pulled to one side. Everything was crooked, off-kilter: wrong. One, where two should have been.

'The blinds are drawn!'

Lucy was right. As the carriage turned, its windows revealed nothing but a blank. Worse followed, for Gadling didn't rein in the carriage at the entrance, by its stone stairs – scrubbed daily – and double doors. Our new teacher wouldn't see the hopeful motto carved above them: *Ex Solo Ad Solem – From the ground to the sun.* He drove on past, towards the back of the building and the stables, and twenty-seven young ladies gave up all thought of sewing and hurried for the stairs.

Sophia called out 'Follow me, girls,' as she pushed her way through to the front. She would already be working out her excuses for leaving the room. No doubt she'd say that we simply *must* greet our new schoolmistress properly, that we didn't wish to appear rude. If in doubt, blame good manners. They couldn't punish us for that.

We were a dark flood of skirts topped by a white froth of muslin. We knew the new teacher must use the servants' entrance, and she'd go in search of a welcome, following a wide central corridor to the entrance hall at the front. We flowed, not down the narrow stairs set into the southern towers – *we* weren't following in the servants' footsteps – but the grand staircase shown off to benefactors, governors, prospective parents and the parson. Two flights down, we reached a gallery, all barley-sugar twists of polished walnut wrapping around the first-floor landing. From here, we could look out and down over the entrance hall. We could see her arrive, even offer our assistance.

No one paused to consider what her response to twenty-seven offers of help might be, where one might be preferred; but who would stay behind? We were destined to serve the needs of fathers and brothers and husbands and children, but we weren't as self-sacrificing as that.

We spread ourselves along the banisters. The only sound was the ticking of the pendulum clock at the foot of the stairs, so miserly in parcelling out the seconds it might have been mocking our haste. And it struck me then that something was not quite right. It was as if we weren't so much a welcoming committee as spectators, ranged around a gladiatorial pit.

I found myself looking at Sophia, wondering if she'd thought of it too. She was the tallest of us, and the prettiest, with only a little coarseness about the thrust of her chin. She was the tidiest, too. There was never a speck on her; specks wouldn't dare. There was never a stray hair from the curls – golden, natural, curse her – pinned about her head. She hadn't made room for her little acolyte, I noticed. Her cousin Lucy, thirteen years old, strived to peer over the taller girls' shoulders, but they were too intent on watching to help her.

I pictured our new teacher walking towards us, all the different versions of her I could imagine: a quiet, gentle creature in need of a friend, feeling her way mouse-like through cold corridors. Or bold and exploring, opening unfamiliar doors, peering into strange rooms until she found a bed she was content to lie in.

The trip-trapping of footsteps approached, as if emerging from my dreams, and we craned for our first glimpse of Mademoiselle Blanc. That wasn't really her name, but that was how we thought of her then. We were in French class when her existence was announced and so a French name was given; our headmistress, Miss Dawson, favoured French fashions and herself preferred to be called Madame Dumont, claiming this to be in the interest of our education rather than putting on false airs. She said Mademoiselle Blanc possessed all the accomplishments that could possibly be required. She'd even lived in Paris – though we weren't told why she was no longer there and I'd begun to figure romantic notions for our new teacher: her heart had been broken and she'd returned to heal. Or she'd had to nurse some ailing, ungrateful relative. Surely it must have been some calamity, to bring her here to us.

Below, foreshortened and cast into shadow, came into view a very peculiar figure.

The first thing I noticed was her hair. It wasn't neatly curled or concealed beneath a bonnet but a disarrayed matted draggle dripping down her back. Her travelling cape was soaked: dark at the shoulders, filthy at the hem. She left a trail of footprints behind her. The maids would be horrified. Madame Dumont was as fond of imaginary servants as anyone but now someone real must be found to scrub the parquet again.

Mademoiselle Blanc turned her gaze upward.

At first, she didn't seem to take us in. Perhaps her vision was fooled by the shadows hanging in the hall or the darkness of the panelling. Perhaps her eyes hadn't adjusted from the outdoors, for there was a hectic gleam in them, as if they were full of rain; almost as if she were drowning.

Then her mouth fell open.

Perhaps it is difficult to imagine the effect her appearance had on us. Mademoiselle Blanc was to be our instructress and our guide, to help form our taste and temper. She was to lead us through the tangled thickets of manners and mores, delivering us safely to the promised land of matrimony. Oh, it's true that schools were expected to do more these days than impart poise and piano-playing, but the accomplishments, for us, were uppermost. We had to catch husbands, after all. Who else would take care of us? Spinster daughters, inconvenient sisters, spare and expensive aunts – none of our relatives wanted that. Worse: we might end up governesses – even schoolmistresses. No: part of Mademoiselle Blanc's role was to ensure we presented ourselves well at all times, to provide glitter with which to dazzle future husbands, yet here she was creeping into the school like a servant, mud on her boots and reeking of wet wool; not a drawing-room songbird but a half-drowned chick fallen from its nest.

She could see us plainly now. And as we watched her, all of us silent, she shivered. Was that some presentiment – or our unwelcoming faces, or simply the cold? I wanted to believe it was that, for cold she must have been in her wet clothes. For a moment, I shivered with her.

A glassy titter sounded somewhere to my left. A long moment of silence followed, but Sophia's laughter hung on the air like shattered crystal: something broken that couldn't be put back together.

Another sound was Lucy, giving an unladylike splutter as the mirth spread. Matilda took up the laughter, and Ruth, and Grace, and it grew, hidden behind hands held to lips. It flew quick as a rumour, relentless as bad news. There were no words. There would be plenty of those later, when we were in our dormitories; then we'd hear them all.

And the shame of it would follow Mademoiselle Blanc, like a shadow. This was worse than standing on a windowsill or bumping one's head against the glass or having a favourite horse. It would cling to her like mud on her skirts, mud that wouldn't wash off no matter how she scrubbed.

Mademoiselle Blanc. Even her name seemed part of the joke, meaning white, spotless; pure.

Her gaze darted into each shadowed corner as if seeking a place to hide, but it was no use. She had to glance upward once more, seeing her own fall, her humiliation reflected in our eyes. For a moment, she looked at me. Blood rushed to my cheeks and I tried to smile at her, though it felt more like a grimace on my lips.

'What do you do there? Idleness!' Madame Dumont's voice rang out, tight with barely contained fury. The new arrival spun to face her, as if she were the one being chastised.

'Girls! Back to your embroidery at once. Miss White, you are most welcome. Pray, this way – step into my study. What an evil day it is!'

If she said anything else, her words were lost. Hurrying away, our stifled laughter broke free, echoing from the walls, the cornices, the sadly besmirched parquet floor. And laughter spilled from me too, though unlike the others, I was not entirely certain why.

$\sim$

I didn't go back to my embroidery, never mind what Sophia would say. Sewing was dull and repetitive and I couldn't see the point in decorating needle-cases or making embroidered circles for china fripperies to stand upon. Instead I sneaked along a quiet corridor, a bare, unpapered, narrow space used by the servants.

The folly was a rather unusual structure. It was only obvious from the outside that its walls curved outward, with each corner softened further by a narrow, circular tower. The impression wasn't so much of a square as a cylinder, with giant pegs thrust into the earth to pin it in place. It was an oddity, and when seen against the flat vale stretching away all around, might almost have been disconnected from the rest of the world.

From the inside, things appeared more ordinary but felt stranger still. I was sure this corridor curved, following the line of the outer walls, yet it hardly appeared to do so. Instead, it felt subtly distorted; without a window to orientate myself, it was difficult to tell if it was the walls or my own self that was not quite true. I was relieved when I reached the door that opened onto the tower stairway, the building's south-west 'peg'. Here was a window: a narrow slit, little more than a loophole, looking out over the outbuildings behind the folly, then fields and copses and villages, the occasional spike of a church jutting from the rest all the way to the horizon.

I still didn't know if it was Captain or Bard who'd come back. Amid the tight-laced, rule-bound, uniformly dull school, the horses were something beautiful. They didn't care for deportment or fine speech or etiquette; they were already perfect. I thought of their proud steps, their shuddering muscles, the dark softness of their eyes. What secret thoughts must they keep behind them? I liked to sneak early season apples for them from the gardens. Sometimes I'd rest my head against Captain's face and feel the bony shifting as his jaw munched – for Bard was too skittish and wouldn't allow such a thing. But Captain enjoyed my company, standing still and quiet after the apple was gone, lipping at the collar of my cloak.

I loved the good smell of horse. It sent me home in a heartbeat: not to my grandparents' house, which I'd come to think of as another prison, but farther still, to my parents' farm. I heard again Mama's voice, distracted and distant, calling me in for tea; the muffled clump of Papa's muddy boots on cobbles. And my sister's laugh – for I was never alone then. There was always another face next to mine, with bright eyes and freckles, the flash of white teeth as she dreamed up some new mischief.

The rasping *fssk* of Gadling's brush came clear across the air as I stepped outside and walked towards the stables. The carriage was abandoned in the yard, its harness hanging loose, the shaft pole forming a triangle with the ground. It seemed terribly still, a sharp contrast to the vigour of his brushing. There was anger in the sound and I hesitated. He knew I visited the horses, of course. I didn't suppose he welcomed such visits; it wasn't done, not by the people who decided what was done, but I think he recognised in me someone who loved the thing he loved and so he tolerated me.

The top of the stable's half-door was open, swaying a little in the breeze, since it hadn't been pinned back. It was Captain's stable and I hurried my steps, the rhythmic brushing growing louder. I told myself Bard had only thrown a shoe, that I needn't feel guilty for wishing him gone. Gadling had left him with the farrier and would fetch him later, and I'd bring both of them all the apples they wanted.

Inside the stable, damp glossy curves gave the suggestion of bulk. The smell was of wet hide and musk, more animal somehow than the usual comforting scent of horse. Carrying his head low, the beast swung his neck around to see who had come, revealing the gleaming whites of his eyes.

It took a moment longer to see Gadling. He stood motionless at the animal's shoulder, glaring at me, the sound of his labour having ceased, though I didn't know when. I felt every inch of my intrusion, its unexpectedness, its unsuitability, and took a step away in spite of myself. *He is a servant*, I reminded myself. *And I will be a lady*.

I didn't feel like one as he said, 'You, is it?'

In reply, I held out my hand to the horse. Although I had no apple he expected one, shifting on his haunches and stepping towards me. He thrust his long nose over the door, already searching, lips smearing my sleeve.

'Captain.' The name slipped from me, soft and crooning. 'There you are. You're all right – you are, aren't you?' I leaned in, the slight greasiness of him just brushing my cheek. Then something struck the side of my head, a hard blow with bone behind it, and I found myself sprawling on the cobbles, skirts splayed and crinoline bouncing, clutching handfuls of flaking muck.

'He'll not have that. Not that 'un.' Gadling's voice was thick with amusement. No: satisfaction.

I scrambled to my feet, grabbing at my crinoline with dirty hands while Gadling stared with dirty eyes. I tried not to think of what he could see – what he'd already seen. Petticoats? More than that? My cheeks flamed. *This*, I thought, *is the reason this is not allowed*, and I hated myself for thinking it.

When I'd regained my feet – with no help from Gadling – I stared at the horse that stood in Captain's stable, looking so much like him and yet not him, not at all. It seemed so obvious now. This horse's blaze began with a star between his eyes, where the hair formed a little whorl, but unlike Captain's the white stripe went right down his nose and spread across the soft delicacy of his nostrils. Bard's markings were finer than Captain's had ever been and I wanted to weep at the sight of them.

Gadling resumed his work, swiping at the horse's damp back with a leather. He had to get the sweat off or the beast might catch a chill. Horses were expensive. No groom could allow that.

'Where is he?' I asked, though a part of me already knew.

'Knacker.'

I stepped back before the force of the word, wrapping my arms around myself. There was no amusement in Gadling's expression now. His face was a wax mask with blank eyes, covering over something else: something I didn't want to see. If I wasn't here, I realised, his look would be different. I thought of a snail stripped of its shell; a lamb opening its new eyes for the first time.

Abruptly, he threw down his leather, as if to say, *Be damned with it; let him shiver*. 'Her.' He gestured towards the school. 'It 'appened when he saw *her*.'

An image flashed before me: limp and draggled hair, darkened from the rain like an animal's pelt, dripping onto a parquet floor. As if he could see it too, Bard shifted on his haunches.

'Spooked at her.' Gadling spat phlegm into the straw and I wrinkled my nose, more from acquired habit than disgust. 'Not Captain – he were right enough, just like always. But Bard – one look at her, and that were it. He shot off – dragged Captain right across t' station yard. Up onto t' pavement. Tripped, he did. Both his knees gone. Poured with blood. Fucking poured.'

The curse was a cold shock. It was as if he wasn't really speaking to me at all, as if he'd forgotten I was there.

Gadling ran a hand across his sweat-streaked face. 'She got a hold of his bridle. Not Bard, he wouldn't have her. She took a hold of Captain's cheek-strap and whispered in his ear. Stood there in the rain while he bled. Soaked, she was. Bonnet in the dirt. Didn't put her hood up to cover her face. But I weren't fooled.'

He stepped forward, into the light. 'Bard knows. Horses sense things – they know what they don't like. Bard knew, but it were Captain who suffered. It were Captain who had to be shot.'

He was crying. I'd never seen anything so shocking. I'd wrung chickens' necks and seen a calf coming out dead from its mother and watched smoke-grey kittens drowning in a pond, but nothing like this. Gadling was a man. He was grown. He was older than me and strong, someone who went out into the world and earned his bread, and he was crying in front of me, nothing but a girl. He didn't even seem aware of it.

He was in his shirt-sleeves. Not even that, for they were rolled back to his elbows. I could see the muscles under the skin, his arms browned by the sun. His shirt was soiled, not with foam or sweat from the horse but with blood. My gaze ran down to his belly where the cotton clung to his body. I pictured the blood coursing warm from Captain's veins, Gadling trying to hold it in, to catch it in his hands as if he could put it back again, undo what had been done.

He saw me looking at him. His expression slowly turned into something else, something I couldn't read. I wanted to tell him I'd seen worse and more, that it was nothing to me, but I swallowed the words, for how could that help? I backed away then turned and ran from him. As I went I didn't hear my footsteps or my own rapid breath; only the *fssk, fssk* of a brush, resuming its work against the hide of a single chestnut horse.

3

I found the other girls crammed into one of our dormitories, spilling into the passage. The younger ones were on the outer edges, their skirts like the calyx of a flower surrounding the petals within. Humming whispers rose like murmuring bees. Their tones told me, without the need for words, that Something was Happening.

It was the room that five girls shared with Sophia: Lucy, Grace, Amelia, Ruth and, more lately, Bea – or *Beatrice* now, at least to me. They drew back as I approached, not to let me in but to let something out.

At first I wasn't sure what it was. The shape was odd and unwieldy, surely too awkward to be permitted in Sophia's room, but then I realised it *was* Sophia. She'd wrested a picture from the wall – and everyone just stood by, watching. No one tried to help, but I saw from her expression that help wouldn't be welcome. Help would detract from her singular glory. She emerged in front of me and took me in. Her eyes were a clear pale blue, like innocence; cold as a winter's sky.

'My, my.' She clicked her tongue against her teeth as she looked me up and down. 'Like teacher, like pupil. Isn't that what they say? Is Mademoiselle Blanc's influence to spread among us so rapidly? Only consider the danger, Ivy. You must mind yourself. One wouldn't want to stoop below one's *natural* level, would one?'

I felt like shivering, just as Mademoiselle Blanc had when she first saw us, though it wasn't cold. If anything it was stuffy, the room's ill-fitting sash window stuck in its frame; there was none of Madame Dumont's *good air* here either.

'Perhaps you might find this useful? Allow me to be your maid.' The others tittered as she spun the object she held in her hands. It wasn't a picture, but a mirror.

It showed me myself, as mirrors will. My face was pale, dirt-smudged. My skirts were rumpled and covered in scraps of straw. My sleeve was ripped from when I'd fallen and before I could stop myself I turned my hands upward, as if with some sudden urge to show her everything. My palms were blood-smeared, like Gadling's arms.

At first I didn't hear their laughter. I saw it, though: flashes of white teeth, the merry brightness of their eyes. Even Beatrice laughed – Beatrice, once my friend, wore an expression same as all the rest.

Sophia lowered the mirror and the spell was broken. *Mirror, mirror, on the wall* . . . But I wasn't the fairest. I wasn't even fair.

'Perhaps you should go to your washstand,' she said, her tone mocking, 'whilst I go about my business.'

A new ripple followed, a chorus of approval, yet when the others moved to go after her she turned on them too.

'No. There is no insolence in it, you understand?' Her smirk gave the lie to her words. 'There is nothing to see. I mean only to be helpful. Do permit me to go alone.'

Their faces fell, Beatrice's among them – they weren't so close after all, then, and I felt a stab of spite that Beatrice had exchanged my warmth for this. I'd never have rejected her that way. My name, Ivy, meant faithfulness, and I *would* have been a faithful friend – but she didn't object to Sophia's rebuff. None of them did. In the end, it was only I who followed her.

Sophia refused to acknowledge me. She went with short little steps, either to be extra ladylike or because of the weight she carried. I stomped along, making sure she heard, but she already knew I was behind her; she must.

Despite her bravado, she took a servants' corridor and went down the servants' stair, as if she didn't want to be seen. Our dormitories were on the third floor, just below the eyrie, along with some cramped little rooms at the back where the servants slept. It didn't seem an especially usual arrangement, but then, the folly was not an especially usual building.

We went down one floor and followed another passage. This led to the teachers' quarters and we stopped at the door separating their rooms from the rest of the school. We were forbidden to enter without good reason and yet she said, 'Open it.'

I didn't. Why should I? She was richer than me, prettier than me, but I was still one of the girls – and a vision flashed before me of what I might have been if my grandfather hadn't helped us, long since sent off into service, perhaps waiting hand and foot on someone just like her, and I pushed the image away.

She turned. The mirror tilted upward; all I could see in its depths was the ceiling, its whitewash long since yellowed. It seemed odd that I couldn't see myself reflected there and for some reason that made me shudder, as if I'd vanished, leaving nothing behind; not even a memory.

'You will open it,' she said.

She'd put on a particularly glassy tone, like the chiming of a bell, and I couldn't match it so I didn't try. 'What're you up to, Sophia?'

The mirror flashed; there was nothing there – and then I started, for as it tilted in her hands, there *was* something. My own reflection, and at my shoulder – for just an instant I'd thought there was someone standing behind me. I blinked the impression away.

'I, you foolish child, am to present a gift to our new teacher. She will by now be making herself comfortable in her rooms. I fancy she is in need of such a thing. What do *you* do, Ivy?'

I'm almost the same age as you, I thought, but my retort dissolved on my tongue as her meaning sank in. She *couldn't*. Was she so bold? Was she so used to having authority over everyone around her, anticipating a time when she'd be above Mademoiselle Blanc or Madame Dumont or any of us?

I didn't want to help her, didn't even want to move, but it was as if something had taken hold of me and I stepped forward. The brass door handle was cold under my fingers as I turned it, doing as she wished, doing as I was bid.

Sophia sailed past me, crossing the threshold.

We knew which room would be Mademoiselle Blanc's. It wasn't as if we'd never seen this corridor before. We were sent here sometimes with notes or errands, with letters that had come from this relative or that. The teachers' names were placed by their doors in little walnut frames, and only one had an empty space where hers should be: *Blank*, I thought. *Blanc*.

Sounds emerged from within: tapping and rustling, the rattle of an ill-fitting drawer sliding out, a dull thud as it was pushed back again. The sounds of putting away, of settling in.

Sophia went to the door, set down the mirror and rapped smartly. It opened almost at once. The voice from within was soft, so low I couldn't make out the words, only the uplift that indicated a question: *How may I help you?*

Sophia nudged the mirror forward. It tapped against the floor as if it too was knocking, eager to make an entrance. She gave her best smile, her most charming, the one that worked on most people. 'Welcome, Mademoiselle. Some of the girls thought we should send this. We have no need of it, you know, but it seems as if you might? We have other mirrors. We were uncertain if you possessed such a thing.'

I tried to swallow down the lump that came to my throat. I waited for the walls to collapse, for the ceiling to fall in. I hoped Mademoiselle Blanc wouldn't look into the corridor and see me. I knew nothing of her, not then, but I didn't want her to think I was one of *the girls* Sophia had referred to. My chest went tight, as if I couldn't breathe.

The teacher spoke more firmly, without consternation or anger or hesitation. 'But of course I do. My rooms are perfectly adequate, thank you. There is a mirror on the wall already.'

Sophia held a hand to her chest, all mock surprise, as dramatic as any showman and twice as shameless. 'Oh! Fancy – however could we have formed such a misapprehension? Never fear, I shall take it away again.'

Just like that, it was over. The door hushed closed. Sophia grasped the mirror and started back the way we had come, stooping as if she only now felt its weight. I jumped in front of her and tugged the door open and she floated through it. What had she done? It had all been so polite. Everything here was accomplished with such good manners, with sugar-sweetness, even the cruellest. Madame Dumont herself could not have faulted it and Mademoiselle Blanc hadn't seemed to see anything strange, not that she had let show.

But good manners could also be lies. Now that Mademoiselle Blanc was alone, it would be different. Sophia's words would repeat themselves in her ears, an insinuating whisper that wouldn't stop, and she'd hear them anew. What would she do then?

As if snagged by the same thought, Sophia stopped dead in front of me. Was she regretting her actions? But no, she stared at the wall, where something had caught her eye. It was a simple nail, jutting from the plaster with nothing hanging upon it. She hoisted the mirror and fitted it into place.

'There,' she said, dusting off her hands. 'Perfect! She may look in it whenever she likes, and I am saved the trouble of carrying it back again. It looks well, does it not?'

She walked away, no longer with such neat little strides, eager to tell the others how clever she'd been.

I stood before the mirror.

It looks well, does it not?

It did not look well. The corridor was too narrow for such a thing. The mirror reflected back the tattered paper lining the walls, the exact same colour as blood drying on a man's white shirt. My outline was there too, hazed with dust, or perhaps only the discomfiting angle. I wanted to peer into it more closely to see what expression was written on my features, but I had to remain uncertain, for I found I couldn't bear to look into my eyes at all.

4

If Lucy hadn't forgotten her copybook, it wouldn't have happened. If Sophia wasn't Sophia, it might not have mattered.

Mademoiselle Blanc paced the room, ready to deliver her very first lesson to our group. Her appearance was faultless. Her steps were dainty, her hands neatly clasped. She was dressed like any other teacher, a plain dark dress covering her from throat to foot. Her bun was secured neatly with a net, her curls kept in place with plain but shining pins. She carried a hint of scent – bergamot and lemon oil – a little fancy for Madame Dumont, who preferred the whiff of carbolic as a sign of cleanliness, but sweet and pleasant. There was nothing to attract either attention or censure and I sensed the disappointment passing about the room in little shifting sighs.

Mademoiselle Blanc was even younger than I'd thought at first glance, scarcely older than myself. Her face was just the shape I'd pictured: oval, with small, neat features and very smooth skin.

Her lips were pronounced in their shape, not quite a perfect cupid's bow. I thought they were suited to laughter rather than frowning, and found myself smiling into the air, at nothing. Her hair was lighter than I'd first thought too; I would have guessed at brown, but it was almost golden where it caught the sunlight from the window. Despite the reception she'd received, there was no sign of tension about her. Her eyes were wide and unafraid, a soft grey with appealing depths and lights in them, and I found it difficult to look away.

She hadn't yet narrowed herself to fit these corridors, that seemed evident, and I wondered if she would. She looked kind where I'd hoped for kindness and I hoped that empty elegance wouldn't take its place. But she must have impetuosity too, to rush into the rain for the sake of a dying horse. How could Gadling have spoken of her like that? Mademoiselle Blanc had been gentle with a gentle creature and I pictured her standing with Captain, comforting him with her whispers as death drew near. She had done what I wished I could do – spoken the words I wished I could have said. I found my eyes stinging with tears and blinked them back.

'Now, girls,' said Mademoiselle Blanc, 'we are here to learn to be well-mannered young ladies, are we not? Well, good manners are precious. *True* manners are what I mean: the kind that ensure any guest feels comfortable in your home, at ease and welcome. Manners are precious, not for their polish or their own sake or to enhance your appearance or position in Society, but as a service you do for someone else. A gift that you give to them.'

She looked from face to face, letting her words sink in, lingering for a moment upon mine. What did she see? I knew

I was plain. My grandmother had mentioned it often enough, with an air of long-suffering, as if I should have tried harder. My face was a little too square, my nose a little too broad, my lips wide but not curved enough, never pretty enough to please her. But I didn't suppose she was thinking of me at all. Her words were clearly meant for Sophia, but Sophia didn't hear them, for Sophia wasn't here.

As I thought of her, the door opened and Sophia and Lucy clattered in. They were clutching copybooks: Lucy's crumpled, Sophia's spotless.

Mademoiselle said not a word, but when she saw Sophia, her eyes narrowed. First the 'gift' of the mirror; now the impudent girl had marched into her classroom fully five minutes late. Silence stretched out and I pictured the walls of the folly swelling with it, bulging further and further outward as if ready to burst.

Lucy curtseyed. 'I'm sorry, Mademoiselle. I lost my book, and Sophia—'

'Sophia may speak for herself.' Mademoiselle Blanc's voice was quiet, but there was steel in it. Perhaps she would be equal to her task after all.

Sophia, taller than the teacher, drew herself straighter still. She gave her most imperious gaze, peering down through her eyelashes. She'd given me that same look many times – she probably practised it in front of a mirror – but unlike me, Mademoiselle Blanc didn't flinch under it. I could have cheered as she pointedly nodded towards the clock.

'I was necessarily occupied.' Sophia was all wounded gentility, no matter that her father was new money. She sounded like a lady lounging on a chaise, waiting to be served. 'I came quite as soon as I was able – and suitably attired.'

It was as if the silence in the room opened its eyes and stared along with the rest of us while Sophia looked the teacher up and down.

'Mademoiselle, it was all my fault,' Lucy interjected. 'Miss Sophia helped me find my copybook.'

Mademoiselle Blanc didn't move. I couldn't blink. There was too much air; a window must surely be opened or the glass would break.

'You,' Mademoiselle Blanc gestured towards Lucy, without taking her gaze from Sophia, 'may sit down. *You*, however, will stand in the corner at the back of the room. Take up the volume of Dr Johnson's *Dictionary* that is placed there. You will memorise the page containing the word *tardy*, and you will recite it for me at the end of the lesson.'

Sophia's face was a blur of fury as she stalked past me, but I saw her hands curl into fists. A soft rustling followed as she leafed through the book at the back of the room. The dictionary was heavy and burdensome. How long would it take her to memorise a whole page? The print was tiny, the paragraphs tight-spaced.

Mademoiselle Blanc went on with her lesson, any discomposure concealed behind incised consonants and well-modulated vowels. Each word was used precisely and in its place, lining up one after another like soldiers at drill. She spoke of the duties of a daughter, the journey of our lives, our guiding purpose, and of what we would all become: hothouse flowers, perfect adornments for any drawing room, the rightful reward for our parents' time and patience and investment.

Everything was just as it should be once more, and yet
I wanted to tear the collar from my neck. The air was too
close, and all my layers of chemise and corset and stockings
and petticoats were suddenly too warm; the fabric made my
skin itch. I tried not to wriggle. Sometimes, when I removed
my inner clothes, my skin was inflamed with scratching. My
grandmother had once wrapped my hands in bandages for
a whole day, pulling them tight, not to heal an injury but to
prevent me from fidgeting.

I forced myself to contain it, to be still, to be the pupil we
all must try to be, but I longed to tell Mademoiselle Blanc that
I knew the reason for her dishevelment when we first met her. I
wanted to thank her for her kindness to Captain, to tell her I'd
loved him too. I wanted to say that one of us at least had thought
well of her and was glad that she'd come to us, and all along she
went on speaking and I didn't hear a word and she didn't look
at me. I found myself wishing she would – but instead she said,
'Now, Sophia,' and something inside me withered.

Everyone turned in their seats. The shuffling wasn't seemly but
Mademoiselle Blanc did nothing to prevent us and I wondered if
she wanted us to see.

Sophia stood defiantly, the book held in her hands as if its
weight was nothing to her.

'Have you carried out your task?'

Sophia closed the book with a snap, as if she were the teacher
and we her class. Could she truly have the whole page by heart,
that *tardy* at its centre? Would Mademoiselle Blanc notice if she
made a misstep?

'Then begin.'

Sophia stuck out her chin and gave us the briefest of glances before fixing her gaze on Mademoiselle Blanc. 'Shabby,' she said.

'Adjective. A word that has crept into conversation and low writing; but ought not to be admitted into the language. Mean; paltry. "The dean was so shabby, and look'd like a ninny, that the captain suppos'd he was curate to Jenny . . ."'

'Enough!'

The girls caught their breath as Mademoiselle Blanc and Sophia stared at each other across the length of the room. *Shabby*, not *Tardy*. Even I knew the two words couldn't possibly be on the same page in the *Dictionary*.

'Come here,' Mademoiselle Blanc said.

Sophia raised her eyebrows, all long-suffering innocence. She put a graceful hand to her chest – *Me?* – as she went, moving closer, too close, until she stood over the teacher.

And Mademoiselle Blanc turned away.

Something sank inside me. Would she retreat – would she do nothing? If she let Sophia win now, she would always win. Mademoiselle Blanc would always be standing beneath us with disarrayed hair and dirty clothes, and suddenly I despised Sophia. What need had she to humiliate the teacher? There had been no need for any of it.

Mademoiselle Blanc opened the cupboard tucked away behind the blackboard. When she emerged, she was holding a cane.

I blinked. None of us had seen such a thing before, not at Fulford. I'd been birched in the village dame school, near the farm, plenty of times: for misspelling a word, for wriggling in

39

my seat, for whispering to my sister; especially that. But here? I wondered, with a little too much eagerness, how many strokes Sophia would have. For me, it was six. Every time, six strokes: enough to smart, often to cut, always enough to humiliate. I could almost see the red lines carved into my skin – but Sophia's impertinence had surely warranted worse than that.

The threat of it had widened Sophia's eyes, showing their cold blue. They looked almost fragile, but she wouldn't beg; there'd only be indignation. She'd say she was here to be finished not thrashed, that her father wouldn't have it, but there wouldn't be tears; never that. She opened her mouth but her voice must have frozen in her throat, for it was Mademoiselle Blanc who spoke. 'Roll up your sleeve and hold out your hand.'

Sophia's fist opened, closed, opened. She wouldn't do it. She couldn't. It simply wasn't possible, and yet it was happening. 'Do you *know*—' she began, and was cut off.

'I said roll up your sleeve and hold out your hand.' Mademoiselle Blanc spoke with unfailing politeness. She gave a rueful smile, as if taking this action caused her pain.

Sophia clawed back her sleeve in quick, sharp movements, thrusting her hand straight out.

'Lower.'

Sophia lowered her hand.

Mademoiselle Blanc made no speech. She made no practice strokes. She altered her stance, turning a little sideways, and I barely saw the cane as it flicked through the air. I heard the sound it made, though, as it met Sophia's flesh. Her shoulders jumped – a reflexive movement, rather than a flinch; angrily, she straightened.

We all jumped as the cane struck her again – as did Sophia, and some caught their breath, but Sophia remained silent. I was wrong about the tears. They had sprung to her eyes unbidden, and she blinked against them as a third stroke fell. I stared, waiting for a fourth, but Mademoiselle Blanc lowered her hand.

Softly, she said, 'That will do, Sophia. Remember it, when next you feel like being insolent.'

Only three? It was over, and Sophia pressed her lips closed so tightly the colour leached from them. Her forehead looked damp – she'd hate that sign of weakness, must long to dab at it with a handkerchief – but she let her hand fall. She should be thanking our teacher, I thought. If she'd had old Mrs Clugston, as I had at the dame school, she'd have had her skirts pulled up and been thrashed across her pale white thighs – but Sophia wouldn't see it like that. She would never forgive Mademoiselle Blanc for what she'd done, even if Sophia herself had forced her to do it.

'Please do wait before rolling down your sleeve,' Mademoiselle Blanc said. 'One wouldn't want it besmirched, would one? One wouldn't want it made *shabby*.'

She stood back, taking her place in front of the blackboard, and looked around at our faces, taking us in one by one.

'Class dismissed,' she said.

41

5

Sophia sat on her bed. She was quivering from head to foot and I knew it was from rage. Lucy crouched in front of her, looking intently into her face, holding Sophia's wounded hand. She looked like a suitor making a proposal and although I told myself I'd come to see if Sophia was all right, I had to bite back a laugh.

Naturally, it was at that moment that Sophia looked up and saw me.

'What do you want?' She spoke as if I was an intruder, not one of the group – but then I wasn't, was I? I never would be, and she'd never let me forget it. The whiff of farming clung. It was in my clothes and my hair and my features and my skin. It was in my flattened vowels, the way I occasionally dropped a consonant if I forgot to concentrate. I'd had to hide all trace of my father's accent, even if my mother's had been acceptable enough. The others were gentlemen's daughters, not folk with straw on their clothes. Their fathers were factory owners, merchants, accountants and lawyers – though not the gentry, however much they dreamed of emulating them.

I told myself my father was an honest man, just like theirs – if they were lucky. He'd owned his own land, at least until his harvests had failed and he'd had to start selling fields. That was why I'd been sent to my grandparents' house, and from there to Fulford; it was the reason I'd left Daisy behind. My mother had gone cap in hand to her parents, who'd been estranged since her marriage. She had apologised for her wilfulness in imagining that she could choose for herself; for her husband and her children; for who she'd become. She was sorry, we were all sorry; sorry creatures, every one of us.

Sophia didn't wait for my reply. Instead, she spoke to those she considered equals. 'How dare she touch me? What is she, after all? Nothing but a little chit who must work to support herself, as far beneath me – *us* – as a cook or a maid. We are here because of our good standing. Why is she here? Because she has nothing!'

Her nose and cheeks were flushed, anger rubbing the polish off her.

'I told you all how it would be. I knew, before she even walked in the door – in that state! – that she would not turn out to be as she ought. This proves I was right. You know I have a certain refinement of the nerves, that I can *sense* things—'

I could not help snorting at that. She sounded almost as ridiculous as Gadling had been. 'Nonsense,' I said. 'You know nothing of her.'

She only grew thin-lipped. 'We'll see. I know more than you suppose, Ivy. I am my mother's daughter, and she has long experienced certain insights into the nature of things. I am touched with the same gift, though I don't suppose you would understand.'

I rolled my eyes. After what I had seen, I supposed that Sophia had as much ability to *know* things as might a horse.

'If anything, *she* ought to come to *me* for guidance – yet she has authority over me? She has no grace, no elegance, no sense of how the world is. She is—' Sophia's words finished in a cry of frustration. She snatched her hand from Lucy, who continued to gaze up at her like a devoted lapdog, and looked down at her palm. It was inflamed, pink as meat ready for the oven, and I glanced down at my own grazed hands. The cause was different but skin was skin, and I hoped she felt it; I hoped it pained her.

'Oh – get out.' Sophia rose to her feet and Lucy stumbled out of the way as her cousin strode towards me, repeating, 'Get out – get out!'

I backed away, step by step, and only realised I'd crossed the threshold when the door slammed in my face. It had happened so quickly. I was cast out from among the *daughters of gentlemen*; I stood in an empty corridor, altogether alone.

I scowled at the closed door. If they didn't want me, I'd go to the stables. I'd breathe in the scent of horse and think of home. Daisy was never unkind to me. She always held my hand if I was unhappy. When my mother was too busy or my brothers ignored us, expecting us only to clean their boots or darn their socks, Daisy was there, thinking up new ways to make me smile. If she were here, it would be different. I'd never felt lost when Daisy was around. I'd never wondered what to say. She'd have laughed in Sophia's face for her silly words, and made everyone else laugh at her too.

My mother had made me a promise: Daisy would be sent along to my grandparents' house in a few short weeks. Mama would make it clear to them that we must stay together. We would be two again, happy again, and I had been content with that: I'd let Daisy go. I had left her behind me.

Then the letter had come from my mother, not a month later, to tell me my sister was dead.

I let out the breath I'd been holding. There was nothing left inside me. I couldn't rid my mind, not of Daisy's face, but Sophia's: so complacent, so haughty, claiming to be something special – and her little cousin clinging to her hand and supporting every action she took, just as they all did. Sophia didn't care for any of them, not really. She only cared for herself. I told myself I was glad she'd been brought lower, and that Mademoiselle Blanc, with her quiet dignity, had been the one to do it. She'd offered comfort to a simple horse; now, in some instinctive way, she'd also comforted me. She might almost have done it on purpose.

Without paying attention to where I was going, I'd reached the south-west staircase. I stopped, looking out of the window towards the stables – to see not one but two chestnut horses nodding over their half-doors.

I shook my head. I must have imagined it. My mind, missing my sister, had striven for balance and completed the picture. Or was I seeing a ghost?

One of the horses tossed his head. That was Bard. This time there could be no mistake, for his blaze caught the sunlight just beginning to gleam through the heavy clouds. The other was strange to me. It wasn't Captain, wasn't a ghost. A white star

45

shone between his eyes, but he had no blaze – only the suggestion of a drip running down his nose. Then Gadling appeared at his side and reached for the horse's face.

He held a paintbrush in his hand, tipped with white. He ran it down the horse's nose, completing the blaze, finishing between his nostrils. He leaned in to examine his handiwork, dodging when this horse too tossed his head – surely in disgust.

There was again a matching pair of horses at Fulford, keeping up appearances, everything as it should be. And I knew I couldn't go to them. I didn't want to see this false horse that had taken Captain's place, and I turned from the window, banishing the sight.

Pretence, I thought. *Pretence, pretence, pretence.*

6

By afternoon there was enough of a change in the weather for us to go out into the garden. And it was Mademoiselle Blanc who accompanied us, since Miss Morrison – or Madame Monette, as she must sometimes submit to be called – had pleaded one of her headaches and declined to take our art lesson. More likely she'd sniffed the opportunity to pass her duties on to someone not yet wise to her ways and was lying on her sofa, eating bon bons and perusing *The Englishwoman's Domestic Magazine*.

If Mademoiselle Blanc had any suspicion, she showed no regret. She led the way eagerly, smiling as she breathed in the free air. As if to show how lovely it was, she gestured towards the sky, which was a high, clear blue save where a few clouds lingered, their edges tinged with darkness.

I caught Sophia's whisper as she leaned in to Amelia. 'See? Striding about as if she owns the place, waving just as if it's all *hers*, and we—'

I rolled my eyes. I didn't think Mademoiselle Blanc was showing off. It was rather as if, now that she'd stepped outside, she felt truly at home. She led us to the narrow wooden door that let into the walled garden and pushed it wide, brushing flaking paint from her fingers. The door had been many colours over the years, all of them visible somewhere as they peeled from the grey wood. It was a story of ruin, but behind it were treasures. For here, besides vegetables for the kitchen, the gardeners raised a thousand blooms for us to snip, snip with our little scissors.

She turned to us, swinging her plain dark skirts. 'Now, girls, we shall pick some flowers. Be quick – it's a little chilly – and we need to return in good time to practise our watercolours.'

I couldn't help smiling back at her, for I loved to paint. After my exile to my grandparents' house, it had become my keenest pleasure. I'd breathed in the exotic scents of the little cakes of watercolour and revelled in the tones that flooded from my brush, feeling almost as if I'd been born to it. When I painted, I could spend hours without a thought for sad things, or anything at all. My only regret was that I'd longed to show Daisy the way of it – and now I never could.

The walled garden was the pride of the school. It reflected its ideals of refined taste and healthful exercise. Its blooms, like us, were carefully tended, preened, watched over. Nothing was permitted that could cause offence to the eye, no weed allowed to flourish.

'Don't forget,' Madame Dumont would say, 'one day it may be one of the greatest pleasures of your lives to select blooms for your home and to know the art of their perfect arrangement.'

48

I preferred to see them here, where they could grow – but I set to with the others, ravaging their petals and severing leaves like so many beskirted and bonneted slugs. We held them out, admiring, comparing, discarding. Still thinking of my sister, I headed for a border crowded with asters, their yellow eyes seeking the sun. The petals were purple or blue or pink rather than white, but they were the closest thing to a daisy I could find here; like my sister, those wouldn't be deemed fit for cultivation. It almost felt as if I were committing some violence as I broke the stems, gathering them in my arms. A shadow fell over my shoulder – was Mademoiselle Blanc judging my taste? Would she find it wanting? There were plenty of fancier blooms here – but I turned and there was no one. She was over with the others, nodding at Matilda's dahlias, making a suggestion to Grace, removing a caterpillar-nibbled leaf from Beatrice's hands.

'You see, it is even more important to consider our choices when they are to be rendered permanent in a picture.' She approached Sophia who, oblivious, grasped at an abundance of blowsy pink roses. 'But then, perhaps we should apply such attention to every area of our lives. As much care as if it were all to remain before our eyes for ever.'

Sophia stilled as Mademoiselle Blanc passed close to her, but the teacher strolled on as if she'd been speaking to us all. Then she turned towards me.

'A nice restrained choice, Ivy. The colours will naturally go together. The word "asters" means "stars", did you know that? The goddess of innocence, Astraea, fled to the heavens when wickedness came to inhabit this world. Those flowers are her tears.'

I stared after her as she leaned in to try the scent of another rose, this one purest white. I could only think of Daisy, gone from this world as completely as Astraea herself, and I felt hollow; not so much like the stars as the spaces between them.

Mademoiselle plucked a few long ferny leaves and, as if noticing her for the first time, stopped by Sophia. She leaned in close so that they were almost cheek to cheek and held out the plain, simple leaves to Sophia's overblown blooms.

'Don't forget the use of foliage. It will soften everything.' Her voice was low, so that I could barely hear. 'These will set off that arrangement beautifully, Sophia. A lovely choice.' She pressed the greenery into the girl's hand, gently, taking care not to hurt her palm. Just as quietly, she moved away.

She was trying to make friends. She wanted to leave the events of this morning behind her. Sophia's eyes glittered as she glared after her and I knew she wouldn't include the leaves in her painting even as she dropped them in the dirt and ground them under her heel. Her picture would only have petals, all the same sugary pink, enough to make one's teeth ache.

Mademoiselle Blanc clapped her hands. It was time to go inside, for our work to begin. She led the way along curving corridors to a south-facing classroom on the ground floor, grandly referred to as the studio. The windows were not as tall as in the eyrie, but at this time of day the room was full of light. There was an easel for each of us, vases set out in front of them. Everyone hurried for those made of ceramic or chipped earthenware, anything transparent being more difficult to portray. I was left to a plain glass jug, but I didn't mind. I arranged my asters, setting taller stems to the back, turning each little eye to the front. Then I saw another arrangement, one of white daylilies on long, slender stems, already in place at the front of the room. They were *Hemerocallis*, gentle shepherds – Miss Peel, Madame Pelletier, sometimes taught us botany and had once told us the name meant *beautiful for a day*. I hadn't spotted any in flower in this year's wet season; perhaps the gardener raised these in his greenhouse, unless it was that their blooms had been too ephemeral for my notice. Their petals were white and soft around their creamy throats and in the light from the window, they glowed. The easel was unoccupied and I realised that Mademoiselle Blanc must have prepared it beforehand, that she intended to paint alongside us.

And I saw what hung on the wall behind it, shining back an image of the white blooms. It was a mirror. No: it was Sophia's mirror, the one she'd tried to present to our teacher, and suddenly the room seemed too small, crammed with furniture and skirts and cloying scents.

'Come girls, we may begin. I trust you will find everything you need.' Mademoiselle Blanc hadn't glanced at the mirror. Had she hung it there? Perhaps the housekeeper, finding it out of place in a corridor too narrow for its proportions, had had it moved.

I took my seat. I wished I could see Sophia's expression, but she was behind me. Had she seen the mirror? With a stab of spite, I wondered if holding a paintbrush would pain her injured hand.

I breathed in roses and lavender, the scents suddenly heady, but the lilies were stronger still. The odour made me think of funerals. Still I took up my brush and dampened the bristles, becoming lost in petals and paint, proportion and colour and form. I tried for exactness, marking the paper with faint indications of where the vase would sit and the highest leaf would reach, ghosts of what would come. Unlike Gadling with his whitewash, I liked to paint my subjects as they were; to reach after the truth of things. I began to add colour. I was no longer certain I liked the shade of the asters. They looked false, as if the petals themselves had been painted. I'd have preferred simple white.

Mademoiselle Blanc left off her own work and passed about the room. I scarcely looked up. I was in that place where I saw only my subject and the paper in front of me. I didn't wish to be reminded that soon I would have to think about other things: all that I did, how I stood and spoke and looked, who I *was*. All the things that were wrong with me. For now, this was as simple as breathing.

'Our time is almost up.' Mademoiselle Blanc spoke softly, as if to wake a sleepwalker; as if she understood. Had the lesson passed so quickly? But it seemed it was not quite over.

'You will notice a new addition to our little room.' She spoke as if she'd been here for years and had just spotted a disruption to the way things were. She moved towards the mirror. 'A gift,' she said. 'One that may be useful after all. Allow me to share with you a little trick. One by one, we shall take our work and stand in front of it. Mirrors always tell the truth. You'll see: it will reveal all our paintings' faults in a moment. And it is only in knowing our faults that we may put them right.'

No one moved. Was this, as she said, a simple trick to help our art, or some other kind?

'Ivy,' she said, 'perhaps you would begin.'

Warmth rushed to my cheeks. Could it be that my picture had stood out from the rest? I harboured a quiet pride in my work. I knew that pride was wrong, but here was something I did well when I was so often found wanting; where the others couldn't look down on me in scorn.

Lifting my painting by the edges, I carried it between the easels. The others watched, full of cold curiosity, and suddenly I didn't want my faults to be revealed in front of them. Still, it was time to hold it before the mirror, to see how the trick worked; to be judged.

'You see.'

I jumped. I hadn't heard Mademoiselle Blanc move to my side. 'The mirror helps distance our eye from what we have done. When everything is cast into reverse in a reflection, we view it afresh. Sometimes it makes us see it all differently.'

Mademoiselle didn't need to point out my imperfections. They were suddenly clear. The jug had harsh outlines that didn't exist in nature. It wasn't even symmetrical. The purples were gaudy and for a moment Daisy's laughter echoed in my ears.

'A good effort, Ivy.'

Crushed, I returned to my easel, paying little attention as the others took their turn. That their creations were clumsier than mine was no comfort. All of the colours might as well have been grey.

Then Sophia glided between the easels, graceful and uncaring, above it all, and held up her work as if it was of no matter in the slightest. Her pink flowers were indelicate. The petals were bold, each barely distinguished from the next. They were as strident as peacock feathers in a widow's bonnet, but she awaited judgement with defiant eyes.

'Very good, Sophia,' Mademoiselle said, and the clock ticked, the moment flowed on, the room breathed again.

Very good, Sophia. The words were like poison in my veins. I was too hot; my skin was aflame. By such a poor standard, was my own picture not good? Yet Mademoiselle Blanc had barely looked at me. I heard her verdict again, this time twisted into a tone of scathing contempt. It didn't comfort me to know that my painting's faults were real. It didn't matter that she was trying to paper over the rift between herself and Sophia. It didn't even help that I knew she'd only told me the truth.

Mademoiselle Blanc went to her easel. She picked up her own painting, carried it across the room and held it before the mirror.

Who is the fairest of them all?

She was. Her work was perfect. Unfinished perhaps, incomplete in its detail, but however she tilted it I couldn't see a fault and my thoughts, in all their littleness, dissipated. Her lilies weren't funereal. There was a joyfulness in them that made me want to laugh. Rendered with the barest delicate touches, I could nevertheless make out some of the individual brushstrokes, freely made yet blending into a harmonious whole.

She turned and smiled. I didn't know what expression she saw on my face; I could only stare. I only admired.

Then chairs scraped and skirts rustled. The bell had rung and she had dismissed us. I gathered myself, then jumped when a voice spoke at my ear. She'd approached me as quietly as before, was standing by my side.

'Your work shows promise, Ivy.'

Her voice was low, meant only for me, and I suddenly didn't care that she'd kept her words for just the two of us. They were heartfelt – and I had a sudden image of Gadling, his eyes full of tears, as shocking as if I'd stumbled upon him naked. Was it because she loved the thing I loved? My heart gave a stutter within its cage of ribs and flesh and corset and bodice.

'If you ever wish for additional tuition, you shall be most welcome. Do come to me. I would be happy to guide you as much as I can.'

I couldn't answer. I breathed in her scent of bergamot and lemon, stronger now even than the lilies, and she went on as if she hadn't noticed my silence. 'I wish to encourage any pupil who would seek to pursue their *particular* talent.'

A light touch on my shoulder and she moved away. Still her words hung in the air. They would return to me later, many times, along with the way she had said them; the way that, when I spun around to look at her, she smiled, as if it was already agreed.

7

It didn't take long for me to go in search of Mademoiselle Blanc. First, I fidgeted through our Sunday assembly as Madame Dumont recounted a dreary parable, thinking of all the things I'd have been doing on the farm: feeding the pigs, milking the goats, letting the chickens out of their coops, gathering the eggs. The whole world did not stop for us to admire God; if it had, we wouldn't eat. We'd show our faces in church to confirm we weren't heathens and then Daisy and I would run off into the fields. We'd chase butterflies and pick cob nuts or blackberries or apples, whatever was in season, and tell shivery tales of ghosts and highwaymen and the terrible things that happened to wayward young ladies. We'd shrieked deliciously over their fate, which could never happen to us; we always had each other. We always swore we'd love each other better than any man who could ever come along.

Why had I wished, even for a moment, to leave it – and her? I had imagined not having to rise at dawn, not having dirt under my nails. Now I wished I could go back, and like my namesake, twine about the house again.

A Sunday at Fulford meant only an interminable drift into an afternoon of *suitable* activities, which meant those involving quiet and the lack of enjoyment. Besides the dictates of religion, we were young ladies at a delicate stage in our lives; we could not be over-taxed in any way. Today we couldn't even walk for pleasure, which at other times was considered the only really healthful exercise we could endure. That was what it meant to be a lady; the servants were permitted to be useful on such a day, but nobody cared about *them*. The only relief from the dullness would be another gathering in the eyrie, when the parson had done with his church duties and came to deliver a sermon to us.

But even at Fulford there must be something that lay between labour and indolence, and so I went in search of Mademoiselle Blanc. I found her easily, since she was ascending the main stair as I went down, though I was surprised when she spoke, since I'd hardly been paying attention. I'd been wondering how much to show her; what to reveal and what to hide; how to present my soul to her in the best light.

'Ah, Ivy. I should scold you, you know, for not giving up the banister to one ascending. But you seem a little preoccupied.'

Here, away from the classroom, her smile was different. I found myself smiling back as I reminded her of her offer and asked if I could show her some of my paintings. Might she be so kind as to give her opinion? I didn't say *today*, but she must be bored too, mustn't she? She wasn't as starched as the rest. Perhaps she wouldn't think it improper.

'Of course,' she said. 'We'll make an assessment. I'll help you where I can. Bring them to my rooms directly.'

I grinned and rushed off, all eager, yet apprehensive too. What would Mademoiselle Blanc make of me? I'd be standing before that mirror again, exposed, faced with only the truth. She'd seen my faults so easily and made me see them, and everyone, and I suddenly wished her miles away from Fulford and all of us.

It was too late for wishing. I returned to my room, which was occupied by two of the girls who shared it. Matilda and Frances had cast aside their books – a volume of sermons and a bishop's biography, edifying reading for young ladies, certainly not a novel in sight – and were primping their hair at the washstands, an activity I assumed was something to do with the handsomeness of the parson's moustache.

I delved under the boxes stored in the bottom of our shared wardrobe. There was no privacy here, not really, but the others were incurious and I'd never suspected them of prying. Why would they? I was beneath their notice.

There, in its canvas wrap, was my sketchbook, its leaves softened and splayed at the edges where they'd been ruffled time and again.

'You're not going out, Ivy?' Matilda sounded incredulous.

'No, of course not. Mademoiselle Blanc wishes to see my work,' I said, trying to conceal the pride in my voice.

'Why on earth would she want to do that?' she snorted. 'Anyway, she can't.'

'Why not?' I frowned. 'She just this moment offered to do it.' I gestured back towards the passage that led to the stairway.

She rolled her eyes. 'Oh for heaven's sake, I don't care about your silly pictures. But we just this moment saw her leaving the school.' She similarly pointed, but in the opposite direction, towards the window. 'You shouldn't make things up. We saw her outside, walking towards the stables, didn't we, Fran? It wasn't two minutes before you came in.'

Frances nodded and looked disapproving, and I looked from her to Matilda and back again, wondering why I felt so crushed. Why would Mademoiselle Blanc rush off to the stables now? And however had she got outside so quickly? But the girls were mistaken – perhaps even trying to play a trick on me. If so, they should have picked a different destination: it wasn't as if Gadling would welcome her. I remembered his tone when he said, *Bard knows*.

His reaction to our new teacher had been no better than the girls'. And yet what could a horse know? Bard had spooked over nothing. Mademoiselle Blanc had done more than anyone else would for him, more than could be asked of her – and Bard was just Bard. Truth to tell, I didn't think he liked me very much either.

'She was all wrapped up in her cape,' Matilda went on. 'But it was definitely her, wasn't it, Fran?'

Frances gave a sly smile as she nodded. 'She seemed very set on getting away, didn't she, Tilly? Perhaps it was the thought of seeing your pictures, Ivy.'

I pressed my lips tight together. *Fran. Tilly.* The two of them were always so familiar, when to me they were Matilda and Frances. There had only been Bea that I could speak to in such a way – but that was over. And not even Bea had shortened my name in friendship; not that she could. I was always Ivy. After all, Ivy shortened only became I, and more alone than ever.

I pulled a face as I turned my back and made my way towards Mademoiselle Blanc's rooms. As I went, I glanced out of the windows – and saw that the outside world was entirely lost. An unseasonable fog had drawn in, concealing everything, and I wondered that it could have risen so quickly. I imagined Mademoiselle Blanc walking into it, being swallowed, and shuddered. How could Matilda and Frances claim to have seen our teacher? There was only emptiness, whiteness; a blank.

I adjusted my grip on my sketchbook, preventing the loose leaves from slipping. In the end, I'd decided to bring everything. Mademoiselle Blanc would see all of me.

I went to the door with its empty sign in place of a name and knocked. At once, an answering sound came from within; I thought it a murmur of invitation. I opened the door and stepped inside.

It wasn't as I'd thought. Mademoiselle Blanc stood in the corner by the window, and she wasn't ready for me. I wasn't certain she'd even heard me come in, for she remained motionless, her head lowered as if gazing out into the fog. I couldn't see her expression. Her hair was down – hanging in her eyes, darkened with damp, just as if Matilda was right and she'd been wandering outside after all. The sight gave me an uncomfortable feeling. I couldn't have explained it; I only knew that something was not as it ought to be, and I opened my mouth to ask if I was disturbing her just as a voice called out.

It was out of place, coming from the wrong side of me. I turned to see Mademoiselle Blanc behind me, just closing the inner door to her bedroom. She was neat, brisk, her hair immaculate, a little smile playing about her lips. 'Ah, Ivy! You have your sketches with you, I see.'

I whirled around. The corner by the window was empty. The figure I had taken for my teacher was gone. There was nothing but a shadow, appearing deeper still by the contrast with the window. Or had I glimpsed her reflection in the glass? The fog confused everything, as if it had crept inside my mind as well as stealing the world away.

'Whatever is the matter?' she asked.

Bard knows, I thought, and shivered.

'Ivy, what is it? Are you well?'

But of course I was. I'd made a mistake, that was all. I roused myself and smiled away her concern, and saw the warmth growing in her expression, and it comforted me. It was like coming in from the cold, though I remembered to make my apology for entering her room uninvited. Was it altogether convenient?

'Of course!' She waved all doubt away. 'I was expecting you. Let's take a look, shall we?'

And so I showed her my pictures – little pieces of my soul, some of which I'd forgotten existed but discovered again as she turned the pages. She said nothing: no murmur of affirmation, no comment, no praise. My heart tightened, shrivelling as she gazed on, and she turned another leaf and was silent. I moved to turn to the next and softly, she caught hold of my hand.

It was a simple pencil sketch of a daisy, not bright and open and joyful but wilting, its petals ruffled, leaves crushed, head drooping on its stem. It was beginning to die.

The sound of her fingertips stroking the paper was a gentle *shush*. I waited for her to tell me that I'd chosen badly, wasting my time on such a tired specimen, and furthermore, nothing but a weed. Instead she breathed, 'This is lovely.'

A lump knotted my throat. I couldn't speak and she seemed to understand, for she moved on, past an unremarkable watercolour of an old church, another of an overgrown well, then one of Fulford itself, until she reached the last: another simple pencil sketch. This was of Captain.

Once more she paused and I wondered what she saw. Was she remembering the horse being dragged across the station yard, falling to his knees? The blood – the way she held him – the words she had spoken? Or was it the way we had looked at her afterwards, judging her for it, seeing only something *tardy*, something *shabby*, standing in her place?

My thoughts must have been reflected in my expression for she reached out and patted my arm. Before she could speak I blurted out, 'He was my favourite.' It wasn't enough and I found myself close to tears, not for his loss but because she couldn't possibly understand. Why did everything I said sound wrong – foolish?

But she nodded as if she did understand, as if she saw everything, then sighed so deeply the air stirred against my cheek. 'This meant something to you,' she said.

I couldn't find the right words and so I replaced them with something else. 'I love to draw,' I said, 'and to paint. It's my solace, I suppose. It's the best way I've found to – well, not to exist, for a little while.'

My words were stupid, stupid, stupid. I'd hardly known I was going to say them, but she nodded and said brightly, 'Your parents must be very proud of you.'

My cheeks flamed. Must they? I had no idea. My mother and father hadn't seen a single one of my pictures. Not even Daisy had. Yet I could almost hear Papa's voice: *You're turning into quite the lady, our lass!* He *would* have been proud, I thought fiercely. He'd have admired them and patted my tamed hair, always pinned down so hard it hurt my scalp. He'd have smiled at the way I spoke, every vowel formed and re-formed by raps on my knuckles from my grandmother's ruler. Would he have been glad that I no longer sounded anything like him? And Mama – would she have been proud too?

Mademoiselle Blanc hadn't realised that I'd drifted from the world again. Or perhaps she had, for she stood and went to the window, looking out into the whiteness. I put out a hand, wanting to pull her back, away from the corner. But I couldn't touch her; I remembered myself and let it fall. She started to speak. She thought she could help me improve my eye. We could try some different approaches that might suit me very well. I had a feeling for detail and for life – I saw that word on her lips, *life*, and gladness blossomed inside me. She said it would be her pleasure to help me and the shadow in my mind dissolved and was banished.

When I left her rooms, my footsteps were lighter than they had been before. I liked Mademoiselle Blanc. I had hoped to like her and I did, and was glad that I did. She'd gazed at my portrait of a simple daisy. She'd lingered over my picture of Captain and had understood. She had *seen*. She had seen *me*, and it was more than

63

gaining a tutor; it was as if a window had been flung open and fresh air had flooded in. I found myself hoping that here was at least one other person in the school who understood what I felt, who might even share a little of it; even if it was only the care for a poor lost creature that had meant something to us both.

8

The fog barely lifted for the rest of the day. At times it was a veil laid over the earth, while at others it was a shroud that swallowed everything. It muffled sound. I didn't hear it when the parson's horse stepped onto the gravel outside, or when the great front door boomed closed behind him. We were at our seats in the eyrie, but the other girls seemed to sense him walking through the corridors below – gazing down as if they could pierce the floor, tracing the path he took towards us.

We knew when he'd reached the top of the stairs by the stir that ran across the dais and through our ranks, ending in a shuffling among the servants somewhere behind us. A dark shape crossed an empty space and vanished behind a screen by the piano. I often wondered if our parson was a little prone to the sin of vanity. For there he waited, only a murmured conversation with Madame Dumont betraying his presence until he could make a more dramatic entrance.

Reverend Aubrey was young and considered handsome. We didn't often see his like at the folly; now everyone seemed to awaken one by one as he stood before us and spoke of love.

He spoke of being kind to the helpless. Of generosity of spirit, of sacrifice and service, of entertaining angels unawares. He spoke of the joy of caring for everything, each creature great and small, and I wondered if Madame Dumont had primed him on the subject. If so, his words fell on stony ground. The girls offered up a row of pretty masks, empty of expression. When it was time for prayer, though, Bea clasped her hands together so tightly that her knuckles turned white, her lips murmuring fervently as she closed her eyes. I rolled mine towards the ceiling. The two of us had made fun of Aubrey, once; we'd giggled about him together.

We prayed to the Lord to make us worthy vessels for His love. To draw close to us, to fill us with His Holy Spirit. The parson said He was here with us always. Was it only me who couldn't sense His presence when I reached out with my senses? I never could convince myself there was anybody there and my words dissipated. Too early, I opened my eyes. Reverend Aubrey hadn't closed his either. He was staring down at us. He was staring at Sophia.

She too had lifted her head. Momentarily, she unclasped her hands and pressed one to her heart. No one else saw. The parson never missed a word and I pushed away the unlikely thought that arose; she would surely wish to reach higher than one such as he. She might have had an itch under her corset. He might only have sensed her inattention.

Eventually, the service ended and we watched as Madame Dumont introduced Reverend Aubrey to our new teacher. He bowed and they exchanged pleasantries; he took her hand and held it for a moment in his.

Sophia pushed past me, her lips twisted in disgust.

I watched her go. Not wrong, then. Well, Aubrey couldn't rebuff Mademoiselle Blanc just because Sophia wished it so. He might not even have noticed the girl watching him. Probably he met with the same fond looks everywhere he went; he'd certainly have spent his whole morning, if not the entire day, being admired.

As soon as I could escape the eyrie, I left – and kept going, finding myself at the foot of the south-west stair, by the door that led outside. A row of capes hung on brass hooks and I grabbed one before stepping out into the changed world. I was walking, but I could hardly be accused of doing so for pleasure, not in this weather. Anyway, no one would see me go.

I relished the air's chill breath on my skin, the cold damp kisses that were all it had to offer. Skeins of mist hung and drifted, now drawing aside to reveal the land around me in glimpses, now concealing it again. There was no sound apart from the grit of my boots on the path. I told myself that Fulford wouldn't be for ever. No: soon I would have to go home again – not to the farm, but my grandparents' house. I already knew what they intended for me. I'd return, having learned to simper, having been primped and polished and pinned down and laced in. Grandfather would have a new gown waiting for me. He'd ensure I was displayed to his satisfaction, like the polished sideboard and gleaming candelabra, and he would present me to one of his cadaverous acquaintances. He'd probably already decided which of them it would be most advantageous for me to marry.

I made no conscious decision of where to go. Whichever way I turned, I was walking into my future – hidden and yet waiting for me, implacable, unchangeable. I tried to tell myself it wasn't so, that I would somehow step back in time instead. I'd reach the stables and there would be Captain waiting for me, the friend sought by a child. And I'd go further still. Instead of Captain, there would be a stolid, blocky mare called Mags. There'd be an old dog called Scampers who'd chase after me when I called, and goats and chickens, and a face I knew as well as my own: Daisy, my sister come to find me after all, reaching through the mist and seizing my hand.

But that was gone, nothing but a picture from a world gone by. There would only be Gadling, eyeing my skirts and leering. And a new horse – one who looked the same as Captain but who wouldn't recognise me, wouldn't nudge my arm for the anticipated apple. If I stroked his nose, would the white come off on my fingers? All paint must crumble eventually.

I stopped. Even the smell of a horse, now, would make me cry. That was in the past. It had gone beyond me and would never be permitted again, because I was a lady; I had a future to think of.

I turned on my heel and found I couldn't see the folly any longer. I was lost. It wasn't just because of the fog; the world felt different, empty, wrong somehow. And it *was* different, I realised. Everything had been, since *she* arrived. It was as if something had been set in motion that couldn't be stopped and I looked down and, with a little start, recognised the cape I'd borrowed. It was her cape; the one Mademoiselle Blanc had been wearing when I first saw her.

I slipped it from my shoulders, the thick grey wool a sudden dead weight in my hands. It was no longer sodden or soiled with mud, only a little damp from the fog, droplets glistening on the brushed surface. I could see her form impressed into the thick fabric and after a moment I wrapped it about me once more, enfolding myself in her garment. And I felt, in the lining, something the maid's efforts had missed.

I knew what it was. I'd seen a similar substance drying on a man's once-white shirt. It was Captain's blood. I swiped at the fabric with my hands but it was no use; it seemed to spread before my eyes until I saw blood everywhere, though no longer blackening and dried; it flowed anew. I blinked and shook the image away. There was only a little blood, and with it, some horsehair – only a memory of what had happened, and that not even mine.

I looked down at my skirt and found it had transferred itself to me. I brushed at the chestnut hairs until they were gone.

When I looked up, I could see the folly after all. It was waiting behind the mist, just as stolid and present as it had always been, and I walked towards it, a little relieved. I went in and replaced the cape on its hook, hoping Mademoiselle Blanc wouldn't notice anything amiss, and followed in the steps she must have taken when she first came to the school. I emerged in the entrance hall and looked up to see Beatrice on the landing. She stared down, her eyes open wide, as if she'd seen a ghost. It was as we had stood when Mademoiselle Blanc first arrived, though now I was in the position of shame and Beatrice in that of judgement.

I swallowed hard. I moved to leave her, but she recovered herself and said, 'There you are. Mademoiselle Blanc told me

69

you'd come this way. She instructed me to watch for you, Ivy. She said it most particularly. You're to go to her at once.'

Most particularly – of course Beatrice would say that. She'd say it because she couldn't say, *I didn't want to be here.* She couldn't say, *I never wanted to see or speak to you or be near you ever again.*

At least Mademoiselle Blanc wished to see me – though Beatrice's words echoed in my ears. How had the teacher known I'd come this way – had she seen me take her cloak? And had she seen the way I'd turned it in my hands before clutching it closer?

My throat dry, I croaked, 'Where is she?'

'Mademoiselle said she'd wait for you. She went into the dining room.' Beatrice spoke primly, as if I were a stranger. But then she cast off her stiffness and pulled a face; her words came in a rush. 'She was so *odd*, Ivy. There was something strange—'

Unbidden, an image came: a shadow standing in the corner of a room, there and then gone. Something that looked like Mademoiselle Blanc and yet wasn't her, as if I'd stumbled across someone else entirely, or some*thing*: downcast, dark, the opposite of the smiling, kind, generous teacher. If it had spoken, would it have sounded like her? What might it have said to me? I shook my head. That had only been a mistake. I remembered Mademoiselle's kindness, her smile, the brief touch of her hand on my back, and pulled myself together.

'Everything is quite all right, Beatrice,' I said, throwing a note of disdain into my voice, showing her she was being tiresome.

She nodded. Her features became neutral once more, as if remembering she was no longer my confidante. She shared a room with Sophia now. She had requested to move *most particularly*. She was Sophia's friend, and somehow along the way that had come to mean she could no longer be mine.

Then she said, 'I'll come with you.'

My heart knocked against my ribs, just once, a reminder that it was there. I remembered the way she had clasped her hands together as she prayed. Was that a sign of regret – of sorrow? But she didn't look at me as she walked down the stairs, only peering towards the dining room with narrowed eyes – almost as if she were nervous.

'She went in there.' She pointed towards the dining room, as if I didn't already know where it was. It wasn't positioned as in most houses. It was entered via a dark corner tucked away behind the stairway and we rarely crossed its threshold outside mealtimes, though we sometimes had lessons there: *Never ask for seconds of soup or fish, since it keeps others waiting. Only the tips of your fingers are to go in the fingerbowl. Young ladies never eat cheese at dinner parties. Withdraw at once if the bottle circulates too freely.*

I strode to the door and opened it. The dining room was empty.

'That can't be.' Beatrice's voice was at my shoulder. 'She said she'd wait for you. I saw her go in. I'd have seen her if she'd come out again.' She peered all around, as if Mademoiselle Blanc might at any moment jump out at us.

I found myself listening, as if a voice might come to me across the empty hall, but there was nothing; only a silence that lay heavily on everything.

There was something strange—

Why had Beatrice said that? Was she remembering our first sight of the teacher, that peculiar figure drenched with rain and blood?

71

But the room only contained its familiar long tables and simple chairs, ones that Madame Dumont would describe as decently plain and others might call cheap. The walls bore a few old paintings, the lineage of a family long since gone. There was nothing else.

I glared at Beatrice. Then I turned on my heel and stalked back into the hallway, but there I stopped, because footsteps sounded on the stairs and I looked up to see Mademoiselle Blanc herself walking towards us.

'But that's impossible.' Behind me, Beatrice plucked at my sleeve. A memory: Bea whispering, stirring my hair with her breath. Bea sobbing hot tears that I stroked away with my thumb. Bea shuddering as I held her close. She'd once told me she hated Fulford too. She'd said she hated everyone in it – except me. She'd been sent away from home because her mother had died. Her father had loved her mother, *really* loved her, and Bea had been the image of her; he couldn't bear to look at her any longer. *I* had looked at her, though. I'd looked into her eyes as she'd clung to me.

Now I pulled free of her.

'Good afternoon, Mademoiselle Blanc,' I called out. 'Did you need anything that I can help you with?'

She paused, one foot suspended above the final step, appearing faintly surprised. She replied, 'Why, no – I'm in need of nothing, thank you, Ivy.' And she went on, entering the outer corridor and passing out of sight.

Beatrice said, 'But how? How can she be here, and—'

She glanced towards the dining room. She was still play-acting then, taking Sophia's part, carrying out some mean trick. Frances and Matilda had told Sophia of my meeting with the teacher and they'd decided to make fun of me. To think that I ever could have thought of Bea as almost another *sister* – Daisy would have pulled out her hair for this. My true sister would have withstood any insult to herself, but never to me.

'How very amusing you are, Beatrice.' I met her eyes at last, but hers were not as I expected. They were wide; they were afraid.

'I didn't make it up, Ivy, I promise. I don't know how – I *saw* her go in there. She didn't walk past me again. Oh – it's almost as if she could be in two places at once, just like Fran and Tilly—'

That was all I needed to hear. I turned my back and stalked away, leaving Beatrice there alone. If she watched me go, I didn't care. Why should I? I'd once held her while she cried, but she wasn't a friend to me any longer. None of them were. And I had a new friend now. Mademoiselle Blanc had looked at my work and seen what it meant. She'd looked at *me*; she had seen me, and she hadn't looked away.

9

Our next lesson was history and geography, but that was more pretence at best. We weren't here for serious subjects. Why learn so much that we'd only have to disguise it later? Our husbands wouldn't like it. We were here to gain adornments, not to learn how to think. And so we were set to recite catechisms from an ancient book of children's lessons. We had read it a hundred times before and knew it by heart, though we were no longer schoolchildren, not really; nor yet were we something else.

'What is whalebone used for?' Miss Morrison croaked in the direction of Ruth, a short, plain girl, who didn't seem to mind the dullness of the question. She was always eager to offer to clean the blackboard or lay out chalk or fill the inkwells.

She stood to answer. 'To stiffen stays, umbrellas and whips.' She spoke in a prompt sing-song and I pictured her in future years reciting these things over the dinner table, all in the same tone, like a canary in a cage.

'Are not umbrellas of great antiquity?' Miss Morrison leaned over to tap her finger on Matilda's desk as Ruth seated herself again. It was her turn, and she must carry out her part with close attention.

Matilda stood. 'Yes, the Greeks, Romans and all Eastern nations used them to keep off the sun . . .'

I drifted away, half listening, just in case the teacher should call upon me. By the time she did I guessed we might have come to Good Queen Bess's thoughts on silk stockings, or more likely, the jewel presented to Florence Nightingale by our own Queen, or some other flotsam snatched from the tide of history. It would supply us with light subjects for agreeable conversation at dinner.

Lucy, having answered the question about whalebone's usefulness to whales, to *form a kind of strainer to keep in the sea-snails and other small creatures upon which whales live*, shifted in her seat. She gazed out of the window and down into the walled garden, perhaps longing to be out there amid the flowers. The folly was never meant for a school, or the windows would have been set higher, removing the temptation. If Lucy wasn't careful she'd be punished; not caned, not in this class, but given endless lines to write. Miss Morrison favoured tiny lettering on large sheets of paper which could be turned, like a letter, and written over again cross-wise.

Our teacher paced towards the back of the room as we shifted from the Eastern nations to the Italians and thence to England with a predictability that made my head ache. Another step and Miss Morrison reached Dick Whittington and his cat, and more importantly what *kind* of cat, for who knew when we might use such a snippet? Whether it was history or fairy tale was of little matter.

For lack of any other variety, I cast my eyes over the objects arranged on top of the cupboards: a globe showing the empire's reach; an abacus, seldom used; a box of ink pellets; and a zoetrope with strips of printed pictures to fit inside its drum. One depicted a ball endlessly passing through a hoop; another, a whale by turns breaching and crashing into the sea; another a girl, practising her *grands jetés* over and over, never anything less than perfect. Zoetrope meant *wheel of life*. When the device was spun, it created the illusion that the images moved, something that seemed almost magical to me; but now it was motionless. I longed to leave my seat and set the wheel in motion, but I could only sit. I could only listen.

I realised the room had fallen silent. Had Miss Morrison asked another question – perhaps of me? But it didn't feel like that. Rather it was as if everything had paused, a brief moment of silence before – what? Everything began to spin? The air was too close. Something must happen. The whale would leap from the zoetrope, demanding the return of its strainer, stolen for stays, umbrellas and whips. The ball would miss its hoop and fly; the girl would overleap herself and run away.

The door at the front of the room opened. It was Mademoiselle Blanc. She stepped in, saying, 'Pardon me, Miss Morrison, but I wonder if—'

And Lucy screamed.

We twisted to look at her, but Lucy didn't notice; she leapt from her desk and went to the window, pressing her hands against the glass. I could hear an odd sound. I realised it was coming from Lucy: a little hiccuping hitch as she caught her breath. I tried to see what she saw – but there was only the garden, only the flowerbeds we had explored so recently. Not even the gardener,

Simons, was wandering the rows with his trug.

Belatedly, Ruth half stood, as if she'd just realised that a teacher had entered the room. She remained there, suspended, with no idea of what to do. No one reprimanded her. No one reprimanded Lucy as she whirled to face Mademoiselle Blanc – then tried to step away from her, pressing back against the glass, her face frozen in fear.

'Goodness,' twittered Miss Morrison. 'Oh my goodness.' She muttered the words as if they were a spell and might repair her lesson, as if she couldn't understand what could possibly have gone amiss.

'Lucy?' Sophia too had stood, though she hadn't been granted permission.

For once, Lucy ignored her cousin. All her manners were forgotten; everything was. She went on staring at Mademoiselle Blanc – who took a step towards her.

Lucy squeezed her eyes tight shut. She whimpered, 'Don't let her. Please, don't let her touch me.'

Sophia moved to her side. She reached out and touched her cousin's arm and Lucy flinched. 'A ghost,' she started to whisper. 'It's a ghost, a ghost . . .'

'Lucy!' Miss Morrison came to herself at last. 'Sit down, at once—'

'It's a ghost of *her*.' Lucy's eyes snapped open. They shone too brightly as she pointed at Mademoiselle Blanc.

'Lu, I'll take you to your room.' Sophia spoke firmly, taking charge of everything. 'You are fatigued. Don't be upset. You can rest a little.'

Mademoiselle Blanc's lip twitched. Then she stepped closer to Lucy. *Don't*, I thought, but slowly, she reached out and touched the girl's shoulder.

Lucy dropped to the floor, a puppet with her strings cut. Her head struck the wall with a sound at once loud and dull; then there was only a horrified silence.

'Get *away* from her.' Sophia kneeled at Lucy's side, lifting her head in her arms, shielding her with her body, as if Miss White would hurt her. But Miss White could do nothing; she could only watch. Everyone was staring at her as if they thought she'd cast some spell over poor little Lucy.

Sophia murmured her cousin's name, patted her cheek. *That won't help*, I thought – but Lucy stirred. She opened her eyes. She raised a hand and touched Sophia's injured palm. I felt sick. What had happened? *Please, don't let her touch me*, Lucy had said, and when she did—

Had Lucy wound herself up to such a pitch that she'd fainted? She would hate our teacher for caning her cousin, but she wasn't bold like Sophia, wasn't impertinent. I didn't know what to think – but the others would, I realised, and the knowledge crept over me of the things they would say. The thing that was, in their eyes, already turning Mademoiselle Blanc into what they wanted her to be, what *Sophia* wanted her to be.

Lucy sniffed back tears. She threw her arms around Sophia, who shushed her. She pulled Lucy to her feet, making encouraging sounds. Lucy stood next to her, red-faced, her hair loose, as dishevelled as if she'd been brawling in a farmyard. Sophia wrapped her arms protectively around her, glaring at Mademoiselle Blanc as if daring her to part them.

Yet the teacher must act, for it was clear that Miss Morrison would not. When Mademoiselle Blanc spoke her voice was faint, and I felt a stab of anger at how they were changing her; how they'd already changed her.

'Do that, Sophia – please. Take her to her room and I shall ask Miss Peel to attend her there.'

Sophia's lips tightened in triumph as she began to lead Lucy away. As they passed Mademoiselle Blanc, though, Lucy stopped. Without looking at the teacher she said, 'You were in the garden. You were in the roses and then you walked in. There were two of you. Only, the other was a – I don't know. A spirit. A *shadow*.'

Then Sophia pulled on her arm and they moved again and a moment later the door closed and they were gone.

Still Miss Morrison said nothing. It was Mademoiselle Blanc who told us to be seated, and then she said she would inform Miss Peel and she too left the room.

We were left to our class once more, and to the quiet. I didn't know what had just happened. Words rang in my ears, ones I didn't understand. Ghost. Spirit. *Shadow*. I looked around at the high walls keeping us in, and gradually those strange words faded until only the old empty repetitions hung in the air: whalebone and corsets and cats, umbrellas and stays and whips, years and years of it, always the same, accumulating in the walls and the cornices and the stale air. We sat perfectly still and we waited for the world to resume spinning, until there was nothing left to do but for Miss Morrison to take up her book, to return to the start; to begin our lesson all over again.

10

When the bell freed us and we went to Lucy's dormitory, Sophia was waiting for us. Seated on Lucy's bed, her hands were clasped in her lap, almost concealing an old and tattered book. Lucy was not there, but Sophia didn't yet explain. She didn't speak until we'd gathered around her, taking the places she expected us to take.

'The answer is here,' she said. 'All of this has happened before. Here is everything we need to know.'

She held out the book. It was bound in green cloth, faded and worn. It didn't look like anything Sophia would own. She was the kind who'd want gleaming leather in a shade that matched the curtains, glistening gold, a cobbled-together crest stamped on the binding. This didn't look clean. It didn't smell clean. The corners were frayed, scuffed down to the boards.

'This is my mother's. She has a collection of such books – she has a special interest in these matters. I have hinted at her gifts,

80

ones she refuses to deny. She is not afraid to look the truth in the face. That is something she has taught me too. We have a certain sensitivity of the nerves. One has to be *capable* of seeing things of this type, you know, or one is quite blind.'

I could only stare.

Then she said, 'My mother is at the centre of a spirit circle. Tea and table-turning, all very discreet and respectable. Many look to her for guidance. I have inherited her delicacy of nature – it allows me to understand things that others cannot.'

I think my mouth fell open. Sophia thought herself something akin to a medium, then, possessed of occult powers, able to speak to the dead and who knew what else. Yet the others didn't seem surprised, and I wondered if I was the only one who hadn't known of this. *Blind.*

She flipped open the book – it seemed to fall naturally at the place she sought, as if she'd opened it there before, many times. And she read:

'A few weeks after *Mademoiselle* first arrived, singular reports began to circulate among the pupils. When some casual inquiry happened to be made as to where she was, one young lady would reply that she had seen her in such or such a room; whereupon another would say, "Oh, no! She can't be there; for I have just met her on the stairway;" or perhaps in some corridor. At first they naturally supposed it was mere mistake; but, as the same thing recurred again and again, they began to think it very odd.'

She closed it with a snap and raised her chin, fixing on each of us in turn. 'You see,' she said, 'it is just like—'

But we were not to hear what it was like, for footsteps rang out behind us – coming along the corridor, louder by the moment. Lucy, returning? Sophia seemed to have forgotten her cousin. But the girls parted, pressing into the corners to move away from the figure who stepped into the room: Mademoiselle Blanc herself.

'I came to tell you that Lucy will stay in the infirmary for a little while,' she said. 'Miss Peel is tending to her, although she is quite well. There is no need for concern.'

No one made a sound. Sophia stared up at the teacher, unblinking. Mademoiselle didn't seem to know what to do any longer, or where to look, until she saw me. She took a breath, gave a little nod and said, 'Ivy, there you are. Come with me, if you please.'

If it were possible for silence to deepen, it did so then. I said nothing, only did as I was told. There was not a single titter or whispered remark behind me as I left the room, but their gaze clawed at my back. I wished I could split in two: to go with her and hear what she had to say and stay with the others to listen to their gossip. But whoever could be in two places at once?

You were in the roses and then you walked in . . .

I followed her, like a ghost or a shadow, and she said not a word. We wound through the corridors in silence until we reached her rooms and she opened the door and stood back for me to go inside. After a moment's hesitation, I did.

The room had changed. Two chairs were arranged in her parlour, small tables set in front of each in place of easels. On the tables were palettes, cakes of paint, brushes and jars of water. They faced a plasterwork stand, though the ugly majolica vase it had once held was on the floor and instead it boasted nothing grander than a simple glass jug – the same one I'd attempted to paint in class.

Now it was full of wildflowers. I recognised enchanter's nightshade, cornflowers, pink and white campion, ragged robin. And there were big, blowsy field daisies, exuberant and unashamed; the flowers my mother called moon pennies. I remembered her naming them all, these wild things that grew in the hedgerows; nothing but weeds, but to me they were as lovely as any other flower.

'I *had* thought we might paint.' Mademoiselle Blanc's voice was apologetic.

When I turned to her, she held out her arms in a helpless gesture, hardly like a teacher at all, and affection for her rushed in upon me. Lucy's words had been nonsense; they were *mad*. She was a child, foolish and impressionable. She'd been in a reverie – or had fallen asleep and dreamed whatever she thought she saw. Miss Morrison had given us little reason to stay awake, after all. Or she'd been playing a trick. She'd been playing a trick designed by Sophia, only pretending to see a *shadow*, a dark figure that looked like Mademoiselle Blanc . . .

My gaze went to the corner by the window. Had something shifted there? I told myself that of course it hadn't, and I hadn't seen anything there before either, only an illusion; only for a moment, and something bright in the corner of my eye drew my focus back to the jug, to where a single lovely white bloom was positioned among the wildflowers. I thought it a lily, then saw it wasn't a funeral flower but a shapely white rose.

You were in the roses and then you walked in.

Had Mademoiselle been outside after all, picking these flowers – for me? But I banished Lucy's words. I banished *her*. I wasn't going to be afraid of my teacher because of a young girl's silly play-acting. Lucy should have a care. Fine married ladies could afford to have vapours; it gave them something to do. Lucy was young and had a husband to secure and couldn't expect to be so indulged. Any suspicion against her mental wellbeing would reflect on her husband or children, and her parents too, since everyone knew that lunacy was hereditary. Even now they might be quieting her with laudanum. Or they'd shiver it out of her with a cold bath.

I smiled up at Mademoiselle Blanc, noting the lines of tension that had spread around her eyes. I said, 'I think we still have a little time.'

She smiled. 'I thought you might like this arrangement,' she said, as we seated ourselves side by side. 'I chose a smaller scale in which to work, hence a sheet placed flat in front of you rather than an easel. I thought it would allow you to focus more closely on the subject. And a pencil, you see, to mark things out, for precision.'

It felt surreal to apply myself to something so ordinary with the echo of Lucy's shrieks still in my ears, but I knew that she was right: this would suit me very well. I didn't suppose I could concentrate, not really, but when I took up the pencil she offered and began indicating the edges of the campion and moon pennies and leaves, taking special care over the shape of the jug, it began to absorb me. This time there would be no error – or not the same one, I was determined of that.

The paper was much nicer than that used in our art classes, almost as thick as a visiting card, the texture luxuriant. I knew it would take the paint beautifully, making the colours brilliant and rich. Grateful that she had provided it, I glanced at her, seeing only the curve of her cheek. She was engrossed; she looked almost like a picture herself.

Behind her, the inner door that led to her bedchamber was ajar. Through it drifted the faint scent of bergamot and lemon, along with the barest hint of sour water from a washstand. All of her furnishings looked as if they'd been in place for decades, everything fringed with ugly shades of pink and salmon, and I wondered how she could bear it.

She stirred and followed my gaze. To cover over my impertinent curiosity, I said, 'How do you find it at Fulford, Mademoiselle?'

She looked startled, as well she might. The events of the last hour played before me again – and she saw it too, for in another moment we both burst into a startled laugh. It all suddenly seemed so improbable. It couldn't possibly have been real.

'Well, Ivy,' she said, 'it is still very new to me.'

She wiped her eyes as we returned to our work. She too was pencilling in the lines, though her design ranged more freely, petals spilling across the sheet. I tried to concentrate on my task, outlining the rose's fringed calyx.

'You have great skills of observation, Ivy,' she murmured. 'A talent for capturing each individual detail, I think.'

I half hid a smile, bending more closely over my work, redoubling my efforts. I would do better still, I decided. I would portray each bloom minutely, faithfully, as closely as possible to the life. My work was already improving, under the direction of her few well-chosen words.

'I very much liked your sketch of a daisy. Anyone else would have tried to make it appear perfect, but there was something about the way you captured its fading – oh, whatever is the matter?'

I shook my head. I couldn't explain to her what the picture meant; about my sister. Now she stared at me, all concern, all kindness, for me. It was so unexpected I found my eyes filling with tears.

'You miss home, perhaps? Is that it, Ivy?'

I agreed that I did, of course I missed home, covering over my silliness. My real home, I meant; the one with the two of us in it, my sister and I. I didn't tell her that, or anything about the farm, for all she had reminded me of it with her wildflowers. To move on to something else, I said, 'Do you miss *your* home, Mademoiselle Blanc?'

'Miss White,' she corrected me, and smiled. She leaned in, conspiratorial for a moment. 'I wasn't sure who they meant by Mademoiselle Blanc at first, you know. That name is only for the classroom, I think we all know that. You may call me Miss White. *Emily.*'

Her confidence was a ray of sunlight striking into me. And I felt how constrained I had been, suffocated by the closeness of corsets and high walls and narrow corridors and all the lives shut away or waiting to begin; by the things I must or mustn't do, all the ways I had been found wanting.

'Where are you from, Ivy?'

I glanced at the moon pennies and away. I told her of my grandfather's house, of his business in Sheffield, of afternoons watching the band play in the grand park to the south of the city. I didn't mention my mother and father and she didn't ask. Possibly she assumed they were dead. I didn't speak of Archie and Tom, my older brothers. I couldn't speak of Daisy. She was mine and mine alone. Those memories were too private, too precious, and I didn't want to dilute their colours by sharing them, like paint washed out by too much water. But for the first time I thought that perhaps, one day, I might. I could hand them to her, those memories, placing them in her hands like delicate blooms, and they wouldn't be spoiled; they wouldn't be broken.

Another memory came to me: Daisy dragging me from the dairy where I was supposed to be churning the butter, shushing me and laughing. Then we'd crouched behind the barn and played another game, one that spoke of all the things we were capable of doing. It had turned into a chant, almost a catechism like the questions and answers in Miss Morrison's interminable book, but entirely ours.

I know I can face down a charging ram.

I know I can pull a wet slippery lamb from its mother.

I know I can glean every last stalk of corn and gather all the apples without bruising a one.

I couldn't remember what Daisy's statements had been. It didn't matter; we would never say such things again. For I was to be a lady and must sit in a classroom with the other girls, knowing that every one of them was better than me precisely because I could do all of those things.

I hadn't been able to see everything that was wrong with me, not then. That came later, after the blighted corn, the bailiffs, the loss of our copper cooking pots and the good linen. It came after my grandparents' first sight of me sitting astride Mags the carthorse, my best frock tucked up to reveal my black stockings covered in straw. It was then that they began teaching me all my faults: how many they were, and how bad.

I wished I could tell her, though. I would tell her that I had been happy. I'd tell her I was named for the place where I was born. We both were: Ivy for the leaves that twined all about the house, Daisy for the little flowers that opened everywhere I looked.

And Emily wouldn't judge. She'd smile on me with those eyes full of depths and lights and even hold my hand as I spoke and she would understand.

For now we sat silently, creating something new, filling in the soft greens, the pinks, the blues. The white petals, however, we left carefully blank, delineating them only by the shadows that lay all around them. For the lightest areas must be left empty; as white as paper, since white was no colour at all.

I didn't realise until afterwards that she never had answered my question. I still didn't know where she'd come from and I didn't care. What could it matter? She might have always been here, the two of us always like this.

When we sat back and examined our pictures I was lost, this time in admiration.

There was a lightness to her work that mine lacked. Her strokes were less constrained; she'd allowed the colours to run into each other and the effect was not chaotic or untidy but wild and beautiful. I couldn't imagine why she'd encouraged me to observe every trifling detail when that was not her technique and her own work was so very lovely. It was as if she'd sensed all my thoughts of freedom and happiness and translated them into something of her own.

Yet she leaned over to look at my work and murmured, 'That's wonderful, Ivy. You've painted it all just as it is – so very like the life. The way that stem is notched, even the wayward petal just there.'

I frowned, seeing only my mistakes. For that wasn't how things were meant to be done, was it? We weren't supposed to tell the truth, not if it made things ugly. I should have left those things out, and I sighed. 'Shouldn't I have tried to make it perfect?'

Softly, she touched my chin and turned my face towards my subject. '*Is* it perfect, do you think?'

I was conscious only of her touch, thinking of Lucy falling to the floor; but nothing happened, and after a moment I said, 'No.'

'Well, then. I think that may be best left to others.'

I was lost. What did she mean? That *perfection* was for others, something I could never attain? If so she was right, but for her to say it . . . I pursed my lips, thinking of Sophia's golden hair, her chiming voice, her spotless dress. Rubbing shoulders with the likes of her hadn't improved me, as was my grandparents' intention. Her company only made me feel my own awkwardness. I was clumsy, untidy, out of place. I was *shabby.* I saw the flowers again, not cultivated, not lovely; nothing but weeds.

'What is it they say of me?' she asked.

I blinked, my mind still full of flowers. *You were in the roses.*

'There is something, is there not?' She paused. 'I know our first sight of each other was unfortunate, but that could scarcely be helped. Perhaps now they will have heard the reason—'

Was this why she had asked me here? I'd been so occupied with the thought of confiding in her, I hadn't considered for a moment that she might wish to confide in me. But she too was alone, wasn't she? And she was scarcely older than I, torn from whatever her home had been and brought here, where she had been set apart, pointed at, laughed at.

'Is there anything else you are aware of, Ivy? I see that you're observant. I don't ask you to speak of it unless you feel you can, though I hope you know that you may tell me anything.'

Anything. I turned to her, and she kept on gazing at me, her expression at once candid and unreadable, like the surface of a painting seen so close it no longer made sense. Her eyes were not simply grey, I realised. They contained hints of green, even of gold, and I couldn't look away. A teacher shouldn't ask me for confidences. That wasn't how things worked, wasn't how they were. Teachers didn't ask pupils to spy for them. But I didn't care for any such rules, not where she was concerned, and I opened my lips to tell her everything just as she turned from me.

'Goodness,' she said, 'how the time has flown! We must clean up, my dear. It's already a little late.'

She stood and vigorously washed her brushes, drawing herself very straight. She looked as if she were separating herself from me, reminding herself she was my teacher, or perhaps covering her own momentary weakness. I hurried to help her push the tables to the side of the room. I was glad of the activity, for I couldn't straighten my thoughts.

If she was similarly discomposed, she didn't show it. She bade me farewell and in the next instant I was standing in the corridor next to a closed door, alone once more. It was too sudden and too quiet and I wished I could fling the door open and tell her everything, anything she wanted: Lucy's silly fancy, the girls' nasty tricks, Sophia's hatred. Why not? She – *Emily* – had been far kinder to me than they ever were.

Yet what had she meant by her comment? *I think that may be best left to others.*

Did she only mean that I saw the truth of things where others didn't? That she too cared nothing for false manners and artifice – for pretence? I remembered the way she had looked at me, the lights that glimmered in her eyes. The way she spoke, so sincere, so guileless, not as a teacher but as an equal. Did she mean that of everyone in the school it was only we who were *not* pretending, who could speak the truth to one another – who had formed a genuine connection between us?

For a moment I reached out and brushed my fingers against her door, lightly, so lightly it never made a sound. And I walked away, carefully composing my features so as not to betray my feelings with an unaccustomed smile.

11

The others moved around me, nothing but blurry shapes in the corner of my eye, figures I couldn't have named. I took no notice, making my way to the dining room along with the rest, until I heard a whisper: 'Where have you been, Ivy?'

I pulled a face, meaning to ignore them, then realised it was Beatrice. I wouldn't have answered anyone else but found myself telling her, 'Miss White has offered to tutor me. We were painting.'

'*Painting*?'

It was odd, I supposed, to spend time on such a thing after what had happened to Lucy, and would seem doubly so if Beatrice actually imagined that Mademoiselle Blanc – Miss White – had meant to hurt the girl. I told myself she'd be a fool to think that, just as she said, 'There's something dark at work here, Ivy. You should be careful. You don't want to be tainted by her company.'

I could only stare after her as she walked towards Sophia's table. *Me* – tainted by *her* company? That seemed entirely unlikely.

I hurried to take my seat and we settled and quieted. We weren't permitted to speak at luncheon unless it concerned the passing of salt or over-boiled vegetables or to say please and thank you. Madame Dumont was very strict on that point. It was an outward show of how well we were supervised, part of the school's assurance that no harm or adventure would ever reach us.

The teachers ate in silence, setting an example of decorous behaviour. Did they never gossip as we did? If so, what did they talk about? Us, I supposed. Perhaps they followed our paths into the future as if running a finger along a map, noting a glittering marriage, the birth of a notable heir, perhaps one day, a lamentable and unfortunate demise.

It was then that I noticed Lucy. She had rejoined us, was seated beside her cousin, and she seemed to have shrunk somehow. A small and unremarkable figure, she raised a spoon to her mouth like an automaton while looking at nothing at all. Was she made docile with medicine or her own shame? She was having bread and milk, I noticed, a child's ration to calm an over-excited constitution. As I watched she cast a longing glance at Sophia's stew and I smothered a smile.

Madame Dumont kept looking at her too. Would she write to Lucy's father about what had happened? I didn't think so, not unless she was forced to it. I doubted she'd even speak of it again. There could be no question of one of her girls being *tainted* – it was Beatrice's word that came to me – for the walls of the folly must stand; they must remain faultless. Outwardly all must appear perfect, while within – who knew?

Our headmistress signalled for the servants to clear the dishes.

One of them wrinkled her nose: Sukie, a vinegar-faced girl of fourteen or fifteen, her features set too close together, a dimple deeply indented in her chin. I might have been standing in her place, if my mother hadn't begged her parents for forgiveness. I'd have been put on a train with my tin trunk, off to earn my keep. Any idea of school would have been left far behind me, as distant as shorter skirts and plaits in my hair. Instead, I was here, setting down my silverware, the knives sadly thinned by Sukie's scouring. I was rising to my feet. It was time for our music lesson, and Miss White was to lead us.

❦

I took my seat in the eyrie, having followed the others up the stairs, up, higher, into the sky. Our chairs were arranged in two semi-circles around the piano, forming a crescent moon around our teacher. Beatrice, on the opposite side, cast me a meaningful glance and I shifted my focus firmly away from her and onto Miss White.

She asked Grace to take the stool at the piano, a good choice, since Grace played better than any of us. The girl stepped forward, though without looking at our teacher. She stared fixedly at an empty space a little to her left. It felt impertinent in an odd sort of way, but Miss White affected not to notice.

'We shall sing "Abide With Me",' she said, 'each taking a verse in turn. You shall begin, Sophia, then Amelia, and so forth around the group.'

Grace brought her hands down hard on the keys. It was the right note yet jarring, and she continued in the same way, correctly but heavily, laboured; resentful. Sophia began to sing. Her voice was fine and clear, and I must envy it, though I told myself her inflection was affected. *The darkness deepens; Lord with me abide.* The notes filled the room, as clear and as fragile as window glass.

Sophia stood as she should, clasped her hands as she should, breathed as she should. Still there was something wrong with the picture: she wasn't looking at our teacher either. The direction of her gaze was subtly wrong, as if the world had tilted. She too was staring at a blank space a little to the side of Miss White. Couldn't she see our teacher – or was she seeing someone else, standing just behind her? I peered, but there was nothing; unless there was something I couldn't see. With all the others staring like that, I almost felt there must be, though it couldn't be a ghost. Miss White was *alive*. Would Lucy's *shadow* appear at any moment and step towards us? But Lucy wasn't here. She must have been coddled after all, exempted from our lesson. Was that for her sake or Miss White's?

Miss White had noticed something was amiss. I could tell by the tiny frown nipping at the skin between her eyes.

Sophia's verse came to an end and Amelia took up the next. *Change and decay in all around I see . . . O Thou who changest not, abide with me.* Her voice was weaker and wavered a little, but her vision didn't. She focused intently on the empty space next to Miss White. They all did.

'Attend!' Miss White rapped the top of the piano with her knuckles and Grace stumbled over her notes, the sudden discordance making us jump. Sophia let out a little sound of mingled surprise and disdain, as if it was the teacher's behaviour that was odd; as if she were not as she should be.

'Next!' Miss White called out, not looking at them either but somewhere over their heads, gesturing towards Honoria. The girl reddened as she sang; the effort of dragging air into tight-corseted lungs, or guilt? Her voice hitched between the lines, each breath an effort, every word a question. She didn't shift her gaze, though. She was drawing strength from the others. I could feel it all around me, something passing between them. Or was it something else I felt – something they could see and I could not?

They were shunning Miss White. They were shaming her, and publicly, yet in such a way she couldn't say a word. They'd come up with this between them; they must have. It was their revenge, for – what? Miss White had done nothing wrong, nothing she didn't have to do. Now they were acting like the children they were. A memory: Daisy whispering in my ear, deciding that we'd spend the day parroting Tom's words or mimicking Archie's movements, fit to drive them mad. This was crueller, a nursery trick but effective still, lent power by their numbers and their innocent, implacable, lovely faces.

I didn't need to wonder which one of them had dreamed it up. I glared at Sophia as if the force of my look could kill, but she never felt it; she didn't falter. She'd already decided what she would see and what she wouldn't.

Honoria's turn ended and Fern's began. The younger girl smiled as she opened her mouth to sing the sweet, gentle words with glee. It almost seemed she would burst with it – she was trying not to laugh.

'Class dismissed!'

The words stunned the room, hanging in the air even as the music died away. Hadn't our lesson only just begun?

Miss White raked the room without meeting anyone's eyes, not even mine. For a moment no one moved. Then Sophia stood, leading the way, showing them what to do.

'Merci, Mademoiselle Blanc,' she chimed in a child's sing-song, the image of obedience, and the others echoed her. They curtseyed, but not to Miss White; they bobbed in the direction of the empty space next to her and we all filed out of the room and down the stairs. I waited for the inheld laughter to burst from them, but it didn't. No one said a word and I wondered if that was because I was there.

I followed them to Sophia's room and she turned to face us, her eyes shining, her smile wide with a job well done. 'Poor Ivy,' she said. 'You don't understand, do you? You don't *see*. But you will.'

She crouched by her bed and retrieved something from her cupboard. She held it up: the book she'd been crowing over, the one with the tattered green cover. There was nothing written there – only scraps of gold clinging to the spine where its title had been stamped, though I couldn't read it. Its unpleasant scent was stronger now. It smelled charred, as if the thing was smouldering in her hand.

Sophia didn't seem to notice, didn't grimace at its touch. 'As I told you, all of this has happened before.' She flipped it open and began to read. It was as we had heard it before, but this time she gave the teacher a name: not Mademoiselle Blanc or Miss White, but someone else entirely.

'A few weeks after Mademoiselle Sagée first arrived, singular reports began to circulate among the pupils.' She paused. 'You know this part. She took up a post at a school in Livonia. Then she was seen in two places at once, over and over, until they knew beyond doubt that something odd was happening.'

I refused to let her see the effect of her words on me. Anyway, I wasn't certain what I felt.

Sophia tossed her head. We were encouraged to read with lively emphasis, to better entertain our future families, and she did it well. I had to admire the performance as she went on.

'She happened to write on a blackboard,' she said. 'While she was doing so, and the young ladies were looking at her, to their consternation, they suddenly saw *two* Mademoiselle Sagées, the one by the side of the other. They were exactly alike; and they used the same gestures, only that the real person held a bit of chalk in her hand, and did actually write, while the double had no chalk, and only imitated the motion.

'You see?' She snapped the book closed. 'A shadow, standing at her side, copying her movements. All the girls in the book saw it. Every last one of them.'

'You saw *nothing*,' I snapped out. 'You all pretended. There was no one there, nothing at all.'

'Of course we did. We *knew* it was there. It may not have materialised, not this time, but eyes aren't the only way of seeing. There are other senses—'

'For shame, Sophia!'

'You'll see it too, Ivy, when you're granted the sight. You'll see everything. There's something wrong with her. We can all feel it. Lu did. She knew it was wicked. How else could it have hurt her with a single touch?'

'Lucy was hysterical. It was nothing to do with Miss White.'

'Nothing to do with her?' Sophia laughed. 'It *is* her, Ivy. You have to see that. Why else does it have her face? Why else would such a thing walk beside her – *abide* with her?'

There was a religious, even blasphemous, ring to her words, and I realised what she reminded me of: Reverend Aubrey on his dais, clutching his Bible in his outstretched hand, gesticulating with it to underline his words.

'She's getting stronger,' Sophia said. 'What will she do next? If that thing would attack Lu—'

The others murmured agreement. I looked from one to the next and saw the same expression in all their eyes. They were like statues ranged about her, or congregants at a sermon, hanging on every word, drinking them in, grateful to be told what to think, what to do.

'And she can go anywhere. She can reach any of us. She may have taken in Madame Dumont, but it's plain that Mademoiselle Blanc and Emélie Sagée are one and the same.'

Emélie – was that Sagée's Christian name? That was unfortunate; but incredulity burst from me. 'You really think that book was written about *her*? Look at it, Sophia! It must be years and years old. How old do you imagine Miss White to be?'

'It was published just four years ago. In 1860,' she said.

I scowled. Could the book have aged so quickly? It looked ancient.

'Anyway,' she went on, 'even if the story happened to be older still, even if Miss White were a hundred years old, do you really suppose that someone with her powers couldn't disguise her true age? She has a *double*, Ivy. She can send out a second image of herself to do what she likes, to go where she likes. Do you think she can't influence how she appears too?'

I could only shake my head. Had she inherited this madness from her mother – did she really imagine Emily to be a wizened old witch beneath her smooth skin and shining eyes? To be sending out a double, to do – what? I couldn't believe Sophia had said such things, and yet no one laughed. They went on staring at me as if I were the mad one. Almost as if they pitied me.

Lucy's hysteria must have spread, not to me, but to all of them. I'd felt it, hadn't I? Something shifting around the room, lending them strength, feeding their stories so that they hardened into certainty. The fiction was becoming real with each word whispered, every shriek and gasp and cry and rumour making it coalesce a little more. Had Sophia considered where this might lead? Her spectre was made of nothing but suggestion, but it could still take on life. Once loose, it would escape her control or anyone's. She would never be able to capture it again.

'And this is who you wish to befriend.' Sophia took up her earlier thread as if I'd never questioned it. 'You should reach towards those around you, Ivy. Your own kind, not that *creature*.'

She held out one hand, opening it in front of me palm upwards, as if she expected me to tell her fortune. My eyes opened wider. It was the hand that Miss White had caned, yet it wasn't as I thought I'd seen it, not at all. I had thought her palm reddened, but this was worse. Her skin was broken. The wound wept; it was inflamed, angry. She had been punished beyond my hopes after all. This must hurt her all of the time. There would be scars. She'd never forgive that – but then, she'd never forgiven our teacher anyway.

'Let me see the book,' I said softly. 'I want to see for myself what it says.'

She snatched the volume back and held it against her chest, wrapping both hands around it. She raised her chin, implacable. She would never let me see it, not now she knew I wanted to.

'This is not for your eyes,' she said. 'But I shall tell you something, Ivy, if only because it is my duty to offer my guidance where I may. Mademoiselle Blanc has a *Doppelgänger*. That is a German word meaning *double walker*, if you do not understand. Such things are a known phenomenon, and they are dangerous. They arise from their originator and tell of great misfortune. They are harbingers of death . . .'

'*No.*' The word burst from me, and I felt the molten heat of tears on my cheek. I brushed them away. I hadn't known I would cry; I couldn't contain all that I wished to say, and yet I could say none of it. It came to me that the others had fallen entirely calm, and they were glaring at me.

There were so many of them. The eyes multiplied around me were so certain and clear and very, very cold. I turned on my heel and walked away from them, so sure their laughter would follow me that I thought I heard it filling the air; but there was only the sound of my footsteps echoing around me as I went.

12

I didn't stop walking until I was outside, in the clear air. The sky was a uniform grey with no sign of the sun, no comfort in it. I started to walk, hoping no one would see me heading off without cape or gloves or hat.

I went past the stables and the gate that let into the walled garden. I didn't want to see the flowers, nor the horses, not today. I was going to a place that few knew of and no one suspected would be of any interest. For that reason it had never been forbidden to us, though if it had been, I'd have gone there anyway. I was a farm girl, after all. They thought me a hoyden; well, a hoyden I would be.

Here was the boundary of the school, separated from neighbouring farmland by a broken-down stone wall. In one place it had crumbled altogether, leaving a gap just wide enough to step through. Beyond, there was no clear path. The edge of the field was lush with long grass brightened with poppies like drops of blood amid the rest. Sometimes I came here to enjoy the air, quickened by shoots pushing through the soil or scented with recent rain. I'd watch the breeze playing in the leaves of distant trees, turning them from light to shadow and back again. I'd breathe in all that was natural and free and without rules and raise my face to the sky. Here I could be alone and myself and no one would see; no one would judge.

My skirts gathered grass seed and pollen as I strode into the damp weeds. I pushed further into the undergrowth until I stood at the edge of the crop, which was ripening nicely. If my father's barley had grown as fine as this, I'd still be at home. I ran my fingers through the silky spikes, smooth in one direction, prickly with tiny barbs in the other.

Then I realised it wasn't barley at all, but rye, cheaper stuff grown for fodder or to lend a little zest to a brewer's ale. Barley seeds grew singly along the ear, but rye seeds grew in pairs: two, where one should be.

I thought of what Sophia had said – *Your own kind* – and wanted to laugh. Could *her* kind tell one grain from another? But I didn't laugh. I stood there remembering each strange thing they'd said and wondering at it all. On the surface, Sophia appeared just as she should be, but beneath – what was she? How did she have such audacity? She could afford it, I supposed. And the wound on her hand must be fuelling her bitterness, bleeding malice and spite.

I looked down at my mussed clothing. This was no place for me to be, not any longer; but I longed for the home I had once so wished to escape. I longed for my sister.

Daisy would have known how to silence Sophia. She'd have known exactly what to say, what to do, just as she always had. I saw again the way she'd dragged me up the coffin steps outside the farmhouse and pushed me onto Mags's broad back. She always was the one to think up mad schemes, even though she was younger. But she always made sure I shared in everything too: the blame, yes, but also the freedom and the joy.

Why had she done it?

I knew why. She had thought she could help her sister become a lady.

It was the day of my grandparents' much-vaunted visit. We'd been told, over and again, what was expected of us: *Seen and not heard. Neat and tidy. Cleanliness is next to Godliness.* We were meant to impress them. Sweet girls to melt their hearts, to smooth the path back into their lives and their purse. My mother had hoped for more than that, of course. We'd heard her talking of it from our hiding place on the stairs: *Do you think they might take Archie? He needn't always stay on the farm. Think of what they could do for him . . .*

My sister's hands had shoved at my thighs, setting me straight on the horse's back. Mags was broad and stolid and slow. She smelled of hay and horse and dung. I'd grinned at Daisy. This was her big idea. She'd explained it all. We would impress our grandparents, but not as we'd been told; not as was planned. That had never been *our* plan anyway.

I saw again the way she had stooped to the cobbles, lifting stems of mucky straw, throwing them over me like rose petals scattered before a bride. The way she'd slapped Mags into motion. Why should our brothers have everything? We spent our days running around after them, darning their socks, doing their errands, and the boys never even noticed us unless they wanted something.

My grandparents were standing at the gate, dark and neat in their city woollens. Their faces grew larger as Mags clopped towards them. So did their eyes. Soon they were as big and round as their open mouths, as big as dinner plates, and how we laughed, Daisy and I. We couldn't have foreseen what would happen. Daisy never imagined the success of her scheme, nor the speed with which they would decide I was wild, wicked and worse: unacceptable. The way they would take me away, but not Daisy – dividing what should never be divided, turning me into something alone. One, where two should have been.

They'd had to take me in hand. Remove me from an environment that was too wild and too free and teach me to be a stranger to my family. They never were content with the results, and after a few years they tired of the effort and sent me here. They thought the school would finish what they'd started.

If they could see me standing in the middle of this field, disregarding all the constraints that Madame Dumont had tried to instil and covered in grass seed, they'd have been altogether disappointed.

Still, I did not turn to leave; I craved just a little longer. The land was turning a deep gold as the sky darkened towards evening. The poppies had taken on a deeper shade, that of drying blood, and an image came: a figure standing in the corner of a room, its face in shadow, its expression hidden from me. *Mademoiselle Blanc*, I thought. Or was it Emily White? I shook my head, reminding myself that there was no difference, they were one and the same and always would be, and that none of this was her fault – was it?

The field left behind me at last, I moved quietly back along the corridor, thankfully meeting no one who might ask where I had been. As I went, though, I heard an odd sound: a low and rhythmic clicking, like that made by a tiny but interminable clock. *Tick . . . tick . . . tick . . .*

And I saw that one of the classroom doors stood open. I paused, waited. There was no sound other than that odd ticking and I crept towards it, then peered in. It was the room where we learned our patchwork history and geography. A kind of premonition growing upon me, I stepped inside and saw the zoetrope spinning on its stand.

Here was the source of the sound, and yet how could it be? Had someone come in just ahead of me and, thinking it a fine jest, hidden themselves? But there was nowhere to hide. The room was empty, as if someone had set the wheel of life spinning and then simply vanished.

Suddenly, I felt cold. Lucy's scream seemed to hang in the air around me. And yet a longing grew upon me to see which image had been placed within the drum. I stepped closer and peered through one of the slits carved into the circumference.

Before my eyes was a little girl, or perhaps a young woman. She held a single rosebud in her hands. As I watched she gave a curtsey and the flower bloomed, opening into a ripe crimson rose before shrinking into a bud once more. The zoetrope clicked as it went, parcelling out its seconds, the *tick-tick-tick* hurling the girl into her future. The rose swelled, turning a deeper, richer crimson, then appeared once more as a bud. Of course, the movement wasn't entirely natural. I didn't quite like it, though I couldn't have said why. I told myself that it was only because she wasn't really one girl, but many; a whole series of little printed pictures, almost but not entirely the same.

Without thinking, I reached out and placed my fingertips against the drum. Its spinning slowed and the illusion of movement began to break apart. The girl separated, becoming not one, not alone, but many once more.

All I could think of was something Miss Morrison had told us once: that the zoetrope was originally called a *daedalum*. It was named for Daedalus of classical myth, not because he invented such a thing, but because he was said to be able to sculpt figures so very lifelike they could move. Their possessors were not content with that, of course, since they could leave their pedestals and walk away. In order to admire and enjoy them, they had to chain their statues to the wall.

Everything was quite still. The zoetrope did not begin spinning again of its own accord, though I half expected it to. I went on staring down into the drum and realised it reminded me of something else – not a story, but something closer still. Looming walls that approximated a circle. Tall windows slashed into them. And inside: young girls blossoming into womanhood, yet always following in the steps allotted to them, doing what Society deemed proper and nothing more; animated by nothing but the semblance of life. Carven statues all, there to be seen and admired and chained to the wall.

The zoetrope was an image of Fulford itself. If I could stand over the building in just such a way, I'd be peering into the eyrie.

I pictured us filing into the room below me, all doing as we should, taking the seats set out for us, our faces like little flowers peeking back at me. And I suddenly couldn't bear it. I turned and, dreading the sound of ticking at my back – the sound of time passing, though not for me, not here – I fled to the familiar surroundings of my room.

The others were there already. They barely looked up when I walked in; they didn't ask any questions, and I was glad of that. Matilda was brushing bandoline out of her hair, a white cloth spread over her shoulders, her lips moving softly as she counted to one hundred. Honoria was polishing her nails with a little leather buffer while Fern soaked her fingertips in a bowl of elderflower water. Frances tapped cold cream into her cheeks, making a sound unpleasantly like ticking as they all carried out the same actions they would do again tomorrow, and the next day, and the next . . .

I buried my thoughts in the shedding of layers of outer clothes and petticoats and stockings, and pulled my voluminous nightgown over my head. I got into bed and dragged the blanket and top-sheet over me. I told myself that what I'd seen hadn't been so very strange. Someone really had been in the classroom just before me. They had spun the zoetrope before they left, and it surely wasn't odd if it had kept on spinning until I happened along. It was something perfectly ordinary that had been made, by circumstance, to feel as if it were not.

I tried to put it from me, as the others made their own preparations for bed. But I could not help thinking of Emily White; though for some reason I thought of her name accented in the French way. *Emélie.* Where had she come from? And could she really appear in two places at once? *Had* she?

I shook the notions away. There must be a natural explanation for that too. What if there was someone here who simply looked like her? Miss White might have a beloved sister, just like Daisy – someone she couldn't bear to be parted from. I pictured her, giving this shadow-sister Emily's features, her figure, her eyes. She stood at her side, mimicking her movements, just like tiny figures in a zoetrope. Perhaps they were even twins. Yes: twins, twined about each other, even if they had few means and only one of them had been able to find a paid position. They'd have been desperate to stay together, and so they'd done it; Emily had cleaved to her sister, refusing to let her go. She had done what I couldn't do, or failed to do; she'd kept her sister close. And so she brought her here, keeping her near but always a secret . . .

It was a dream of an image and I wished I could believe in it. Like a shadow dissolving before the light, like my own sister's face, it faded. A sister would have been found. The maids would have discovered her. Or she'd have kept herself better hidden altogether; she wouldn't have been caught standing in the corner of a room or wandering among the roses.

It's a ghost . . . It's a ghost of her.

I saw her again, standing in the entrance hall, dripping to the parquet; her hair a damp rope, her face pale, her eyes cast into darkness. I pushed my blanket away as if it were a shroud, smothering and heavy, weighting me into a grave. I felt cold right through. Emily was young and vibrant and alive. She was *here*. She'd touched my arm. She'd smiled at me and I had lived in that smile, just for a time. She couldn't simply stop, couldn't vanish – but Daisy's face rose before me, as if to give the lie to my thoughts.

I peered into the corners of the room, where the shadows lay deepest. I half expected a figure to be standing there, darkness spooling from its heart, like paint spiralling from a brush in a jar of water. I fervently wished it away.

A new thought came to me: if Miss White truly had a double, why wasn't she aware of it? She hadn't even been the one to see it. It was others who'd done that. Miss White didn't seem conscious of any such thing; she hadn't listened to any of the stories.

But if it hadn't come here for her, the one whose face it had borrowed – of whose *great misfortune*, whose *death*, had it come to tell?

13

When I awoke, the dread that I'd felt during the night hadn't so much vanished as retreated, seeping into the ragged wallpaper, the crumbling cornicing, the cold floorboards under my feet. All of them seemed to whisper that something was going to happen – but what? Surely nothing could, not here. The whole place was designed to prevent it. This was the result of Sophia's silly stories. I shouldn't have listened; I should be more rational.

We began the day with morning prayers. We took our places in the eyrie, surrounded by an expanse of emptiness where the shadows of the past danced their fading waltzes. Our teachers were a sombre line, their white lace caps like antimacassars ranged along the back of a seat. The servants were ranked behind us, a presence felt yet invisible, just as Madame Dumont said servants should be. Our voices combined in a soft murmur, the words falling from our lips without attention, a ritual we knew a little too well. And all the time, I heard a small sound beneath them, coming from everywhere or nowhere: *tick . . . tick . . . tick . . .*

We prayed for God's help to be good.

We prayed for the Lord's light to be revealed to us.

We prayed for the strength to love one another.

Madame Dumont stepped forward, bowing her head then shaking her shoulders, as if to cast off the funereal air. She said it was her pleasure to announce that something special was going to happen. There was to be a fete in Snaithby Dun, the nearest town, and since it would be an opportunity to show everyone what well-conducted and irreproachable young ladies we were becoming, we were to have the treat of an outing.

All around me gasps were gasped and glances exchanged, bright eyes shining their pleasure. I felt separate from any of it. I couldn't bring myself to be glad. I glanced at the tall windows as a cloud slipped past; did the world seem to be spinning?

Madame Dumont smiled, looking from one face to the next, drinking in our gratitude. She said that some of us could even take the carriage, and a faint pulse of interest threaded my veins. I'd be able to see if the horses moved in step, a perfectly matching pair once more. Miss White could take the carriage too. The others would be reminded of her kindness to Captain. It would be a new day, a happy day, and they might reconsider their silly stories; they might decide to like her after all. And we could all process through Snaithby Dun together, Miss White arm in arm with each of the girls in turn, at the heart of us as we walked and talked and laughed.

I hurried along the corridors after our assembly, not caring to be ladylike, only wanting to see Miss White ahead of our next lesson. As I'd hoped, she arrived before the rest of the class. She looked surprised when she saw me there, catching my breath.

There were lines of tension about her lips. I was sure they hadn't been there before and I imagined them sinking into her, deepening into creases and folds. I wished I could reach out and smooth them away.

'Miss White, may I speak to you? I must tell you—'

'What is it, Ivy? I have a class at any moment.'

'I know. But you asked me – before, you asked if I could tell you anything. About the other girls. To make some confidences. I wanted you to know that anything you require of me – well, I would be happy—'

'Well, now!' She gave the kind of indulgent smile that might be bestowed on an infant, dismissing my words, or perhaps the memory. 'That would be entirely improper.'

I opened my mouth and closed it again. I was sure I hadn't misunderstood her. *What do they say of me?* Those were her words, though I could understand if she'd decided she should not have spoken them. I said again, 'I would tell you everything.' For she had to know the things they said about her, about the book and the doppelgänger and what it meant. Would I tell her that too?

'Everything?' she exclaimed, mock-scandalised. 'Why, you are a dear little thing. Whatever could there be to tell? Schoolgirl tattle? I assure you, I have no need to hear it, Ivy. Now, I must ready the class.'

I could only watch as she stepped past me and went inside. I should have planned this better. I should have made her listen. Of course it wasn't the place of a teacher to be guided by her pupil, or to make a friend of me – but still, I *was* her friend. The circumstances weren't ordinary, so why should we be?

The others were in the corridor, making their way towards me. There was nothing I could do other than take my seat with the rest. Miss White was adjusting the placement of a book on her desk: a German dictionary. She picked up a piece of chalk.

No, I thought. *Not this.* What would the others say?

To their consternation, they suddenly saw two Mademoiselle Sagées . . . They were exactly alike; and they used the same gestures, only that the real person held a bit of chalk in her hand, and did actually write, while the double had no chalk, and only imitated the motion . . .

Miss White turned to the blackboard and began tapping and scraping, spelling out the vocabulary we must write into our copybooks.

Tanzen – dancing

Singen – singing

Klavier – piano

Accomplishments all, to embellish the charms of any young lady whose father was of a certain income. She hadn't written the German word for painting, I realised, and I tried to think of it, but all that came to me was—

Doppelgänger

Doppelgänger

Doppelgänger

I realised that Miss White had stopped writing. She stood before us with her back turned and her hand raised, entirely motionless.

Amelia and Beatrice, seated in front of me, exchanged glances. We weren't permitted to speak unless we were called upon, but Sophia, a row further forward, shifted in her chair and I felt the energy in the room shift too, becoming bolder, more potent. Amelia smothered a grin; Sophia put up her hand.

Miss White didn't turn. She didn't even twitch. She might have been a carven statue, so very like the life. Would she simply walk away from us?

Sophia called out, seemingly without a care, 'Have you ever been to Livonia, Mademoiselle Blanc?'

Livonia. Miss White wouldn't understand the significance of the question, though she must feel the impertinence of Sophia asking it – but our teacher didn't move. Then she did, a tottering step taking her to the desk, which she leaned upon. She opened her lips, but she had no voice; it took a long moment before she could whisper, '*Faites attention.*'

A plea, not a command. French, not German.

A titter ran about the room, light and fleeting, before dissolving.

Miss White raised her hand. The movement was languorous, almost as if she were sleepwalking. She still held her stub of chalk. Did she mean to write on the air? If she did, would words appear, words we couldn't utter or understand?

Then Amelia pointed towards the window and said, 'Look!'

Heads swivelled at her command. Sophia half rose. 'It's here,' she announced. 'It must be. Can't you feel it? It must be here somewhere.'

Miss White didn't countermand her. She didn't seem aware of it as Sophia left her seat and went to the window. Seeing that, the others were released; they followed Sophia.

Miss White did not speak. She only leaned more heavily on her desk, her head drooping as if at any moment she might fall asleep.

A voice: Sophia's, tight with triumph. 'I *told* you.'

Slowly, I stood. I too was drawn to the window, as if under a spell. I knew that something must happen, *had* to happen, and at once I saw what they saw. A figure stood in the yard, staring up at us. I could only see a little of her face even though her head was tilted back, because of the hood of her cape – one I recognised. I felt again its brushed surface, the shape of her in its folds. It was Miss White's cape.

The figure held an armful of plucked flowers. Suddenly their scent was all around me: heavy, cloying, dizzying. White lilies for a funeral, the same as those Miss White had chosen for herself, the ones she'd gathered for our art lesson. A wave of disorientation washed over me. Had time spun backwards?

But this was no illusion, no glimpse into another time. It surely wasn't a spirit or a ghost. Her shadow stretched across the ground.

Doppelgänger

Doppelgänger

Doppelgänger

I didn't want to look away but I returned my gaze to the teacher in front of us. I could hardly see her face either, since it was downturned, but her cheeks were pale. White. *Blanc.* Was she in some kind of trance? Was that because she was so caught up in the effort of appearing in two places at once – not just where she had to be, with these nasty, gossiping girls, but also out there, where she wished to be, in the garden and the clean air?

I told myself that when I looked again, the figure holding the flowers would be gone. And yet I took a deep breath and turned my head and it didn't vanish. It didn't even move. Miss White had become the shadow – nothing but a shape in the corner of my eye, dark, *there*. I turned to her again. She didn't vanish either – of course she didn't. She was *real*. It was simply that there were two of her: two, where one should be.

Grace let out a little cry. Beatrice was praying as she had in the eyrie, clasping her hands, as if she'd done some terrible sin and must atone.

Miss White raised her head, though only a little; she remained suspended over her desk, as if caught in some place between sleeping and waking, life and death. I wanted to go to her. I wished to shake her out of wherever she was, to restore the light to her eyes. To have her look at me and know me. If only she'd listened to me . . .

Sophia called out, 'She's leaving. Look!'

She was right. Outside, the figure was walking away from us. We could see nothing but the back of her cape, though her arms were still laden with those heavy, sweet-smelling, somnolent flowers. *Beautiful for a day.* As we watched, she dropped one of them to the ground. After a few more steps, another. Funeral flowers.

A harbinger of death.

She was going towards the stables and from somewhere beyond her, a whinny rang out. It sounded almost afraid, unless it were only that everything seemed tainted by our own fears, but at once Sophia said, 'Hear that? They *know*. Dumb beasts can sense things. Unnatural things.'

Her words were almost like Gadling's. They were nonsense – they couldn't be true. But I couldn't help thinking the horse had sounded just like Captain – who was *dead*. He'd died when Miss White came here. Death had spread its wings over the school from the moment she arrived.

I shook the wild thoughts away. I wasn't like the others; I didn't think like this. I'd been with our teacher more than any of them and I wasn't dead; I was *here*. I'd sat at her side and painted with her. She was alive. She loved the things I loved and she'd been kind to Captain when I couldn't. I'd looked sidelong at the curve of her cheek and thought about the day when I might tell her about the farm, about Daisy, about everything, and known it would be safe in her hands. She wasn't wicked, wasn't cruel. She wasn't any of the things they painted her as. She wasn't Mademoiselle Blanc or Emélie Sagée. She wasn't even Miss White, not to me: she was Emily. She had given me her true name, like a gift.

I found I could move once more. I hurried to her side and leaned over her, reaching for her, hesitating only a moment before I touched her. Nothing happened to me. I didn't sink to the floor or lose my senses. There was only the soft touch of her simple cotton dress as I wrapped my hand around her shoulder. Speaking softly, I asked, 'Are you quite well?'

She gave no sign of hearing me. She hardly gave a sign of being alive – but I felt the swell of breath under my fingers, the warmth of living flesh.

Behind me, Sophia said, 'It's gone.' And suddenly, Emily stirred. She rose to her feet. She raised her head and saw me, though there was no recognition in her eyes. She shivered, then restored her expression to her habitual calm, coming back to herself, stronger by the moment.

'Class – sit down!' This time her command was firm and we scurried to our places as she stood up straight again; herself again. 'I felt unwell for a moment, nothing more. The remnant of a little chill from my journey here.'

That would be something I could understand, although she had hitherto betrayed no sign of it, and I did not suppose she'd have put us in mind of her damp clothes and hair if she did not still feel weakened. But as if nothing had happened, she turned to the blackboard. She still held her stick of chalk and she raised her arm and began to write, new words appearing vigorously and quickly, as if she could overwrite our behaviour; as if they could make us forget.

I closed my eyes, listening to the click and scrape of chalk. It sounded almost like something else, another sound, that slowly took on distinctness in my mind: the *tick-tick-tick* of the zoetrope. I pictured a little figure within it, a young lady moving, spinning, dancing: *Tanzen, Singen, Klavier*, each step foretold, decided upon, never permitted a moment's deviation.

When I opened my eyes, Miss White was gazing directly at me. She showed no annoyance, only curiosity, and I realised I had raised my hand, as if I too were about to write on the air; or as if I were about to reach out for her and grasp her shoulder again. I roused myself and let it fall, and the moment passed. The seconds ticked on; she opened her lips to speak, and my reverie was subsumed in the new vocabulary we must learn.

14

The flowers weren't in the yard where I had seen them fall. That was hardly a surprise. I hadn't been able to sneak out of the school for hours, but still I stared down at the grit and sniffed the air. There wasn't a trace of their scent, but of course there wouldn't be. It didn't mean they were never there. Simons the gardener might have come along and cleared them away. Maybe Gadling had.

Turning to look up at the folly, I took a few steps backwards. Was this where she'd stood? What had she been staring at? I couldn't see through the windows. There was only the blank sky reflected back at me. I shivered and reached to pull my cape more tightly around me – but I wasn't wearing a cape. I'd only borrowed that – and I frowned. Was that what someone else had done? Taken Miss White's cape, picked the flowers she had chosen, positioned herself outside her classroom? Would they stoop to that?

Tilting back my head, I stared at those shining windows. I could read no answers in them and I sighed. From here, the folly's curved walls made it look more than ever like the drum of a zoetrope. And the school had the same purpose as a zoetrope, didn't it? It was designed to spin all the girls into one thing: the image of a perfect wife and mother, the angel of the hearth, all of us almost but not quite the same. It contained us within its walls for others to admire and approve. It laid out the steps that we must take. It made us look as if we were alive, when all we did was move in endless repetitive circles . . .

My grandfather had taken great pains to impress upon me the horror of not following the prescribed path. He had told me of the things I should fear: marrying an indolent man, a drunken man or an ungodly man. Worse: not to be married at all. Those were the terrors he understood. To be of a certain age and a certain class and alone – I'd be good for nothing then. The best I could hope for was that one of my brothers would take me in and allow me to tend his children. Or I might have to become a governess, fated forever to live in a world between: above the servants, beneath the family, unfit for the society of anyone. Always alone, nothing more than Ivy. *I*.

No: we must all learn our steps. And yet here, in the very grounds of the school, something else had come to us, or perhaps *someone* else. For here was a mystery that lay outside the things we had been taught. Not everyone here was chained to the wall, for it seemed that one had broken free: a figure who looked like Miss White, moved like her, yet wasn't her; one who wasn't constrained, who wasn't bound to follow the rules.

Of course, I was outside it too, at this moment. I was out of place and I felt a certain strength rising from that. I could almost hear Madame Dumont lecturing us: *Young ladies should have no desire to wander about, just as if they were independent creatures* . . .

Well, perhaps one independent creature should seek out another. And so I went to see Miss White again.

☙

Emily answered my knock so promptly, she might have been waiting for me. I had hardly stepped inside the room before the words burst from me. 'I wanted to apologise,' I said, 'for the behaviour—'

'Why?' She sounded as if she knew what I meant and at the same time didn't know why I meant it.

'They are trying to cause some mischief.' I paused, feeling like a child tattling on a naughty sibling. What must she think? My words weren't enough. The tale was too mad for my telling. I was trying to cling to reason when reason had been left far behind.

She tilted her head, quizzical. 'I think I know that already, Ivy,' she said.

I didn't know where to look. It was something about the way her eyes met mine, full of gentleness – of understanding. She didn't look at me as the others did and yet I was everything that I became in their presence: awkward, clumsy, inferior. Miss White would have done better to make a friend of Beatrice, I thought, or Amelia, or Grace; one of them might have been able to change the other girls' minds. None of this would have happened.

'We should paint,' Emily said, and she caught my eye again, and this time she smiled.

And so we took our seats and uncovered our paintings. We

had little time left, I saw; the wildflowers in their jug had begun to soften. They weren't fully wilted but the stems were less sturdy, the petals not so bright. We must hurry and finish before they died. I breathed in the scent of pigments, of paper, of petals just beginning to rot, and raised my brush.

'Really consider the forms, Ivy,' Miss White said. 'Try to sharpen the sense of their structure, the way the leaves grow from the stem, how the petals unfold. Think about how they *work*. Miss Peel sometimes gives botany lessons, does she not? Use them. Try to understand what it is you see before you begin.'

I gazed at our subject, searching for what she meant, and remembered what she'd said to me last time about perfection. I marked the small rip at the edge of a leaf then added a suspicion of brown to the base of a petal. She was right: imperfections made the image seem more real, more lifelike. A soft murmur told me she saw and approved.

We went on working side by side, and I didn't look at her, though I was conscious of her in every moment, her wrist moving across the page before she rose to wash her brush clean. It should have been easier to tell her all that I wished without looking at her, without seeing the expression in her eyes, and yet I kept opening my lips to begin only to close them once more. It wasn't just the oddity of what I had to say; I didn't want to break the moment. It was such easy companionship, almost sisterly, though I couldn't allow myself to admit that hope, not now, and pushed the thought away.

Yet the shadows in the corners of the room were darkening, and I knew I had to begin somehow. 'Miss White, the others are saying something very peculiar.'

There was silence at my side. I opened my mouth and the rest flooded out. 'They seem to think they've discovered proof that you had another existence – another life – one that no one could have imagined. They say you were in another school before this, and that untoward things happened there, that you were accused of – things. So you came here to leave it all behind, but it has followed you—'

Emily dropped her brush. I turned to see her eyes wide and unblinking and filled with horror. In the next moment she gathered herself, stooped and recovered the brush; then she fussed with her skirts as if to compose herself, or hide her discomfiture. 'Is that – really, Ivy? What odd ideas you have, to be sure.'

'They think—' I had to tell her everything. I had to say the word I didn't want to say, the one that might make it real: *Doppelgänger.*

'Enough.' She spoke firmly, although the colour had left her cheeks. She looked less like herself and more like a teacher, stern and distant, who wouldn't stand for idle chatter. 'Girls will have their pranks. I am perfectly well equipped to deal with them. And I *shall* deal with them as I see fit, Miss Ivy; this needn't concern you.'

Miss Ivy? In a moment, I was transported back to my grandparents' house. My grandmother was leaning over me, reaching out with her ruler; I'd spilled ink on my fingers, or misspelled something, or added the figures and reached the wrong answer. Quickly, I withdrew my hand, before she could rap my knuckles. But of course, it wasn't *her* . . .

I blinked back tears. My teacher had dismissed me with that *Miss Ivy.* She'd turned me into what the others all made of me; she hadn't seen the things I wished her to see.

'Ivy?'

I tried to focus. There was a shadow standing over me, leaning in, close to my face, and I started.

'Ivy, I told you, it's all right. You don't need to think of such things. *You* don't need to take care of *me*.'

She had changed again, becoming herself again, Emily, who stood not as a teacher but as a friend to me. She peered anxiously into my face and I forced myself to smile up at her. She made me feel that it would be all right. Those things I had come here to speak of – all the mad stories – seemed as distant and unreal as a fairy tale when she was standing in front of me.

Her returning smile told me that she wasn't dismissing me. She was only telling me it would be all right, that she would see to everything. *She* was protecting *me*, I realised. It wasn't that Emily didn't want to listen, or didn't believe a word I said. She only wanted to shield me from the others' prying eyes and nasty tricks, and my eyes welled with tears.

'Perhaps we should finish there.' She stood back, shifting to stand at my shoulder. 'You're improving, I think. You've done some lovely work today, Ivy.'

Ivy once more. Not *Miss Ivy*, spoken with that horrid formality. She gestured towards my picture, following the path my brush had taken. She was right, it did look better: the flowers stood out in sharp relief. The shapely white rose almost appeared like the real one sitting in its vase in front of us. The *originator*, I thought, but pushed that word away.

As I moved to leave, I looked at her picture, ready to make a complimentary remark – and paused. How long had we been working? Yet there was nothing different. Her painting didn't

A . J . E L W O O D

seem to have progressed at all and I leaned in closer. There
wasn't even the lingering glisten of moisture on the paper, and
an image rose: Miss White standing before a blackboard, her
hand skipping and jumping as she wrote; and *another* Miss White
standing beside her, a shadow-figure that held up her arm as she
did, moving as she did, forming the shapes of letters and words
and sentences as she did, yet nothing appearing there.

But Miss White was here in front of me. If I stretched out my
hand, I could touch her. What would I feel? Soft skin, delicate bones,
the tender give of her flesh – or something else, something that was
too giving, *too* soft, my fingers sinking into her as into the fog?

Emily reached out and grasped my arm. 'Are you really all
right, Ivy?'

I looked down at her fingers – solid, corporeal, wrapped
about my flesh. I assured her that yes, I was quite well. And I *was*.
Sophia's words were insidious, that was all. They took on shapes
in the minds of anyone who would listen, solidifying, assuming
form even as she tried to turn Miss White into a ghost.

But I wouldn't listen.

Of course Miss White had been too preoccupied to paint.
She'd been taken up with helping me, watching me, offering her
advice. I felt nothing but gratitude as I smiled up at her. She was
my friend. She was *Emily*. I could see that plainly and soon the
others would too. And tomorrow, *tomorrow*, I needn't be afraid of
the other girls' silly notions. Even Sophia must put them aside,
for they wouldn't risk anything to prevent the outing they had so
longed for: it was the day we would go to the fete.

15

Clouds greyed the sky, but we knew it wouldn't rain. It wouldn't dare. The sense of holiday would keep it at bay even if our glances didn't. Our best day-dresses were brushed and ready, picked out the moment the outing was announced. The girls had long since decided the important questions of which hats and ribbons and feathers to wear, with seemingly endless discussion, and for once I hadn't minded it. Even the teachers had lent their advice. We didn't wear uniforms at Fulford; making ourselves appealing through dress was as important as any other lesson.

We donned the many layers required to make young ladies respectable, ensuring that the air couldn't touch our skin, that we could scarcely draw breath in our corsets, that no one could possibly suspect we possessed ankles or legs. Garment after garment added to the weight. My skirt was my most flounced and cumbersome, my crinoline a cage for a bird. Daisy would have crushed or torn or muddied everything on purpose; she'd never have allowed herself to be so constrained. She'd never had to learn that the more we grew, the more we must be held in.

The others seemed to welcome each additional weight they must carry, their excitement growing with each layer until finally we were ready. Then Frances and Matilda said we must see if the girls in Sophia's room were ready too. I sighed inwardly, though they seemed inclined to include me, at least today, and so I went with them.

'Do you think there'll be amusements?' Ruth called out when she saw us in the doorway, her cheeks flushed at the thought.

Naturally, we were certain there would be; lots of them.

'Young men would be better,' Amelia joked, and we all laughed. I couldn't help it; the spirit of the day was contagious. Perhaps, today, we'd all get along. We'd forget what had gone before and never think of it again.

'What do *you* wish for, Ivy?'

I was surprised by the question, which came from Beatrice. She was a little behind the others in her preparations, only now pulling on her stockings. I bit back a sarcastic response – something about not having enough mirrors for everyone, perhaps – but found I had no answer. I didn't know what I was looking forward to other than escaping Fulford for a day, but I said, 'A ride in the carriage,' and realised it was true. I'd be able to see the horses again. Furthermore, I'd see Emily with the horses. She might even stroke them – and nothing would happen, nothing *unnatural*, and Sophia would have to admit that her words about dumb beasts had been ridiculous.

'Well, we can't all ride,' Beatrice said. 'Are you sure of a seat? Some of us must walk, you know, if it isn't to take all day.

Mademoiselle Blanc offered to accompany the walking party, though, so I don't suppose anyone will jump at that.'

She sniggered and my smile faded. I should have thought of this. Of course Emily would have offered to shoulder the more onerous task; she was new, after all. But footsteps sounded at my back and everyone made themselves busy grasping reticules and gloves. I turned and saw Miss White. She'd come to chivvy us along and she smiled around the room, but something in her expression told me that she'd heard. Mortification crept over me. Would she think I'd been gossiping about her with the rest?

She looked sombre next to our bright colours, a mourner at a feast. Her usual plain dark dress was fastened to her throat, her hair tucked out of sight under a bonnet rather than a more seasonal trimmed straw hat. Still she smiled sweetly. 'Girls, if you are quite ready? Those who are, go downstairs and assemble by the turning circle. The carriage is waiting.'

The girls rustled past her, thanking her or saying good-day before moving off down the corridor, smothering laughter as they went. I went to follow them, and Emily affected not to notice me – or perhaps it was only that she'd seen Beatrice. The girl had pulled on her dress but was fumbling over the buttons, even though they ran down the front of the bodice and should be simple enough. Haste was making her clumsy.

'Be still, Beatrice, why don't you?' I heard as I left. 'Stand before the mirror there and I'll help you.'

So I left her, following the others down the stairs to the front door where Madame Dumont awaited. And there was the carriage, two chestnut horses stamping in their harnesses, with matching blazes; one real, one painted. They looked so alike I could only recognise Bard by the way he tossed his head, frothing at the mouth, already fretful. The other was motionless save a twitch that rippled one gleaming shoulder. Gadling stood by, not troubling to hold them. He was pinch-lipped and sour, as was his way when in the presence of people rather than beasts.

'Into the carriage, girls.' Madame Dumont clapped her hands. 'Now, where is Madame Monette? She is to accompany you.'

Gadling touched his cap and went to open the door for us. I opened my mouth to say I'd walk, I'd much prefer it, but at that moment Miss White rushed from the door, so discomposed I never spoke the words.

'Madame Dumont, you are needed!' she said. 'There has been a – an incident. Beatrice has fainted.'

Sophia, next to me, put her gloved hand to her mouth, a theatrical gesture. She ran her gaze over Miss White, lowering her head so that I couldn't see her expression. An image came to me: Lucy, staring at Miss White as she reached for her shoulder; then dropping to the floor, the life suddenly gone from her limbs.

'Where is she?' asked Madame Dumont. 'You left her alone?'

'I did, Madame, though only for a moment. There was no one else, and I had to fetch someone. I thought it best to find you at once.'

Madame Dumont sighed, more with annoyance than concern, and she turned to Gadling. 'It seems we cannot wait. You should set off directly – take these girls to Madame Pelletier. She will meet you by the buttercross. Quick as you like, then return for the rest.'

I found myself crammed into the carriage, my hand briefly in Gadling's as he helped me up the step. Was it my imagination that he squeezed a little too tightly? Ruth sat next to me and we fumbled to arrange the hoops of our skirts. Sophia, opposite, gave a discreet little bounce to arrange the back of her crinoline, something I'd never caught the trick of, though Amelia, next to her, reached around to grasp the topmost hoop of hers. A sharp whistle from without stirred the horses into motion. And just like that, I left Miss White behind.

We faced forward once more, Sophia and I doing our best not to look at each other. Despite its outward polish, the carriage was old and creaked and smelled of mildew. Gravel spat from the wheels, striking the underside of the carriage, and Sophia grimaced as we jolted onto the unmade track. She reached out to steady herself with one gloved hand, but there was nothing to hold onto but each other and in that moment no one cared for her. Everyone began to exclaim at once: 'Whatever happened?' and 'What on earth could be wrong?' and 'Did Bea say she was ill?'

'She was so looking forward to this,' Ruth added, as if that should have prevented anything from happening to her.

'She simply fainted,' I said. 'Perhaps it was the rushing about. She should have been ready earlier.' If she'd been in my room, she might have been, I thought but didn't say. I would have helped her. Miss White needn't have offered to fasten her dress; we could all have walked together.

'Nonsense,' Sophia snapped. 'She was quite well before Mademoiselle Blanc entered the room. She didn't feel ill in the slightest. All of us saw her.'

'We don't know that,' I said. 'She might have felt ill all morning but said nothing in case it meant she couldn't go.'

Sophia tossed her head as if I was being unreasonable. 'She felt perfectly all right.'

There was nothing to be said to that, nothing that wouldn't take us full circle, and so I remained silent.

'We shall no doubt see her soon. When the carriage goes back again,' said Ruth.

Sophia pulled a face as if to say that, since Beatrice had been left to Mademoiselle Blanc's ministrations, the girl would likely be dead in a ditch by now. Then she looked at me. 'Well, this *is* an adventure,' she said. 'It is fortunate you are with us, Ivy, since we may need you to translate.'

Translate? We were hardly likely to encounter French or German today, and if we did, she was more proficient than I. But it was clear that she meant some insult by it, so I didn't speak.

'Where *are* you from exactly, Ivy?' Sophia went on. 'A grandfather in trade in Sheffield, was it? Or was it somewhere else – somewhere a little more quaint? You will be able to guide us all admirably amid the farm folk, I am certain.' Her accent broadened as she went on. 'Aye, thee can 'elp us, since we shull all 'ave ter learn it.'

I felt my cheeks turning slowly red. I'd tried so hard to hide any trace of my father's speech in my own, but she'd heard it anyway – of course she had. I suddenly didn't know what to do with my hands, so clean and neat in their white cotton gloves they might hardly have belonged to me. When I pictured my hands they had rough skin, dirty nails, calluses on the palms. Sophia had managed to turn me into something clumsy again, ungainly, coarse; unacceptable. Alone. She had reduced me to what I truly was and I hated her for it. I wished Daisy was here. My sister never would have stood for it. She'd have scratched Sophia's eyes out like a spitting cat, and I would have laughed.

Amelia giggled. 'Have a care, Sophia. Your father won't like it if you go home speaking like that.'

Sophia snorted. 'Then he shouldn't have sent me here. Of course, he imagined I'd find good influences at the seminary – that I'd be mingling with my betters, making advantageous connections. Can you imagine?'

Amelia wrinkled her nose – Sophia's words were hardly complimentary to any of them – but she only asked, 'Why *were* you sent here, Sophia?'

And I realised that I didn't know. Sophia simply *was*. I knew why the others had come here rather than be educated at home by a governess, as most young ladies were. Beatrice was banished by a father who couldn't bear to look at her. Amelia's mother was taken up with a new baby, and thought her eldest daughter more hindrance than help. Ruth's father, a widower, had gone to India with his regiment. I was here to be tamed of course, and we all thought that Lucy had followed her cousin, but what of Sophia? She had sisters, we knew that much, though I didn't think they'd been sent to Fulford. With yet another female to make arrangements for, I'd supposed she needed some extra polish to enhance her prospects. Many parents envisaged their daughters rubbing shoulders with their social betters at a seminary, as she'd hinted.

But Sophia only gave a heavy sigh and stared down at her hands. Eventually she said, 'It *was* somewhat remarkable, one might say.'

I rolled my eyes at that – what about Sophia did she *not* think remarkable? – though she didn't seem to notice.

'I have told you of my mother's gatherings. I have explained how I share her gift. It was she who helped me to seek a more enlightened path.'

I glared at her, but still she deigned not to see me.

'My father's sight, however, remained clouded. Though in every other respect he is a very fine man, of course; very fine.' She paused. 'He discovered that I had been attending the circle – even, on occasion, bringing the spirits. He did not understand. He thought it best I should be sent away, at least until I'm a little older.'

Bringing the spirits? Did she think she could summon them, have them come at her will? I wanted to laugh. Of course her father sent her away. He'd want the whole thing kept hush-hush until she was married off to some unsuspecting pigeon who hadn't heard about her *gift*.

'He instructed me never to speak of it,' Sophia added. 'He thought it best that the matter was buried. But how can I, in all conscience, remain silent now? I prefer plain-speaking. I always tell the truth.'

Well, here was an admission. Sophia had been sent away in disgrace, at least in her father's eyes, and she was disobeying him still. She ought to have been put under the care of my grandfather, not her father. He wouldn't have asked her to respect his wish for secrecy; he'd have given her the buckle end of his belt, and that would have been the end of it.

Now she was indulging her silly pretensions to supernormal powers with her tales of Miss White. What is a medium, after all, without the uncanny? She *needed* Miss White to have something strange about her. Sophia's ability to see it was what made her special, after all. It set her apart from everyone, above even those who had authority over her. More than that, it offered proof that her father had been wrong in setting his will against hers. Miss White did not just provide a way of gaining attention and admiration; she was the means to rid Sophia of her shame. And shame was not something Sophia McKenzie Bideford was accustomed to feeling.

'So Fulford was my punishment,' she murmured. 'Well, look at us now! Perhaps we shall all be terrified to death, and my father may see what his money has bought him.' She looked down at her hands, or perhaps at something more distant still. Then she began to pull at her glove, which was of silk rather than plain cotton like mine; she loosened the fingers before removing it and held out her hand.

The wound Miss White had inflicted hadn't yet healed. If anything, it was worse: the welts were livid, as if at any moment they might bleed. Was it infected? In spite of myself, I felt a pang of sympathy. This looked painful, even pitiful. I'd *wanted* Sophia to be pained, to feel every stroke of her punishment and more, but this was too much. Could Miss White really have done it? I pictured her face smiling down at me, the gentleness in her eyes. She couldn't possibly have meant for this to happen. She *hadn't* – but that wouldn't matter to Sophia. She'd say the teacher did this to her deliberately. She'd say that she was monstrous, and everyone would believe her.

No one spoke and Sophia sat back with a sigh. She looked away, tilting her head towards the window so that her eyes filled with the cold grey clouds. What could anyone say? Even Sophia was silent and I wondered if she could hear whispers in her ear even now – whispers from another world. Did she hear spirits rapping out messages amid the carriage's rumble? Did she hear their unearthly moans beneath its creaking?

She raised her head, peering into my eyes. I couldn't read what I saw in hers – a question? An accusation? I tilted back my head as if I could see the sky through the roof of the carriage. There was only a lining of pale blue satin, like the lid of a coffin, frayed and speckled with mould.

Then music emerged from the world outside – the one I'd almost forgotten existed. It flooded in, the sound weaving through the clatter of wheels and harness and hooves. The lively air of a fiddle rose, its rhythm lent emphasis by the clapping of hands, interrupted by a distant cheer. Barkers shouted their wares; animals brayed or snorted or stamped; and underneath it all came the unintelligible murmur of a thousand conversations. The horses slowed their pace. We were in Snaithby Dun, and the fete was all around us.

We tried to peer out of the breath-smeared windows. We'd seen the town before, but not like this. It wasn't large – even catching a train meant going on to Lundby Bridge, another five miles distant – and I hadn't suspected there'd be so many people. We must be close by the green but I couldn't see an inch of grass for all the colourful print dresses and smocks and gaiters and velvet coats filling it, though the buttercross jutted from it all, its ancient stone much eroded by the elements.

The door flew open. Gadling handed us down one by one, clinging a moment to my arm, and I avoided his gaze. I was looking for Miss Peel, but she was nowhere to be seen. Gadling didn't remark upon her absence or offer to wait with us. He'd been ordered to return and seemed intent on doing so as quickly as he could, for he caught Bard's head and turned the horses around. In another moment the equipage was moving away, leaving us surrounded by strangers.

'How very odd,' Ruth said. 'I suppose we'd better wait for her.' Disappointment weighted her voice and she gazed across the green towards the inn, from whence the music rose quick and merry and just a little wild. She could long for it all she liked. We were young ladies and couldn't join in the dance that reeled about the yard, couldn't even clap our hands. Still the rhythm of it found my feet, making me tap my toes inside my boots.

'Nonsense,' said Sophia. She took hold of her skirts, lifting them above any threat of mud. 'Miss Peel has perhaps been called away on some errand. Or the carrier took her back to the school; I'm certain we passed him on our way here.'

I didn't know how she possibly could have noticed, but I didn't say it, for just at this moment I admired her boldness. I even welcomed it. Would she defy Madame Dumont? Well, then perhaps we all could.

'I believe it is our duty to ensure everything is proper for when the younger ones arrive,' she said, and with that she walked away from us and into the throng. She threaded between farmers with their walking sticks, women with willow baskets over their arms, labourers with bright cloths tied about their necks, gamekeepers in their bowlers. A small boy, grinning, rolled a hoop between them without once brushing her skirts. The others followed and I too hurried after her.

Sophia's back was straight as a board and her head turned neither to left nor right as she led us past what would ordinarily have been the market. The pens were full of livestock ready for judging and the roof echoed with braying and bleating. Farmers leaned over the railings to inspect their rivals' animals, dipped and scrubbed and anxious for the loss of their fields. One fellow was leading out a heavily muscled bull by a rope passed through its nose-ring. Its collar bore a red rosette; curls spilled over the top of its head, like a child's.

Sophia saw none of it. Casually, as if without noticing, she made for the centre of the fete. And here were Ruth's amusements. Wooden boat swings flashed high as children squealed. Skittles scattered with a deafening rattle. Children cheered as a grinning, frowsy-haired puppet was flung from a booth. A man on a soapbox lauded a cure-all tonic for sixpence and Sophia marched right under his nose; it was he who fell silent for a moment, he who followed her with his gaze. We scurried in her wake and I began to wonder if we'd be permitted to look at any of it. Would she simply reach the other side, find Miss Peel still missing and march us back again?

Next came rows of booths and carts loaded with an array of goods: raisin wine and gingerbread, stuff shawls, tin soldiers, carved horses and cows and elephants, trumpets, skipping ropes, boiled sweets, boots and caps. Brightly painted whipping tops were arrayed next to a barrow-load of watercress, the sudden peppery scent sharpening my senses. Another fellow had a box of terrier puppies at his feet, noses twitching, bright eyes blinking against the clamour as they squirmed and climbed over each other. He nudged one back into the box with his foot and glared at me, as if daring me to pet them with no intention to buy. A woman sat next to him with a fleece for spinning, dirty white, badly washed; I smelled the lanolin, saw her fingers shining with grease as she plucked fibres from the teasels of her carders.

But here was something more acceptable for Sophia: the pure whiteness of lace collars, followed by a riot of bright ribbons. She paused to run her hands through gleaming crimson strands while the others dived in, wondering whether apricot was better than chartreuse. When they'd counted out their coins, we saw a printer with his samples: visiting cards, black-bordered letter paper for mourning, blotters, sealing stamps and wax. Amelia seized on some writing paper with a fancy border but Sophia declared it vulgar and she shame-facedly put it back. Sophia selected crisp white sheets and I remembered the paper Emily had given me for my watercolour, the way it had taken the paint so beautifully.

Was she here by now? But Miss White had meant to walk. She might only be halfway along the lane, though surely getting closer every moment. Miss Peel might have returned to the buttercross and be waiting for us but I could see nothing of that; a parade had come, blocking the road. Wagons bearing a brewer's insignia approached, drawn by huge and stately shire horses with feathered feet, bedecked with shining brasses. Perhaps this was where the rye would end up; an image came to me of the field, everything quiet save for the crop shushing in the breeze, and I wished I was there again and alone after all.

When I turned, the others had moved away. I didn't know how they'd left me behind so quickly. They appeared to be strolling, their heads turning as they chirruped at each other. They were approaching the inn. Its sign swung and creaked in the breeze, displaying a simple picture of a tree: The Royal Oak. The benches outside were crammed with ruddy-faced men, lifting brimming tankards to wet lips, banging on tables in time to the music rising from the yard. The fiddler curled around his bow, picking up his rhythm. A boy on a penny whistle threaded its tones with his own, quicker still, pure as a chattering stream. Both watched Sophia pass by with appreciative gazes, though I observed with spite that they didn't miss a note.

I hurried after the others. The green was crowded, pulling and pushing them away from me. Where had all these people come from? It felt as if they'd emerged from the hedgerows and woods, rising from the rivers, from between the stalks of rye in the fields. The constant motion made me dizzy. Once, I'd have thought nothing of it. I'd have gone to market with my mother and shouted our wares along with the rest, making sure our eggs and butter sold first. Had the farm and its ways so quickly become strange to me? Was the only result of my grandparents' meddling that I no longer belonged anywhere?

A glimpse of light blue skirts might have been Amelia and I started towards her. Then I saw Sophia, but in the opposite direction. The crowd parted and she became clear – her face not composed, nor determined, but soft; almost gentle. She peered up through her eyelashes as she reached out and touched a young man's arm. I recognised the flat-crowned hat of Reverend Aubrey.

The crowd closed around the pair and they were gone. I couldn't see any of the girls anywhere. We should have waited by the buttercross. Madame Dumont had instructed us to do so and we'd ignored her and this was the result. She'd never let us out of the school again. I might not even be able to go to the fields. Even here Fulford's walls were closing in around me, shutting me inside and spinning, spinning; faces flowing past, images in a zoetrope. I recognised none of them. They laughed and grinned and leered, staring at me with eyes that all looked the same. People spilled from the inn, bringing their dance onto the green. A flare of skirts, a loud whoop; a girl's flying hair whipped into my face and her laughter echoed in my ears. I tried to find Sophia again, a fixed point in a world where everything was whirling, but she was gone. I wasn't even sure I'd seen her at all.

But I didn't want Sophia. The person I wished to find was Miss White: Emily, who would calm everything, make it all stop. I searched the mêlée of strangers for her face, but of course she wasn't there; she might have vanished into the spaces between them. I thought of Beatrice with her dawdling and allowed myself to hate her. This was her fault. We should all have been here together, a day of pleasure, a holiday; for a time we could have forgotten the school and everything in it.

A touch on my shoulder and I spun around to see a young woman, a stranger, in front of me. And everything stopped.

She was a fortune teller. I could tell by her darkly purple scarf, spangled with stars and crescent moons, and the coins dangling about her forehead. She raised a hand, jangling the wire bracelets along her wrist, and waited for me to place mine into it. She would say something about meeting a man, I supposed, then demand payment, but I found myself removing my glove and holding out my palm anyway. What did she see as she peered into it? But her stare faltered – her gaze flicked to my eyes and she frowned, stepping away from me. She shook her head as if she'd changed her mind, or seen something she didn't like. Then she spat into the dirt.

I moved away, colliding with someone behind me. A labourer leered from under his shapeless felt hat and I muttered an apology, then a hand grabbed my arm and dragged me into a spin – another young lad, his red hair a little like mine, his breath sour with drink. I pulled free. How dare he? Couldn't he see I was a *lady*? Or had he taken one look at me, all dressed up like a peg-doll in a fancy frock, and known exactly what I was?

I swiped at my eyes. I wished any of the girls would appear. I wished again for Miss White, then, fiercely, for Daisy. If doppelgängers really could be conjured from the air, why could my sister not have had a double-walker? If she had, she could have stayed by my side always. If wishing could do it, she would come to me; she'd take my hand and make me laugh in the face of it all.

The green was a maze of unfriendly, unkind, unfamiliar faces, without walls or paths or any way out. The sound of the fiddle was maddening. I lowered my head and pushed between tall backs, broad shoulders, grasping hands, and there – was that a cluster of wide dresses? I hurried towards them and they dissolved. There were only four or five sheep being herded into a pen by a stealthy dog, a whistle lowering him to the ground.

Then I saw the buttercross, and in the next moment a carriage standing by it; a carriage with two chestnut horses.

I hurried towards them. I didn't look for Gadling, simply pulled open the door and hauled myself inside.

Sophia gazed steadily at me from the opposite seat. She appeared quite settled, as if she'd been waiting for some time. My breath caught; my face felt damp, strands of hair clinging to my forehead. I tried to gather myself as she coolly adjusted her skirts, ensuring they made no contact with mine. I think she murmured, 'Goodness.'

Goodness. There was none of that here. There was no kindness or warmth, not even the pretence of it. I pressed against the hard seat and stared back at her. She refused to look at me, then broke into dimpled smiles as Gadling opened the door to admit Amelia and Ruth.

The others filled the space with excited chatter as we started on our way. Ruth had bought soft pink ribbons, while Amelia had chosen virulent shades of emerald and azuline. They held them up to their dresses and declared the result most becoming. Sophia watched over it all like a queen – or did she look a little sad? She said nothing of where she'd been, and I opened my mouth to ask about the reverend then closed it again. Possibly I hadn't even seen her. I'd been so confused. A headache still pulsed at the back of my eyes.

The thrumming of gravel announced that we were turning into the track. I hadn't expected to be grateful to hear it, but now I longed for the folly's confining walls and stifling corridors. Soon we were there, and found they were waiting for us: Miss Morrison and

Miss Peel stood at the entrance, and at their centre was Madame Dumont, tight-lipped. The carriage halted. For a moment, none of us moved. I couldn't hear a sound, only an echo of all the clamour of the day, the strange voices and wild music.

Then a man appeared in the doorway, someone I didn't know. He wore a stiffly starched collared shirt under his waistcoat and carried the scuffed leather bag of a doctor. Suddenly I couldn't breathe. There was a shadow behind him, as if warning him of something – but it wasn't a shadow at all. It was Miss White, though it didn't altogether look like her. Her skin was stretched too tightly over her bones, so that she seemed almost a stranger. Her lips moved, though I couldn't make out the words, and my gaze went to her hands; I caught my breath.

Her hands were stained with paint. Or had she cut herself?

I couldn't move. I was a statue; I was chained to the wall. I could do nothing as Sophia stepped down. The doctor murmured to Madame Dumont, gesturing inside. Miss Morrison and Miss Peel didn't seem to know where to look or what to do; they hadn't been waiting for us at all. Miss White made to wrap her arms about herself as if she were cold, then gazed down at her hands as if she couldn't quite recognise them.

Sophia walked towards her, though the teacher didn't notice until she stood right in front of her. I didn't know what Sophia meant to do but suddenly I could move and so I went after her. Sophia was staring with wide, unblinking eyes – as if she were the one cast into a trance – and she began to raise her arm, to do what I didn't know, but I grabbed her hand, seizing her injured palm and twisting it hard.

Sophia cried out, as much in surprise as pain. She pulled free and looked down as blood began to seep through the silk of her glove.

'Inside.' Madame Dumont seemed oblivious to it. 'All of you. Go directly to your rooms and do not leave them until I give you permission. Doctor, to my study, if you please.'

After the bright day, the hallway was shadowed and cold. It felt as if something were moving among us, chill fingers brushing our skin. I half imagined the sound of weeping drifting along the corridors – but as we approached the dormitories, I realised the sound was real. I pictured us as we had been earlier, walking in the opposite direction, tripping along, thinking of our special treat. We had been foolish – we had been innocent. Were we so much younger then?

We found Lucy sitting on her bed, her eyes puffy and swollen. Grace was there, pushing a glass of water into her hands, though Lucy spilled it when she tried to drink. Her hands were shaking. She seemed barely conscious of us as we gathered about her. Everyone started to speak at once. Whatever could have happened? What was wrong with Lucy? And where was Beatrice?

'The window,' was all Lucy said. We turned and saw that the sill was filthy, covered in flakes of paint and scraps of dirty cobwebs.

Sophia pushed me aside, and I was suddenly glad I'd hurt her. I wished I'd broken her fingers.

She knelt in front of her cousin and rubbed Lucy's hand, making comforting noises. Neither seemed to notice the blood on her glove. Lucy sniffed and wiped her nose on her sleeve. No one saw that either, or chastised her for it, or cared.

'I didn't get to go to the fete,' Lucy said, as if that was what mattered, and I wished I could slap her – all of them.

Lucy took in a great gulping breath. Then she started her tale.

'There weren't enough places in the carriage. Sophia, you said you'd go first so I was the last to leave, apart from Bea of course. I was in the hall and I heard her talking with Mademoiselle Blanc but then I went down and stood by the clock. Then there were footsteps, but fast – as if something bad was coming. And it was – it was *her*. Mademoiselle Blanc ran down but she didn't see me, she just went outside and I heard her say that Beatrice had fainted.

'She came in again and went back up the stairs and I was worried for Beatrice so I followed her. Sukie was on the landing and she came too – she said she was there to polish the banisters, though I think she wanted to see us all in our best.'

Sukie: the servant who hauled our warm water and emptied our slop-pails. The one who scowled at Madame Dumont's commands, the one prone to grinning and winking as she listened to our conversations.

'So Bea was with Mademoiselle Blanc when she was taken ill?' Sophia prompted. 'She was supposed to be helping with her dress. Were they quite alone?'

Lucy nodded.

'So no one knows what happened between them. Only that Beatrice was supposed to have fainted and Mademoiselle Blanc left her.'

'Oh – yes,' Lucy replied, 'but she didn't leave her for long, as I said. When she saw me, Mademoiselle told me Madame

Dumont was bringing smelling salts as soon as she could. She said everything would be quite all right.'

Sophia snorted and I shot her a look, but my voice had left me. It felt as if everything was spinning, too fast and out of control.

'Mademoiselle Blanc and Sukie and I were a little way along the passage,' Lucy said. 'But then we stopped, because there was a noise, and Sukie shushed us. I thought that was rather rude, but Mademoiselle Blanc didn't say anything so I didn't either. Then there was another noise, louder; scraping and rattling. The window, being pushed up. We never open that window. You know how it sticks, how dirty it gets on the other side. The maids never can clean it.'

I glanced towards the scattering of paint and filthy cobwebs littering the sill where the sash must have been forced open.

'Mademoiselle would have gone in then, but we heard something else – someone talking low and fast, or as if they were babbling. I couldn't make out any words. But then there was a scream, loud, as clear as anything. We all moved fast enough then, but it was Sukie who got there first. She didn't see anything though, because the room was empty. You see?'

I shook my head. What did we see? It only sounded like another trick. It seemed that no one had really seen anything.

Then Lucy said, her voice faltering, 'Bea fell. There was just the open window. I'd never seen it so wide. It jams, you see.' She had told us that already, though she seemed to have forgotten it.

Her words sank into me, bringing pictures with them; unpleasant, horrifying pictures. Impossible pictures. I closed my eyes and pictured Bea's soul, not falling but rising into the air, moving away from the confines of the school and any of us, free to be whoever she wanted at last. *Ex Solo Ad Solem – From the ground to the sun*. Was that where she had gone? I imagined the light making her face gleam pale, paler, until it dissolved into the white blankness.

But other pictures pressed in, more awful still, and more real: a long fall through the air, grasping for something, anything solid, and finding nothing at all. My friend lying on the ground beneath the window, her face bleached as white as I'd imagined it, not in beatification but the coldness of death. Her pretty limbs all twisted in unnatural ways; her head cracked open, her brains bashed out. And blood – there would have been lots of blood, wouldn't there? I shook the images away and a whirl of faces flew past, as if I was back at the fete, nothing around me I could recognise. A hand seizing my arm. A girl's hair whipping into my face. A puppet: Judy, fallen from her booth – or was she flung out? And then I pictured Miss White standing by the door, her face pallid, her hands steeped in red.

Lucy covered her face. 'Sukie started to shriek fierce loud,' she said through her fingers. 'It frightened me worse than anything.'

We stood there, able to do nothing, to say nothing. I looked around at the others' faces – shocked – frozen. Even Sophia looked stricken, all her composure forgotten. It came to me then that I would never see Bea again. We would never make up our misunderstanding; we'd never renew our friendship. *Almost sisters*, I thought fiercely, and had to fight back tears.

'It was our fault,' said Sophia. 'All of us.'

She was right, I thought. We should have looked after Beatrice. We should have kept her close. The doppelgänger had come to warn us, after all.

Sophia pushed herself up. She no longer appeared stricken but calm – deathly calm. She went to her cupboard, bent low and withdrew something: a book of textured cloth, scuffed, *shabby*. With dismay, I recognised it. She held it out, as if all the answers we needed were contained within.

'We knew what she was,' she said. 'We all knew.'

I stepped forward and tried to snatch the book, but she clutched it to her. 'This told us everything. I told you it holds the truth, didn't I? It's all here. It always was.'

'Don't even begin,' I said. 'Miss White left Beatrice alone. She was quite well. If Bea did something – something *mad*—' And why would she have done that? She had needed a *friend*. She'd needed *me*. 'You can't blame Miss White. She was with Sukie when whatever happened happened, and Lucy too. She wasn't even in the room. There is absolutely nothing you can say of her.'

But Sophia didn't heed my words. She simply began to read. '"Soon after, one of the pupils, a Mademoiselle Antonie de Wrangel, having obtained permission, with some others, to attend a *fête champêtre* in the neighbourhood"' – She glanced meaningfully around. 'They were going to a fete, you see—'

I wanted to slap her. I wanted to grab her hand again and twist, harder this time. I wanted to see the blood drip from it, but what could I do? There was only me to fight them. I needed a sister – I needed Daisy, but she couldn't come to me. I needed Bea, but Bea was *dead*. And the others were all Sophia's, hanging on her every word.

'". . . being engaged in completing her toilet, Mademoiselle Sagée had good-naturedly volunteered her aid, and was hooking her dress behind. The young lady, happening to turn round and look in an adjacent mirror, perceived *two* Mademoiselle Sagées hooking her dress. The sudden apparition produced so much effect upon her that she fainted.'''

She snapped the book closed. 'You see, it is all here. It is just the same!'

And it was. It was exactly the same and entirely different, and I wanted to snatch her words out of the air. But she hadn't finished.

'Bea saw Mademoiselle Blanc fastening her dress in the mirror, just like the girl in the book. And behind her, someone else – her doppelgänger. That's why she fainted, but for her that was only the start, don't you see? It's plain in front of our faces. Mademoiselle Blanc rushed off to fetch Madame Dumont, *apparently* leaving Bea alone – but she wasn't alone, was she? Because the doppelgänger was still there.'

I opened my mouth, but I couldn't speak.

'Bea came to, but there was nobody who could help her. We had all left already. Even the real Mademoiselle had abandoned her. There was only the *thing* that comes out of her; that she *sends* out. Mademoiselle Blanc's double.'

'Her *opposite*,' Amelia murmured.

'Perhaps. Yes – just as if it really was an image glimpsed in a mirror.' Sophia liked this notion; she went on, warming to her theme. 'It would be a simple matter for her to appear respectable, all that a teacher should be, if she were to cast all that was unacceptable in her character into that thing – her *reflection*. It is quite clear that she has such undesirable impulses, from what she did to me in class.'

In spite of myself, I heard the echo of our teacher's words as if they floated across the room: *Mirrors always tell the truth. You'll see: it will reveal all our paintings' faults in a moment . . .*

'That's what frightened Bea into leaping from the window,' Amelia said.

'Yes!' Sophia replied. 'Bea saw the doppelgänger and recognised it for what it was. She knew it was unnatural. She knew it was *evil*. She saw its true nature.'

An image: a shadow-figure in the corner of a room, its hair hanging loose and damp, its eyes hidden. I blinked the image away. That was not her, not our teacher. It wasn't the person I knew; it wasn't Emily White.

'She must have tried to get away, but there was nowhere to go.' Sophia's words were relentless. 'It had her trapped in the room. There was only the window – that was the only way to escape the abomination, and so she took it. Who wouldn't? She would have been overcome.'

'Sophia, listen to yourself,' I said. 'Beatrice is *dead*. You can't *use* that in such a way, just because you dislike—'

'*Dislike?*' She waved the book in my face. 'Do you imagine that's what this is about – something so trivial? This is about all of us, Ivy. It's about our safety and our morals and our sanity. Would you let such things crumble around our ears? Are we supposed to listen to you instead – Mademoiselle Blanc's *pet?*'

I could only shake my head. All I could think of was how, that very morning, we had been happy. It had been a holiday, a little taste of freedom. Mademoiselle Blanc – Miss White – had been so kind. She'd offered to help Beatrice, and Beatrice had been glad for her help. Well, almost – for I remembered what she'd said about Miss White as she entered the room. But that didn't mean anything . . .

Sophia had poisoned her mind – against me; against Miss White. Could Beatrice have been so bewitched by Sophia's words that she really thought she'd seen a doppelgänger? She had learned to follow Sophia in everything, after all, just like the others – like everyone. Beatrice might have read that very page in that very book and, when a similar situation arose, taken it as her cue.

I imagined her trying to flee, scrabbling at the window. It must have been so heavy. Did fear give her the strength to open it? 'What came after the hooking of the dress? What does the book say?' The words were out of my mouth before I could stop them.

'Nothing.' Sophia didn't so much as glance at me.

'*Nothing*.' I emphasised the word.

'The book speaks no more of that incident, only of others. It barely needs to, does it?'

'It's perfectly clear that Mademoiselle Blanc was to blame,' Amelia cut in, to murmurs of agreement.

'Unless it was more than that,' Sophia said softly. When she went on, she spoke as if we were stupid not to have seen it before. 'Bea could never have opened that window by herself. But doppelgängers have powers we can't imagine. It might have done anything. What could have prevented it?'

She paused. 'Why would Bea even want to open the window? It offered no kind of escape, not really. I don't suppose she'd *entirely* lost her mind. She might not have jumped from it at all.'

I pressed my eyes closed and opened them again, half expecting the whole mad scene to have vanished; but there they all stood, Sophia's words sinking into them. What did they see? A dark shadow of Mademoiselle Blanc, pointing at the window, making it slide upwards with the force of her will? The cool air of day rushing in − and then what? The doppelgänger seizing Beatrice and pushing her towards the drop?

I opened my mouth to say *That isn't her, it's not Emily*, but it wasn't any use. Was Sophia too sending out a part of herself somehow − using her force of character, her will, to make everyone see what she wanted us to see? Perhaps she had powers after all. She had created madness with her words. She'd created a kind of shared hysteria, a fear that could leap from person to person like a shock of electricity. It was a contagion of the mind rather than flesh and blood, but it was real, and it was here; it had reached out and touched us all.

Cruelty curved Sophia's lips. 'That's the truth of it,' she announced. 'The doppelgänger is a kind of projection sent out from the originator. Something like a reflection, but one that refuses to vanish. I knew I had felt such a thing. I sensed it growing in power through the vibrations in the atmosphere. I *do* have something of my mother's gift, you see? Mademoiselle Blanc has created this creature. She lends it her strength, though it weakens her in the process, and she directs its actions with her will. It can touch things, *do* things, but it can't think; it can only carry out the originator's wishes.'

The originator. Sophia had referred to such a thing before, but now she wielded the term as if it were a scalpel and Emily a specimen pinned to a table. The girls' eyes gleamed about me in the dull light, half mesmerised. They really thought that Miss

White had sent that thing to Beatrice. They thought she'd *wanted* to hurt her. For a moment I couldn't breathe – it was as if my throat had constricted – then I strode forward and snatched the book from Sophia's hands. I threw it from me as hard as I could, along with its vile words and insidious ideas. It fell just short of the window and Lucy scrambled after it with a little cry, as if it were the Bible or something that might save us all, and she seized it, cradling it in her hands.

'She wasn't even there,' I said. 'You know that. You heard it from Lucy's lips. Miss White would never dream of doing as you say. Why should she?'

'How would you know?' Sophia's voice had triumph in it, as if the last blow had already been struck. 'She showed no sign of liking her. She must have heard what she said of her when she walked into the room. And perhaps she wanted to punish her – for being *tardy*.'

She stared at me, they all did, and I turned and ran from them, not stopping until I was in a distant corridor; I wasn't sure which. It might have been any of them or anywhere, and I was bursting with rage, or perhaps tears. How had things grown so dark so quickly? It came to me that we'd been instructed not to leave our rooms, that I shouldn't be here, and then I remembered that Beatrice was *dead*, she was never coming back, and none of that mattered.

If there was a doppelgänger, it had been a harbinger after all. It was under no one's control; it had brought its message and it was gone.

Had it gone?

Cold fingertips caressed my neck, stroking my hair, and I shook away the thought that came: that it had come to me too, a shadow standing in the corner of a room, yet more solid than any shadow should be. I peered along the corridor, at the windows that slashed the walls with light. I strained for any sound, sending out my senses to detect any presence, but the corridor remained silent and no one came. Still I found myself glancing down at my hands, remembering the fortune teller I had seen that morning; the way she had gazed into my palm as if seeing something terrible there, then had let my hand fall, as if it wasn't even worth the attempt at telling my future.

16

Reverend Aubrey's voice was a monotone that wouldn't stop. He said how terribly sad this was for us all, what a tragedy. He didn't say *wicked*; he didn't say *unnatural*. Naturally he didn't venture close to the word Sophia had hinted at: he didn't say *murder*.

But Beatrice wasn't murdered. She was defective.

That was how he explained it. We were lined up in front of him wearing our most sombre clothes and meekest expressions. Behind us, Sukie's showy sobs reminded us of her part in the matter. It seemed she was basking in the attention it brought her.

The parson didn't use the word *defective* either, but we understood him well enough. The doctor had weighed the evidence and decided that epilepsy was the best possible explanation to give for Beatrice's fall. It was more likely than fear, less shameful than taking her own life. It wasn't without taint of course; it still carried the whiff of madness, and by rights madness called for asylums, not schools. Like God, it moved in mysterious ways, and like God it didn't invite too many questions.

The explanation was easier for everyone, except perhaps Beatrice's father – but then, he hadn't even been able to look at her. Beatrice was the image of his poor beloved dead wife and now she was gone. Would that be a relief? Or would guilt eat away at him, the guilt that he'd sent her away and this was the result? But if she'd been *tainted*, he'd have done the right thing. There never would have been any choice. All to the good if Beatrice quietly vanished before she came home, ready to cause embarrassment as well as pain.

It was easier for Madame Dumont too. The corridors of the school would remain free of scandal, her reputation spotless.

But judgement, like death, had spread its wings, and Miss White had fallen into its shadow. She was already condemned, though she didn't know it yet. I looked at her downcast face and saw that she was beautiful. The gleam of a tear brightened her eye before she dabbed it away, delicately, with the back of her fingers. I should have told her everything. I should have made her listen to me. If I had, perhaps none of this would have happened.

Reverend Aubrey turned the benevolence of his gaze on us, the only gift he could give, and surely all we could wish for. 'Beatrice has been returned to her father, to be embraced in the bosom of her loved ones so that they can say goodbye to her. The funeral will be a quiet affair.'

I imagined it would be. They'd bury her and tamp down the dirt before word could spread. Beatrice was defective and now she was dead: may the Lord make us truly thankful.

We stood to sing 'Amazing Grace'. Sophia's voice was like crystal, *How sweet the sound*, and Reverend Aubrey looked towards her and quickly away.

I found myself wondering what Daisy's funeral had been like. But then, I hadn't even been there for her last days. When I had pressed my mother in a letter to tell me more of what happened, she had written again and said she'd died of a fever. There was nothing else; she was plainly reluctant to write of it, and I to think of it. Now I wondered what hallucinations might have come to my sister – what fears? I hadn't even known the cause of her illness, but perhaps no one did. There were so many things that could kill, after all; so few that could make things better.

The parson made his final remarks to close our gathering. He said we should be happy for our friend and companion, since she was with God and would be troubled no longer. She had gone into *the love that passeth all understanding*. He said he was a humble channel for that love and indeed he spoke lightly, as if the words didn't quite touch his insides. He released them and they flew into the air like birds seeking the light.

When it was over, the teachers closed around the parson and herded him between them like a prize sheep. But he refused to go. He paused and they divided around him, a river flowing around a rock, as he turned to Miss White, who had faltered. He offered her his arm. He leaned his head towards hers until they were almost touching and uttered what must be words of comfort, words that were only for the two of them.

Sophia stood stock still, glaring with poison in her gaze. Did she really imagine herself in love with him? There was no love in her. I saw again the way she'd reached for his arm at the fete. I could only think that she desired to be admired – worshipped – by everyone within her reach. Or maybe she'd wished to turn Reverend Aubrey against our teacher, leaving no one in whom Miss White could confide.

But she had me.

My name, I reminded myself, meant *faithfulness*. I didn't suppose Sophia knew that. Ivy bound and twined and clung. It was a symbol of friendship. Beatrice would have learned that, if she hadn't fallen away. And ivy was a symbol of *life*. I saw again the fortune teller's confusion and banished her from my mind. Ivy remained green when all around it died. Even when the trees lost their leaves and faded to grey and succumbed to winter, it alone thrived.

Alone.

But I wasn't alone any longer, was I? Nor was Miss White.

The two of us need never feel alone again.

17

I will stay awake. I will stay awake. The distant church bells had struck two hours after midnight some time ago and I peeked at the sleeping girls around me, pale shapes limned by the moonlight creeping in at the edges of the curtains. They looked like statues reclining on their tombs, and yet they weren't entirely still. Matilda muttered in her sleep, as she so often did. Frances shifted and kicked as if someone had grabbed her ankle.

I placed my feet on the floor, relishing the chill. I didn't light a candle. The curtains were thin and I could make out all I needed to see. A candle would only send strange shadows into the corners, making the dark darker. I stood for a moment sensing the weight of the school around me, the depths that lay behind the blameless face it turned to the world. I felt the texture of the silence that swelled to fill the room, the corridors, the stairways and all of the empty spaces beyond.

A floorboard creaked beneath my foot and I paused to see if anyone stirred. If they did, I'd just say that I'd heard something too. After what happened to Beatrice, it would be natural to be unsettled. A lie wasn't a good way to use her memory, but why should she care for that? At least it meant I hadn't forgotten her.

I tiptoed to the door and listened. It wouldn't do to be caught by a teacher on her rounds come to check on us or by a servant roused from their bed, but no lamplight glowed beneath the door and I quietly opened it. My movements were as practised as any burglar's, which was fortunate, for I intended to steal.

Cold air moved across my arms as I stepped into the passage. It was darker here but I knew the way blindfolded and it was only a few steps to the door I needed. When I opened it, the sleepers within looked just like those in my room, except that here, one of the beds was empty.

I tried not to look at it, instead approaching Sophia, making out the golden gleam of her hair. She slept like a princess in a fairy tale, her lips slightly parted, no sneer in them. She was at peace, almost a child, her curled hand resting beside her cheek on the pillow. She made no sound. Was she waiting for her prince?

I bent, my face almost touching hers, and, reaching out with one hand, opened the cupboard next to her bed. Here were her intimate things: cotton inner clothes, her stockings and garters, hair oil and dusting powder alongside letters from her parents, the treasures she hadn't been able to leave behind. I ran my fingers over them all, seeking something dusty and rough and shabby, unlike the rest: the book she hadn't wanted me to read. Well, I must read it. And it was there, grimy under my fingers, making its mark on me, its thief. What did I care? The others already thought me beneath them; well, now I was.

The green cover was rendered colourless by the moonlight. It smelled of burning and my fingers tingled at its touch. Could they sense the secrets within? No doubt Sophia would claim such a thing was possible. If so, perhaps she'd sense it now – being stolen away by tainted hands – but she didn't stir as I slipped from the room.

Instead of returning to my own, where the girls might wake and see me, I continued along the corridor. Here there was a corner, though it led nowhere; another of the folly's oddities, there was only a little stretch of passage ending in a storage room used for bed linen. Next to it was a single narrow window.

The moon was almost whole, only a little piece nibbled from its edge. I leaned against the windowsill, all the better to see by its light. I held up the book and smelled its burning, acrid at the back of my throat. Had the cover blackened since I'd last seen it? I couldn't be sure, but I thought it had. Willing Sophia to sleep a little longer, lost in whatever dreams she dreamed, I opened the book and saw its title.

Footfalls on the Boundary of Another World, by Robert Dale Owen. I'd never heard of him. He hadn't won fame or even notoriety with his book, then, despite all the Sophias and their mothers in this world.

I let the book fall open naturally at a well-thumbed page. The covers sagged apart, loose threads jutting from the binding like pale hair. I began to read, but there was nothing as Sophia had described: the section opened with the account of an intelligent, accomplished, diligent teacher, one who delighted the school with her good nature. Sophia hadn't mentioned that. Yet as I continued, it struck me that the book's Emélie Sagée and Miss White were somewhat alike. Both were of fair complexion, with a neat, medium-sized, slender figure. And Miss White's grey eyes could perhaps be taken for Sagée's blue ones, in a certain light.

Something wasn't quite right, however, and I scanned the lines again. In the space of a single sentence, Sagée was described as both blonde and having chestnut hair. Had Sophia noticed such an obvious mistake? If so she hadn't chosen to mention that either. Then I saw that the events described in the book were said to have happened, not when it was published, but earlier still: in 1843, and even then, Sagée had been thirty-two years old.

Shaking my head at Sophia's misrepresentations, I read on. I'd heard this part already: as she went about her duties, the teacher was reportedly seen in two places at once. In the book, the matter was set before the headmistress. She dismissed it as 'fancy and nonsense', and quite right too. Despite the difference in years, there was a certain satisfaction in picturing her with Madame Dumont's face.

Next was the incident with the fete and I was struck again by the similarity to what had happened with Beatrice. Sophia must have loved this. Each sentence must have been as a seed planted, each re-reading supplying the water it needed to grow.

But it was too much of a coincidence, wasn't it? And I found myself wondering just why Beatrice had been so tardy that morning.

It wasn't like her. She wasn't one to linger so long over the washstand, even if her room was short of a mirror. She didn't need help to fasten her dress, not really – we were all used to shifting for ourselves, since there were no maids to be spared at

Fulford. And we'd all been so excited – except perhaps me, but even I'd been ready to step into the day.

Could she have done that on purpose? The similarity might not have been chance at all. The incident in the book might have been noted, studied – copied. Not a coincidence but a guide.

Beatrice might have lingered because she expected that Miss White would come and fetch us. She had offered to walk us into Snaithby Dun, after all, willing to accept any irritating duty that presented itself. When it happened so perfectly, would it have been so great a step for Beatrice to pretend to faint? Especially if Sophia had schooled her in her task.

I remembered what Sophia had said, seemingly an age ago, when she'd spoken of the way she could sense things, and I'd accused her of being ridiculous: *We'll see*.

And the two of them had grown close, or so Beatrice liked to think. But Sophia hadn't been so very great a friend to her, had she? Perhaps Beatrice was desperate to win her approval, willing to follow her in anything. I couldn't believe she'd have dreamed up such a scheme herself – but it was Beatrice who'd paid for it. Little wonder if Sophia couldn't confess her part now; probably she couldn't even admit it to herself.

Miss White wasn't the originator but the victim of their trick. The similarity to the book wasn't proof of her guilt but her innocence. Yet she *must* be the evildoer – or Sophia must shoulder the blame.

It still didn't explain how Beatrice fell from the window. Had her fantasy run away with her? Fear might have grown upon her, becoming something else, something she couldn't control. Maybe she really thought she had seen a doppelgänger. And so she'd leapt to her death, to escape nothing more than her own fevered imagination.

Poor Beatrice. She had been foolish – more than once. She should have remained my friend. I would have helped her; I never would have driven her to this. Now Sophia was trying to pass the blame. Did her hatred for Miss White run so deep? But of course it did. She'd held out her hand and showed it to us, festering in her skin.

I peered again at the book.

Months passed by, and similar phenomena were still repeated. Sometimes, at dinner, the double appeared standing behind the teacher's chair and imitating her movements as she ate – only that its hands held no knife and fork, and that there was no appearance of food; the figure alone was repeated. All the pupils and the servants waiting on the table witnessed this.

Well, here was a scene Sophia couldn't hope to re-create. It was impossible, and so she'd skipped over it. Yet if the doppelgänger was real, why shouldn't it appear to everyone? There would be no limit to what it could do. Eagerly, I read on to see what that might be.

Once, the book said, when the teacher was confined to bed with influenza, the doppelgänger appeared to the girl who'd been sent to read to her. When it had, something odd had happened to the teacher.

Suddenly the governess became stiff and pale: and, seeming as if about to faint, the young lady, alarmed, asked if she was worse. She replied that she was not, but in a very feeble and languid voice.

That was like our German lesson: Miss White being overcome with weakness, just when the doppelgänger was glimpsed outside. Sophia would say that, in lending the double her strength, our teacher had weakened herself – but how had Sophia managed that?

Of course, she hadn't. It was surely a coincidence. Miss White had taken a chill from her journey, that was all. The timing was unfortunate but meant nothing; it was only a pity that events had played into their hands so well. Or perhaps Sophia had taken advantage of the teacher's sudden faintness, playing upon it, only making us all *think* we saw her standing in the yard, her hands full of flowers . . .

Then I read, *But the most remarkable example of this seeming independent action of the two figures happened in this wise.*

I was never to read it, because along the corridor, someone cried out.

I stared towards the sound as if an answer would come to me from out of the dark. I stepped towards it – and stopped, suddenly not wishing to turn the corner. I had the sense that someone would be standing there, just out of sight, waiting for me; peering up at me through loose, damp, twisted hair, their eyes full of nothing but darkness.

It's not her, I thought, the words as nonsensical as everything else, connecting with nothing, and I forced myself to move. The corridor was empty. It only seemed darker still, after the light from the window. I stepped into it, my white nightgown and white hands floating like those of a ghost. It was so very easy to leap to the thought of spirits; little wonder that wild stories spread so fast. The moon was high, the school dark and quiet, so who wouldn't give way to such suggestion? Who wouldn't dream of them?

When I reached Sophia's door, sound returned. I hesitated a moment before I pushed it open.

Sophia was sitting up in bed, surrounded by shadows – the other girls gathered about her. 'I told you,' she said, 'there was someone here. I have a sense that they were watching me sleep. I *felt* it. I'm not a fool, I know the difference between a dream and – and—'

A scrape and flare came from the corner as Grace struck a match; there were no gas lights, not at Fulford. She set it to a cheap tallow candle and shadows went darting across the wall, growing huge and distorted before shrinking once more. In the glow, the girls' eyes were lurid; fascinated.

'I awoke,' Sophia snapped, as if someone had contradicted her. 'I'm absolutely certain of that. I didn't open my eyes all at once but I could hear you muttering in your sleep, Amelia, and I sensed someone leaning over me. I didn't *dare* open my eyes. Then I felt fingers brush my lips.'

She broke off with a shudder. 'I opened them then, quick sharp, and I *saw* her. Only for an instant – she was all darkness and I couldn't see her features, just loose hair hanging down, *touching* me, but I knew it was her. That's when I cried out, Lu.'

'You scared me half to death. I sat up straight away, though I didn't see anyone.'

'Well, of course not,' Sophia snapped. 'She'd vanished by then.'

With a start, I realised she might have been describing *me*. I'd stood over her in just such a way, a short time ago, though Sophia had muddled her account, hadn't she? When I'd reached for the book our faces had been so close. I was sure she hadn't awoken – but had she somehow sensed me, becoming conscious of my presence? She'd claimed to have special powers, after all . . . but she would call her *insight* whatever suited her. She'd call it Mademoiselle Blanc or Emélie Sagée, and everyone would gasp in horror. And Sophia would have what she craved: their admiration.

She stirred and looked around. Her eyes widened when she saw me, then narrowed in anger. Lucy chose that moment to fling herself onto Sophia's bed and wrap her arms around her. The others followed, drawing in, saying how awful it was, that no one and nowhere was safe. I edged nearer too, so close that I smelled the trace of rosemary water in Lucy's hair, and I crouched and slipped the book under Sophia's bed. It wasn't where I'd found it but perhaps she'd think that, in some moment of distraction, she'd put it there herself.

'Someone's coming!'

Grace was right; a bright glow came from beneath the door, then the sound of footsteps, louder by the moment.

The girls raced for their beds, pulling covers up to their chins. Grace huffed out the candle and suddenly it was pitch black. I had nowhere to go, the only one who did not belong, and then I realised there was one place; I pulled back the covers of Beatrice's bed and slipped beneath them.

It was ice cold, as cold as if it had never been slept in, as if there were not even the memory of her to warm it. I closed my eyes tight and thought of my friend. The way I'd pulled her closer even than these covers, the way she'd cried until my shoulder was damp. The way I'd comforted her. The way she'd looked up at me, her eyes so candid, so open; the way she'd whispered that she hated everyone but me. It had almost been as if Daisy had returned to my side, she was so dear to me in that moment – and more memories came: Sophia stalking in, tall and haughty and furious. The way she had looked at me; the way they all had, their eyes fascinated and horrified and all of them the same.

I shook my head. They had *lied* about me. Sophia had lied . . .

An echo of her voice: *I always tell the truth.*

But she didn't. Miss White was proof of that: Emily, my teacher and my friend, who knew me better than anyone.

And if it was Miss White approaching us now, expecting five occupied beds and finding six, what would she think? What would she think of *me*? What would anyone?

The footsteps grew louder, then stopped. Another, stranger sound resolved into the fizzing drone of a paraffin lamp. The light grew brighter even through my closed eyelids. At least the smell of paraffin would cover the stink of scorched tallow.

I tried to make myself still. I stopped breathing, becoming silent. Everything was, and I realised that would give us away. No one muttered in slumber or shifted or turned in their bed. There were none of the usual small sounds of sleep, nothing as it was supposed to be.

'Is anyone awake?'

It was no more than a whisper and I couldn't identify the voice: Miss Morrison or Miss Peel? Even Madame Dumont? But I felt it must be Emily and I willed her away. At least she might be new enough not to have learned which bed ought to be empty. How had I left mine in the next room – the sheets mussed, the pillow dimpled with the shape of my head? I couldn't remember.

I opened my eyes. Every shadow in the room stretched itself before beginning to fade as the footsteps moved away. The door closed on the sound and left us to the merciful dark. I stared upwards, allowing my vision to adjust and my heartbeat to slow. Gradually, the sounds of sleep began to resume around me. No one ordered me to go or hissed insults through the space between us. Had they forgotten I was there? Perhaps they thought I'd rushed from the room before the teacher came, that she'd somehow failed to see me in the passage. Perhaps they never thought of me at all. Breaths lengthened and beds creaked as bodies relaxed into them. They had forgotten me and for a moment it felt good to be forgotten.

Eventually, I uncurled and pushed the sheets back. They were scarcely warmed from my body and the cold returned, making my legs stiff and slow. I stood and yet I didn't immediately leave. It was an odd feeling being the only one awake. All the nasty expressions I was used to were prone and helpless around me, even Sophia's.

For the second time that night, I went to her side. I bent and peered into her sleeping face.

She didn't stir. She couldn't sense me standing over her. So much for her *gift*. I wrinkled my nose with scorn as I bent close, closer – and felt for the book under her bed, then replaced it just as it was before, in the cupboard. There: she'd never know. She couldn't even see what was right in front of her eyes.

Now I could leave – and yet I didn't. A strange certainty flooded me that they wouldn't wake, that I had somehow become a part of the night and might go wherever I liked. It was an odd kind of freedom, one I wasn't used to, and I wondered if this was what a doppelgänger might feel; if, of course, they felt anything at all.

It can touch things, do *things, but it can't think; it can only carry out the originator's wishes.*

What nonsense! But then Sophia always did speak nonsense. Nothing she'd ever said about me had been true . . .

I stepped past the sleeping girls and went to the window. The curtains weren't fully drawn and I looked out, trying to see where Beatrice had fallen. I couldn't see the ground below. I could see the moon, however, swathed in a nebulous mist but still bright, still gleaming. It touched the slate roofs of the outbuildings with its glow but beyond them, where the fields lay, there was nothing but the dark, nothing but my own shadowy reflection. It went on looking and looking, unmoving, and I could not see its eyes.

What would it be like out there now if my mind could carry me wherever I wished to go – if I could take on some ethereal form and fly? Was it really possible for anyone to be in two places at once? Of course I remained motionless, bound to the cold ground – though I almost fancied I heard the breath of the wind in the distant trees, could make out each leaf as it stirred them, watch the path it made as it flowed along the hills and rushed through the empty fields.

18

When I stepped out of the back door it might have been into a world alone. The sky was milk-swollen, not yet bright enough to dispel the early morning haze, and everything was veiled in mist. I was the only moving thing in the landscape. I felt as if I were following in the footsteps of my half-sleeping thoughts. I'd risen early, leaving our room while the shapes around me slept on. I couldn't bear the thought of getting up with the rest, filing down to breakfast, sitting and eating while looking at Beatrice's empty seat. I didn't want to be near the others; and it was more than that, for the strange longing that had come over me when I looked outside last night had remained, as if the world was calling to me – or perhaps my home. I had barely slept since then but I didn't feel the lack of rest, only that of clean air.

No one had raised an alarm last night. Either the unnamed teacher hadn't noticed my rumpled bed or it really had been Emily, and she'd known it was mine and kept silent.

I hurried across the yard, too exposed and too visible. No one had seen me go, though I'd heard the clatter of a maid laying a fire somewhere close by as I'd left, and hoped I wouldn't pass anyone as they took out the ashes for scattering on the paths. I hated the sound of my footsteps, surely loud enough on the gravel to be heard through the folly's thin windows. Even now anyone might be looking out of them, watching me go, wondering what I was doing.

I didn't stop until I stood at the edge of the field, breathing in the scent of rye. Everything was very still. No breeze stirred the crop, though I sensed the memory of its whispers, like secrets just beyond hearing. I began to feel like myself again. This was like home, like *me*. I understood it. Here, everything was as it seemed; nature didn't pretend to be anything else.

After all that had passed, there was comfort in the touch of the rye against my fingers. Each ear was fat and healthful, and the silk pricked at my skin like memories. As if to root myself in the world again I plucked an ear of grain, tugging it from its stalk.

It wasn't perfect after all. It wasn't even golden.

I turned it in my hands, peering closely. Some of the grains were darker – rotten, as if decaying even as they grew. They were too soft and too yielding, turning to smears on my fingers. I brushed the residue away and frowned across the field, which from this distance appeared perfectly golden once more.

I knew it to be an illusion. So much of this field wasn't even rye. Something was growing here in its place, tended and nurtured just like the crop, but bringing with it only the promise of death. Had I really imagined that nature didn't pretend? It had taken a farmer's daughter to see it: the field was full of ergot, a fungus that flourished in poor summers, clinging to the stems of rye and mimicking the shape of its grains, yet dark – poisonous. The difference would only become plain if it were to be eaten.

Hallucinations. Hysteria. Madness.

Lucy, screaming in a classroom. Beatrice leaping from a window. It had all been blamed on Miss White, but there was never any need to blame anyone. There was no need for spirits or doppelgängers. Ergotism caused strange visions. It could even give the sufferer the sensation that they were being touched. Some felt it as heat – I remembered Sophia's hand, seemingly more inflamed each time I'd seen it. Was this the reason? Did she have the burning touch of what some called St Anthony's Fire?

If she did, it would get worse. The pain would turn into a black rot spreading through her limbs. She might fall into a poisoned sleep and never wake again.

It could kill me too. I was here in the field after all, where they had never been. I pulled my skirts free of the clinging barbs, not wanting them to touch me. I brushed at my hands again, then at my neck, my skin that was so often inflamed. I itched all over. Every shadow in the field seemed sinister, an imposter lurking. It was full of tiny doppelgängers. I had tried so hard to banish such notions – now it felt as if they were all around me, stronger than ever. But I hadn't eaten rye, had I? Not from this field – of course I hadn't, it hadn't yet been harvested – or from anywhere around here. I pictured myself running my hands through the grain then inadvertently touching my lips. Would that be enough? I hadn't had any hallucinations or delusions. I hadn't seen anything odd, in the corner of a room . . .

I turned and Miss White was standing behind me.

She was at the gap in the wall, the borderland between the field and the school. I blinked but she did not vanish. She only said, 'Ivy, whatever is it? Have you seen a ghost? What are you doing here, and at this hour?'

Have you seen a ghost?

But it was only Miss White, only Emily, who had been kind to me, who even now wasn't angry with me. I smothered the thought that had come, unbidden and unwanted; the offspring of Sophia's fevered brain, not mine.

'Come,' she said. 'Explain to me on the way. You shouldn't be here.'

Nor should you, I thought but didn't say. Anyway, it seemed she wasn't going to punish me. She reached out a hand, dropping the flowers she must have been picking – more moon pennies. Had she planned for us to paint them? Now they lay scattered, little eyes looking at me from the grass. I thought of Daisy, but it was all right: at this moment I didn't need my sister. I knew exactly what I had to do.

I took Emily's hand and she drew me back across the gap in the wall. Her skin was warm, a little damp, perhaps with sap from the flowers.

We stepped back into a yard that was full of the brightening day and returned to the school. She didn't lead me into breakfast with the others but towards her rooms and I was relieved when she closed the door behind us.

'Now, Ivy, whatever is the matter? Please tell me.'

I stared down at my skirts, still covered with residue from the rye. I looked at my hands. There was no redness or swelling; they

175

didn't burn. Was the madness in me too? Would I come to think Emily a monster, as the others did?

'Are you ill? You're quite safe here, Ivy.'

I roused myself and told her everything. I described what I'd found in the field. I informed her of Sophia's hand and the delusions spreading among the girls. I was glad I hadn't said these things before; now I could explain it all. 'This proves it,' I finished. 'It shows that their ideas about you are nothing but false. They really are poison.'

Her expression was solemn, giving away nothing. If she was glad that the girls' odd sightings could be explained so neatly, she didn't show it. She reached out and clasped my hand and a tingle passed through my skin.

'But when would they have eaten rye, Ivy?'

I paused, for I didn't know. The school didn't claim to spoil us with luxuries but we did have good wheat bread. English farmers mostly sold rye for fodder. Few savoured the taste of dark rye bread; in France they might, but even Madame Dumont hadn't adopted that custom. She would think white bread more suited to our delicate feminine tastes and constitutions.

An image came to me: a large wagon drawn by shire horses, bedecked in ribbons and brasses. I remembered the men outside The Royal Oak, their reckless laughter and glazed eyes, the infectious notes of a fiddle. The way it had made my fingers twitch and my feet tap, wishing I could join in the madness of the dance.

I realised that ergot could make people do that too. In the grip of its poison, in pain and delirium, they would twitch and fling themselves about in the effort to be rid of the thing inside them. Some blamed it for the dancing manias of medieval times, where one after the next would join in the horrid semblance of gaiety until they danced themselves to death.

What if ergot-infested rye had been used to brew the local beer? I asked Emily as much and she started back from me, raising her eyebrows, and I realised what she was thinking. *Sophia?* But that was impossible . . .

'She wandered off alone at the fete,' I found myself saying. 'I saw her on her own, very near the inn. I remember thinking it was strange that she'd managed to leave us all behind. What if she did that on purpose?'

I remembered the way she'd grasped the parson's arm. If Sophia was so free as that, so disregarding of what she ought to do, what she ought to *be*, what else might she have done? I decided not to mention him. If I did, Sophia might appeal to him herself; she might even persuade him to vouch for her somehow. For once, I would model myself on her. I would say only what I wanted the others to see and nothing more, nothing to muddy the picture.

There was something wrong with Sophia's hand. Emily could never have done that to her. She *hadn't*.

Miss White drew in a sharp breath and said, 'I shall think upon it carefully.'

Yes, I imagined she would. I had given her the means to prove herself innocent of anything that had happened; but the cost would be to blacken Sophia's name entirely.

Of course, it might also save her life.

19

I was dancing in the eyrie with Sophia. Her injured hand was clasped in mine and I was careful not to squeeze too hard. The gloves she wore must have been new; the others would never have washed so clean. She had taken the part of the man, since she always did have the propensity to lead, though she contrived not to see me for all that I was directly in front of her. I half expected her to start flinging herself about maniacally, but of course she did not. Her every step was perfect. It was I who was out of time, *tardy*, Miss Peel clapping to remind me of the rhythm, twirling her hand in the air, trying to teach me grace. I was not certain grace was something I could learn, but still I tried to ape her movements.

This was an important lesson for us. We must dance, for by so doing we might entrance a future husband; there could be no tangles or trips to spoil the picture. I wondered what Sophia saw behind her eyes. Was she dreaming of attending balls like the gentry, of wearing a white dress for her coming out, all swansdown and artificial lilies of the valley to show her innocence? Who did she picture herself dancing with – Reverend Aubrey? I almost laughed in her face.

And should I too wish for merriment and dazzle? I'd rather have thrown up my heels for the fiddle at the fete. Besides, it was pointless wishing. There would be no glittering moment for me, no crowd of handsome fellows offering their hands. The question of marriage would arise with one of my grandfather's dull old friends amid talk of stock and trade and prices, all equally unfit for my ears, and that would be that. Besides, who should I dream of dancing with? I knew no young men. There was only the parson, but he was a milksop – and an image came to me of Gadling: his bared arms, muscular and tanned, casting off his bloodied shirt and bedding me in the straw, nothing but a farm-girl after all . . .

I shook the image away and returned to what I always was: alone. I followed the steps set out for me, spinning in my prescribed circle, and wondered if there were nothing better I could wish for – no other kind of life.

Then a voice said, 'May I interrupt?'

It was Emily. I hadn't heard her emerge from the stairs but she stood at my side, just like a rather forward gentleman come to cut in on the dance. Something like disappointment went through me as her gaze went to Sophia.

All around me the dance frayed, grew ragged, unravelled. Honoria stopped punishing the piano with her clumsy fingers. Someone else was standing behind Miss White, a shadow at her shoulder: Madame Dumont. Her expression grave, she said, 'Sophia, would you kindly remove your glove and show me your hand?'

My heart thudded louder than Honoria's clumsy playing, than my graceless feet. I didn't know where to look, or whether to be thrilled or horrified; perhaps I was both. What had I expected? Sophia's life might be at stake. Had I thought Miss White would do nothing?

Slowly, Sophia loosened each finger of her white glove and eased it from her hand. She held it out for inspection, palm upwards. Madame Dumont took hold of her fingertips, gingerly so as not to pain her, or perhaps in fear of being tainted by Sophia's touch.

'Come with me, if you please,' she said. 'I have sent for the doctor. I would have him examine you.'

It was so indiscreet. Everyone stared. That wasn't like our headmistress and I wondered how concerned she was beneath her calm. This would reflect on her too, of course, and on the school and all of us. And the farmer – with a start, I realised I had forgotten him. How could I have done that? Now I wondered what would happen to him if his crop failed. Had I grown such a stranger to my past that I could ruin a man like my father without a thought? It was blighted harvests that had brought me to this place. Would this farmer too have daughters and sons – and did they have rich grandparents who could help them? What would happen to them if they had not?

I felt the ripples of what I'd done spreading outward, further and further, through the eyrie's tall windows and across the land. I wanted to take it back – I wished I could spin the zoetrope, not forwards, but against itself. All the seconds and minutes would be gathered in again. All that had passed would be undone. The full-blown rose, crimson and ripe, would shrink into a bud. I would stand in the field and see nothing but gold. The whole folly could return to the way it was before I'd spoken, and back – further. Beatrice and I could be friends again. I'd wipe her tears away; they'd melt back into her eyes. She would never even cry them. But instead we were here, everything spinning forwards quicker and quicker, all of us hurled into the future, never quite fast enough to fly from our confines and be free.

Sophia's look turned to incredulity, then anger. She stalked towards the stairs at Madame Dumont's heels, not waiting for Emily. She should have allowed both teachers to go ahead of her, but no one objected or apologised to Miss Peel for the interruption. In another moment, they were gone.

Then, as if nothing had happened, the dance began again. Everyone took their positions and I had to follow their steps in order to keep my place, though there was no one to take my hand in theirs. I held my arms out in front of me anyway, describing with outstretched fingers the place where they should be. It must almost have appeared that I was dancing with a ghost.

20

Sophia didn't return to our lesson. When the bell finally released us, she wasn't in her room. I looked in at the empty beds and something twisted in my stomach. It almost felt that the sight was another harbinger and I wondered what the doctor had found – had it always been poison threading her veins, rather than malice? Somewhere outside, the breeze would be stirring the rye, lifting spores of ergot from things that only looked like husks: doppelgängers all, carrying death in their wake.

I breathed in and even the air seemed bitter. I sniffed – it wasn't just in my mind. The odour made me think of Sophia's book, shut away but still spreading its darkness. Yet the smell intensified as I stepped into the corridor. It was like snuffed candles; like sulphur.

I followed it, stepping towards the corner that led to the little store room. And there, in the stretch of corridor leading nowhere, stood Sophia. Smoke rose from her – she was bent around her book, holding a match to the cover.

I called her name.

She jumped, as if startled from her habitual calm. She fought to regain it, though her eyes were teary gleams, her face rendered unfamiliar by its expression. She was changed: no longer the perfect pupil, the carefully tended flower. Was this what guilt had done? She'd accused Miss White and urged Beatrice towards her death and rejected all sense – and me. Now she might be dying. She must want to set things right before she looked into God's face – perhaps into Beatrice's. She was trying to undo all the harm she'd done, by destroying the book.

She must know what it was, now, to be alone and unhappy and afraid. Somehow I couldn't triumph over her; instead I stepped towards her and held out my hand. *Faithfulness*, I thought. I would show that I possessed it where she did not – and yet she remained focused on the match as it burned lower.

The book's old, damp cover wouldn't catch, which was fortunate, for what would she do if it was set alight? I leaned in and blew out the flame. Thicker, blacker smoke rose between us and she blinked against it.

'That doctor's an ignorant fool,' she snapped, as if she weren't conscious of the book at all. She spoke as if continuing a conversation we'd been having for some time – perhaps, in a way, we had. She cast the spent match onto the windowsill and wiped her face with her sleeve like one of the younger girls, her fine manners forgotten. 'He said such awful—'

She shook her head, recovering herself. When she spoke again, her haughty manner had returned. 'He asked such ridiculous questions.'

I waited for her to name them, preparing myself to appear surprised, but other voices reached us: it was the other girls, her friends, and Sophia strode to the corner and began to take charge.

'I cannot imagine what I've done to warrant such treatment,' I heard her say. 'One would think it was *I* who'd done something terrible. Mademoiselle Blanc has accused me – *me*! And of such things!'

I followed, her silent shadow. They didn't look at me, only gazing up at her, wide-eyed, expectant, and she didn't disappoint them.

'They asked if I'd been wandering in the fields like a ragamuffin. They asked if I'd consumed *drink*. Can you believe that? They seem to think I ran away from you all at the fete, as if I would – off to dance with farm boys at the alehouse. As if I'd ever have anything to do with such types!'

Such types. I looked down at my skirts. Fragments of rye still clung there. I couldn't quite bring myself to brush them away.

Sophia hadn't been sorry. She hadn't taken my hand; she never could have wanted to be my friend. What, then, had she been doing? I remembered when I'd taken her book. It had smelled charred then, hadn't it? I'd looked at its faded covers and imagined they'd grown darker since I'd last seen them. But of course they had. She'd never wanted to destroy the book; she'd only wanted to make it look as if it were smouldering of its own accord, as if there were something unnaturally powerful about it, as if it were potent with its own dark magic – or perhaps a teacher's wickedness.

I realised that, sure enough, Sophia was speaking of it to the others, waving the book around, giving out some muddle about how it wouldn't burn and yet it *was*. She was confident they would believe her; she didn't even trouble to conceal her box of matches. Then she said, 'This is all *her* fault.' She sounded stronger by the moment, fed by their rapt attention. She didn't need to tell them who she meant. 'She accused me of having some ailment, a *weakness*, but of course the doctor couldn't find anything. He merely gave me some ointment – for the pain of what *she* did to me.'

She didn't mention what *I'd* done to her – the way I'd grasped her hand and twisted.

'He proved me innocent of any of it. It's Mademoiselle Blanc who was made to look a fool.'

My cheeks flushed with fresh guilt. For I'd told Miss White everything – but not quite everything, had I? I'd so badly wanted to present her with a solution, all tied up in a shiny bow, so that she'd be happy – so that she'd be safe. What had I done? Of course Sophia hadn't been off drinking in the inn. She'd been speaking with the parson. That had been her object.

I always tell the truth, Sophia had once said. And in a way she was, but she was lying too. If I was guilty of omission so was she, pretending to explain to them without explaining at all.

She turned and gave me her sweetest smile, her eyes innocently blue.

I opened my mouth to tell them about the ergot, but I couldn't speak. What difference would it make? I may have given her the means to do it, but it was Miss White who'd accused her, and Sophia wouldn't forget that. If I told them of my part in it, both of us would be cast out – and how would that help Emily? Instead, I could become like the ergot: outwardly one of them, but really something else. I would watch them as closely as I could and await my moment. I might still be able to do something for our teacher, something to make up for my mistakes, and I must; for all of them would want to punish her for this. And so I listened as they rattled on, feeding their hatred, and felt myself slowly turning invisible.

21

Sophia's defiance was the armour she'd adopted and she was still wearing it at luncheon, her back very straight and her chin in the air. A cursory glance might have taken it to be her usual composure, but I recognised the artifice in it by her failure to blink.

Her calm demeanour soon cracked. Partway through our reheated hash, Sophia dropped her knife with a clatter and then just sat there, her hand resting on the table, palm upwards. From where I sat, her wound appeared to be purpling with bruise-like shadows. How could the doctor not have seen anything wrong?

Staring fixedly at her plate, Sophia said, 'I have decided to write to my father. Perhaps he will have me withdrawn from this place.'

Speaking was not permitted at luncheon. This was clear impertinence but the teachers turned towards her, saw who had spoken and looked away again. Miss Peel made some casual remark to Miss Morrison, as if to cover over Sophia's words. They must think she'd suffered indignity enough for one day.

187

I half wished Sophia *would* write to her father, though I couldn't bring myself to hope he'd take her away. He had chosen a place in which she could blossom, and he couldn't possibly have chosen badly, could he? That would reflect upon his judgement. He'd tell himself she was nothing but a child and prone to tantrums.

Sophia half closed her eyes, seemingly oblivious to my attention or anyone's, content to let her words take root where they may. And they *would* take root. Madame Dumont wouldn't be so disdainful of the threat – she couldn't afford to be. If Sophia was withdrawn, others might follow: Lucy, certainly. Sophia's father might have other connections among the parents. Beatrice's death must have them all on edge – or had that been hushed up?

No one at Sophia's table spoke. They didn't dare look at her. She sat there, accused, wounded, suffering; beautiful. As if she'd heard my thoughts, she raised her head and gazed at me, drinking in my look like a draught of cool water. Then she pushed herself up from the table and, without waiting to be dismissed, walked from the room.

The rest of us waited until the bell rang and went on our way, with nothing having been said of Sophia's behaviour. It seemed, today, she could get away with anything. The school had changed immeasurably since Miss White had come to us.

I left the others and followed a corridor towards the outer wall, taking a circuitous route towards class. Could I smell smoke again? I stifled a cough as I neared a window – just as a wraith of it drifted by.

But someone was approaching. They hurried towards me; not Sophia, as I'd half expected, but Lucy. 'What are you doing hovering there, Ivy?'

I scowled at her rudeness – I was older by some years, after all, never mind how her cousin spoke of me – and said, 'Is Sophia setting matches to her book again? Don't you smell it?'

She looked incredulous. 'Why ever should she do that? She'd have the greatest difficulty showing the book to Madame Dumont if she burned it, don't you think?'

'What? But she can't mean to—'

'Of course she can. She's decided to tell her everything. It was that, or she really would have to leave – and why should she? It's Mademoiselle Blanc who should go, not Sophia. Anyway, Sophia will see to that. She's going to have her dismissed.'

I stared at her in horror. Then I pushed past her, not towards class but Madame Dumont's study. What was Sophia saying at this moment? If Madame sent Emily away, I realised, everyone would be happy. No parents need be involved. The girls could return to their dull, passive, unthinking ways – but Emily couldn't. Who was she next to Sophia? She had no connections, no one to defend her. With such a slur on her character, she might never find another position. She'd be ruined, with nowhere to go, no one to take her in; nothing to do but starve.

I raced past another window as a skein of smoke unfurled against the glass. Lucy was right; the fire, whatever it was, was outside, the smell seeping in around the badly fitting sashes. For a moment I couldn't see the sky for the smoke sliding past, though it was the folly that appeared to be moving, spinning on its axis.

I pictured it tearing free of its moorings, coming loose from the world, and I began to run.

At the door to Madame Dumont's study, I stumbled to a halt. Voices came from within, or rather, one voice.

'You may see for yourself how the pages have charred. It's worsening by the day. One can smell it, smouldering. She's trying to destroy it, you see? Mademoiselle Blanc doesn't want its story to be told and so she's making it burn with the power of her will. She's trying to hide the truth.'

A murmur in return, then Sophia's voice became more insistent. 'The cover is turning black. The whole thing is. It's like with my hand – Mademoiselle Blanc wanted to wound me and so she did, but then she went *on* wounding me, with her unnatural influence. She has powers. Who knows what she can do? It's her malevolence that's hurting my skin. There's something very wrong with her. There's no poison inside me; there never was. My hand is *burning*.'

My mouth fell open. Where was Sophia's truth now? These lies were blatant. I'd seen her scorching the book herself, shielding the flame as it burned lower – shielding it with her *hand*. She hadn't done that because of guilt – she'd done it so that she could place the blame on Emily. What if she'd damaged her own skin on purpose too?

Sophia had claimed to be able to *bring the spirits*, and perhaps she had: conjuring them from the air and pretence. The flame must have hurt, but if anyone was capable of doing such a thing, it was Sophia. She would have closed her eyes to the pain, thinking of Mademoiselle Blanc, because she hated her; because she so badly wanted her revenge.

I grabbed the door handle, the brass so cold it almost felt as if my own skin was burning, and I opened it as Sophia said, 'It's a sign. A portent of what will happen to the whole school, if Mademoiselle Blanc isn't cast out of it.'

The whole school. I stopped dead, still smelling the smoke, feeling its prickle in my throat. What else had Sophia done with her matches? What *wouldn't* she do?

'I've heard enough,' said Madame Dumont. They were standing by the fireplace. Our headmistress was nearest, her back turned. In one hand, she held the book. 'I find it difficult to believe that a young lady like you would be taken in by any such notions, let alone make such outrageous claims. I have shown you far too much leniency of late. I have placed too much trust in you, Sophia.'

'Madame, the book is proof of what we say.'

Madame Dumont, still without noticing me, opened the book to its title. '*Footfalls on the Boundary of Another World.* For shame, Sophia! I should think it far better if no one had ever trodden there at all, don't you? Robert Dale Owen is plainly an enthusiast. You must realise that when such people find *proof* of the marvellous, no one is to be doubted more. You should know better. Think of the place you will take in Society.'

Sophia had no answer to give. Nor did she mention her mother's table-tilting and spirit circles.

The headmistress had noticed me at last. 'You too, Ivy?' she sighed. 'Are you here to speak of ghouls and goblins? I warn you, you'd do better to hold your tongue.'

I dared do nothing else as she went to her desk, opened the drawer and retrieved something: her own box of matches.

Tucking the book under her arm, she shook one out. 'Mademoiselle Blanc is trying to burn this with her special powers, you say?' She went closer to the hearth, in which a fire was neatly laid, ready to be set alight. It was not the hour but she struck the match, bent and held the flame to the tinder; a little golden light took hold and began to grow.

Madame adjusted her grip on the book. Sophia reached out as if to snatch it from her, then let her arm fall. 'Madame,' she said, 'please, pay heed to what it says. The teacher's presence did terrible things to their school. It even warns us: "Either the teacher or the institution must be sacrificed."'

Madame Dumont flipped the book open with one hand, exposing its inner pages – no doubt at the very section she most wished to destroy. The match, still held in the other, brushed lightly against the paper. With a sudden rushing sound, it ignited. Fire enveloped the book, swallowing it whole, then Madame Dumont's hands. She cried out and flung it into the fireplace. It was too late; her sleeves were alight.

I whirled around. A shawl had been left hanging on a coat-stand just inside the door and I grabbed it and flung it over her arms, patting at the flames. Smoke billowed through the wool and we both started to cough. She tried to pull away but I grasped her arm, making sure the flames were out; and then there was nothing but her hitching breath, the shock whitening her cheeks.

Slowly, I peeled back the shawl. There were her fingers, swollen and cracked. Then her wrists – but the wool stuck to them. I tried to ease it away and her skin came with it, pink and seeping. Blisters rose as I watched. There was a smell: not the sharpness of matches or burning paper but something else, reminding me of meat singed in the oven, and I had to swallow my nausea.

'The doctor.' My voice was hoarse. Something inside me had gone very still.

Sophia, though, was loud. 'This is proof! Look at it! The book was bewitched. Like this whole place, like all of us.'

'Sophia, *shut up*.' I had to speak for Madame Dumont, since she couldn't say a word; she was shivering all over. 'Go and fetch Miss Peel. She's taking deportment class. Tell her we need the doctor, then go to the other rooms and have every teacher take her class outside. Tell the servants too – go to the kitchens, or send someone. Get everyone out.'

Madame Dumont shook her head as if to rid herself of the smoke. It billowed around us, and I realised the book was burning still; its pages were smouldering in the grate, malignant flashes of light like eyes opening one by one to look at us. The fire spat its disgust, gave a sigh of fragmenting paper.

'Not necessary.' I could barely hear Madame's voice.

'Forgive me, but it is. Sophia, you need to go *now*. Madame Dumont, there's a lot of smoke. Outside I mean, not just in here. Fulford may be on fire.' I glared at Sophia and put an arm around the teacher's shoulders. 'Your hands will be all right, you'll see.'

After another moment, Sophia stalked past us and out of the door, her expression blank. I led Madame Dumont after her, though Sophia was already lost to sight. Madame's steps were like those of an invalid but she moved with me, along the corridor and towards the entrance hall.

Girls were already pattering down the stairs. Sophia must have acted quickly, unless it was that the other teachers had noticed the smoke. I put out a hand to prevent one of the younger girls running into Madame Dumont, who was paler than ever; her breathing was shallow and quick.

I guided her onto the steps. Hands grasped at mine: Miss Peel, taking charge. I relinquished my grip and she tried to lead the headmistress away, but after a moment Madame Dumont pulled free and sat down right on the steps, in front of everyone.

Miss Morrison stood below us, on the turning circle. She called for the girls to line up in front of her, shortest to tallest, and they did, wafting smoke from their faces, some starting to cough. Sophia was there too, already pouring her version of the tale into Amelia's willing ears. 'Mademoiselle succeeded in burning the book,' she said. 'Perhaps she wanted to burn us all.'

'Go back inside!'

One by one, everyone fell quiet. Miss White stood in the doorway, looking around at us all. 'Return to your rooms!'

No one moved. The girls were motionless; even the teachers stared. Did Miss White want us to walk into the fire – to burn along with the book, as Sophia had said?

Even Madame Dumont wore a new expression. She looked down at her hands, then back at Miss White. I wished I could turn her head away and stop that gaze. A look like that would lead to questions; decisions.

I knew what she was thinking. The way the book had burned wasn't natural. It wasn't *right*. I had smothered the thought amid everything else, but it came back to me now and I couldn't quell it. I had seen Sophia trying to scorch the book and it had only been blackened, not burned. So why such a conflagration when Madame Dumont touched it – when Sophia had spoken against Mademoiselle Blanc? What would they think – what would anyone? Sophia had even told her that Miss White was trying to destroy the book with her powers, to prevent the story being told.

'The school is quite safe,' Miss White called out. 'The fire is in the rye field – you see? It is the crop burning, nothing more.'

She pointed into the distance. From here, none of us could see the field, but we could see the black smoke rising into the air, and she was right; it was coming not from Fulford, but beyond it.

The first of us to move was Sophia. She walked through the throng, not stopping to speak to anyone. Her head was held high, as if all this was exactly what she'd expected; as if she alone understood what it meant. The others followed her, of one mind again, already anticipating the moment when she would tell them what to feel; when she would explain to them what it was they had just seen.

22

'I saw Mademoiselle Blanc in the field.' Sophia looked around defiantly, daring anyone to disagree. 'I saw her double from a window, moments before I knocked on the door of her classroom and she came out of it. She was both inside and out, standing in the middle of it as it burned. That's how she knew what was happening – because she caused it! There were flames all around her, although *she* didn't burn. It was she who sent the fire to us.'

Outside the window, smoke hung thickly in the air. Now and then it parted to reveal glimpses of the field, its once deep gold turned black. The fire was smouldering, giving out flashes of light as vivid as malice. Miss White had been right: they were burning the crop. There never had been any danger to the girls, though from the way they gasped and put their hands to their mouths, that wasn't how they saw it.

'Why would she do that?' I said. 'She had no reason.' I didn't mention the ergot, since Sophia had not. That would rather give Miss White a purpose in destroying the field, though it was one of protecting those around her, nothing dark; nothing wicked.

But Sophia had an answer of her own. 'Poor Madame was injured when she tried to burn the book. The way it burst into flames was horrifying. Mademoiselle Blanc knew we were speaking of her and she wanted us to stop. Whatever the cost.'

'And you were such a help, weren't you Sophia, in putting out the flames?' I said.

She fell silent and glared at me, and so I pressed her. 'Perhaps you'd like to tell us what you did.'

She looked outraged. 'What *I* did? I did what I should have done ages ago. I went to Madame Dumont. It's hardly my fault if it ended badly.'

Of course, the others echoed with their eyes. *Of course, it wasn't your fault.* Outside, a flurry of sparks caught and lifted on the breeze, rushing towards us like ill intent.

'Wasn't it?' I said.

Silence, as heavy as smoke.

'You went to her to have Emily dismissed just because you dislike her. You played tricks against her to blacken her name. You pretended to explain everything while telling half-truths, if not outright lies. But those things don't matter now. I'm speaking of what you did to Madame Dumont's hands. What you did to the book. You put something on it to make it burn like that, didn't you? You must have.'

Her mouth fell open. 'How dare you? I would never do such a thing. *I* wouldn't even think of it.'

197

'Tell the truth! It wouldn't burst into flames like that before, even when you put a match to it. What did you use? Paraffin, or something else? What was your plan? I suppose if Madame Dumont hadn't tried to burn the book, you'd have suggested it yourself. Were you going to say you should destroy its influence? I suppose *you* would have been the one to throw it on the fire, so that when it went up like that, so violently, she'd have to believe you.'

Sophia straightened. When she spoke, it was slowly and with emphasis on every word. 'I have done nothing wrong.'

She turned to the others; their opinion mattered more. 'I could never have burned that book. As I explained to you before, I *did* set a match to it, to make an experiment, to see why it was smouldering as it was. But as Ivy has so rightly pointed out, it wouldn't burn, not for me. *I* have no special powers. It was only Mademoiselle Blanc who could set it aflame like that, and she did. She wanted to keep her secrets – or possibly she wanted to hurt *me*.' She held out her hand to display her wound again, and we saw the way it had blistered – just like Madame Dumont's.

'Our headmistress was injured because I told her the truth,' she said. 'I feel terrible about it, but what could I do? I had to try. I had to stop Mademoiselle Blanc, for all our sakes.'

'Don't go on with this, Sophia,' I said. 'You've seen where it can lead. You'll damn yourself with your lies. You have to tell the real truth—'

'I cannot say what didn't happen.' She pressed her lips closed. And of course, it was impossible for her to admit anything. Her plan had gone awry; her trick was too successful. Beatrice was dead. Madame Dumont was hurt. Those things were unforgivable and if she admitted to them she'd be the one cast out; by the school, possibly even her family.

But she hadn't finished.

'You will see,' she said, drawing herself straighter, 'that I am doing what I must. I am being exactly what I ought to be. If you don't understand that, Ivy—' She took a deep breath. 'I have been taught by my elders and betters to protect the younger girls from elements that are not desirable – even wicked. And I shall. Do you think I act for my own sake? I mean to show them what is decent and acceptable in Society, and what is not; what must be shunned.'

I could only stare. She really seemed to believe her words. I remembered her stricken face when we'd found out about Bea; then the way she'd so quickly recovered. Of course she'd had to persuade even herself that the cause of it was some wicked spectre, never her. She was so unused to being anything less than perfect.

'You should listen too, Ivy.' She sighed. 'I offered you my friendship. We all did. We know what you are, but still I've tried to protect you and all the girls. Such is my duty and I'll do it still. Will you let me?'

Offered you my friendship? I hardly knew how to answer that. She had never been my friend. I remembered the sneering way she'd spoken of my family, my *natural level*. We were from different worlds. She was nothing like me.

No, a little voice inside me whispered. She was everything my grandfather would have wished to see in me and couldn't. She was everything my father had sent me away to become. She was exactly what the school would make of us all, and she *wanted* to be those things – but then, that was why I despised her.

'Do you think me ignorant, Ivy?' Sophia said softly. 'Of course I know all about you. But there's still decent blood in you, is there not? That will out, if you let it. If you surround yourself with what is right and proper.'

She held out her uninjured hand, healthy and smooth. I stared at it for a long moment. I pictured taking it and Sophia smiling and all the girls gathering about me, not *I* any longer but one of many. I could do what my grandfather had sent me here to do. I could learn to be just like them. To belong. I could have sisters again, of a kind. I pictured us in future years, married ladies paying morning calls on one another, sitting in drawing rooms just like my grandfather's and pouring tea, gossiping about that awful teacher we once had. How we would laugh about her! Wicked Mademoiselle Blanc, starving on the streets, just as she deserved! And the walls would be full of paintings of hothouse flowers, all beautiful and entirely perfect, never a daisy to be seen among them, for such weeds could never have a place with any of us.

After a long moment, I shook my head.

She let her hand fall and sighed. 'Very well. I won't offer again.' She looked down at me as if I were a child too wayward for her help.

'I suppose Mademoiselle Blanc has some unholy influence over you – is that it? It's you who cannot see what is before your nose, Ivy. You are under her spell, or perhaps simply as bad as she is.' She paused, a new light in her eyes. 'Or is it something else?'

The others straightened too, staring at me with new interest. They all knew what she meant and I could only shake my head as warmth spread through my cheeks.

'Perhaps Bea could have told us.'

My mouth fell open. 'You dare talk to me about Bea? It was *you* who placed her in that room, by that window! She was my friend, my *friend*, and *you*—'

She strode towards me. I barely realised she'd slapped me until the heat in my cheeks began to burn.

'How *dare* you, Ivy?' She looked around at the others, their faces identical in expression. 'Your friend? We had to pull her from your arms. She was crying and crying, and you – what *were* you doing, Ivy? You'd wrapped yourself so tightly around her we couldn't get her free. You were smothering her. Choking her. Worse.'

I shook my head. Of course Bea had been crying. Her father had sent her away and she was alone and I was her only confidante. I'd comforted her. I'd held her. She'd stopped crying then; she'd blinked the tears away.

Sophia leaned over me, her eyes full of scorn – or disgust. 'I always knew there was something wrong with you, Ivy. *Unnatural.* We all did.'

'They were talking of *you*.' This new voice was small, yet clear and childlike. It was Lucy, and she was addressing me.

Sophia turned to stare at her. 'What do you mean?'

'When Mademoiselle Blanc was fastening Bea's dress. I heard them talking, before I went downstairs to wait at the door. Bea didn't raise the subject of Ivy, of course.' Her lip curled. 'She wouldn't have liked to do that. But Mademoiselle did. She started saying how Ivy needed a friend and perhaps Beatrice could help, that maybe they'd be suited. She couldn't have known they really used to be friends, of course. I didn't think about it at the time.

I was looking forward to the fete. I imagine Bea was horrified, though. I wonder if her reaction made that *thing* even angrier?'

Sophia's head snapped around to stare at me again. I had to get away; I couldn't look at any of them. I turned and ran from the room.

23

I leaned back against the door, squeezing my eyes closed. Words whirled through my mind, shifting like smoke, changing everything. *Unnatural*, I thought. *Unnatural, unnatural, unnatural.* Is that what I was — what we had been to each other? My name meant *faithfulness*. I would always have been faithful. I was her *friend*.

Behind my closed eyes, I saw Bea. She was in the eyrie, saying her prayers, her knuckles white with clasping them so tightly. She hadn't been praying for Sophia's sins; she'd been praying for mine. For hers. Because we'd cared for each other, hadn't we? We had loved one another and we'd been alone and Sophia had seen something ugly in it. She'd told her lies. She'd enjoyed them. She'd accused me of things — as if my thoughts had ever been for myself. Yet Bea had given way before their words. She'd started to look at me through their eyes, her expression changing, as if I was becoming something else in front of her.

I shook my head. I'd only longed to think of Bea as a sister.

Even if it was more than that, surely it would only have been *love*. It couldn't be so very unnatural, although I knew it was *unacceptable*, at least by those who decided what was unacceptable. Is that why Bea had leapt from a window – because Miss White had put her in mind of me and brought it all back to her? Lucy had spoken of hearing Bea speaking low and fast, words she couldn't make out. Had she not been *babbling*, as Lucy had said, but praying? Had she reached out with her senses, trying to find some presence who would grant her the forgiveness she had never needed, and finding nothing, no answer at all, become desperate? If so, I thought fiercely, what happened to her still came back to Sophia: her ugly accusations and uglier looks.

I pressed myself against the door's hard panels and listened to the silence. I saw my true sister, Daisy, her face pushed up close to mine and a grin on her lips, and felt all the emptiness of this place, all the lonely abandonment of its corridors, the sighs that had been breathed here, the tears it had swallowed. I wished I could turn into nothing but my namesake: stem and leaf, nothing but ivy, and forget.

Then I thought I heard a sound after all, a soft shifting coming from the room behind me, and I turned and pressed my hands to the door. After a moment, I knocked.

It didn't open but an answer came, for someone was approaching along the corridor and I straightened, not wanting them to think I was eavesdropping. But it was Emily herself walking towards me, and the scent of smoke came with her.

'Ivy, I cannot help you now, I'm afraid. Our lessons must wait a little longer.' She summoned a smile, then faltered as she looked into my face. Quickly, she opened the door and let me in. It hadn't been locked. And the room was empty, not even a shadow to make me imagine anyone was there; I couldn't have heard anything after all. Two draped paintings appeared abandoned, the flowers in the corner left to wilt. We might never finish our pictures. We'd have to start again – if we could even have that.

'I wanted to apologise to you,' I started, 'for the way they treat you. It is unjust and unfair, and—'

She held up her hand to stop me. 'You don't need to apologise to me, Ivy. Girls enjoy a little gossip, that's all. They enjoy making up stories.' She let out a sigh. 'You're clearly upset, but please, don't concern yourself on my behalf. I'm quite all right, you see. I always am.'

'But you *don't* see.' I tried to gather myself. 'Sophia is trying to have you dismissed. She went to Madame Dumont and told her everything – all her outrageous tales. She wants to see you cast off, sent back to—' But I didn't know where Emily might go. I didn't know where she'd come from. 'I hate her! I tried to stop her but she won't change, she just lies and lies, and I'm sorry, I really am.'

Miss White stepped towards me, then stopped. She stood there watching, as if she were frozen.

'What did Sophia say exactly, Ivy? Do you know the substance of her accusations?'

'She claims that you were at another school. That things – happened there. That you are not all that you seem.'

She turned pale; she sat down heavily upon a chair. 'She knows of that? Is this what you hinted at before, Ivy, when you spoke of my having another life?'

Miserably, I nodded.

'And now she has told Madame Dumont.' She started pulling at her collar, as if she couldn't breathe.

I went to help her, tucking my fingers inside the fabric to unfasten the button at her throat. 'It'll be all right, you'll see. Madame Dumont won't listen – she didn't entertain Sophia for a moment. She burned the only account of it that Sophia possessed. She threw it on the fire.'

Miss White wasn't reassured; instead she pulled away from me and hurried to the cupboard at one side of the room, crouching to rummage inside. She withdrew something: I half expected Sophia's infernal book to have appeared again, but instead there was a bundle of letters, tied with a ribbon. The faint scent of bergamot and lemon arose as she clutched them, pressing her eyes closed with what appeared to be relief.

I tilted my head and made out a name written there: Not Emily White or even Emélie Sagée, but *Emeline Jones*.

I had no idea what to say. I couldn't think. Emily, Emélie, Emeline . . . the names spun into one. Who was this person I didn't know and hadn't suspected existed until now?

Who *was* she?

It's you who cannot see what is before your nose, Ivy.

I knelt down next to her. I wished I could reassure her, tell her I would always approve, reach out and touch her shoulder – but I couldn't. Those names prevented me. *Emily. Emélie. Emeline.*

She seemed entirely lost, in some other world – or perhaps in the past. Speaking half to herself, she said, 'I had to leave that life behind me.'

Which life did she mean? I no longer knew – I couldn't see any of it. I almost wished to be back in Sophia's room, her hand held out to me. If I'd taken it, perhaps the world would make sense. It wouldn't be spinning around me, nothing solid at all. But now I reached for something else – I put out my hand and ran my fingertips over that strange name. *Emeline*.

All at once, Emily roused herself, as if the life had flooded back into her. She pushed the letters back into the cupboard, under some linens.

'I was Emeline then.' She sniffed, an ugly sound. The tip of her nose had turned red. 'I was born Emeline. Do you understand, Ivy? You do, don't you?'

I didn't. I understood nothing, but I did not reply.

'I was imposed upon. You already know how things are, Ivy, I see that. I had to change my name and leave my real self behind, because of all those who would have judged me without hearing a word I said. I know it was an untruth, but it was in a just cause. I had to keep my good character. I have no relatives, nowhere else to go. I have to work.'

I always tell the truth, Sophia had said. I couldn't seem to banish the thought of her.

Now Emily wasn't even Emily any longer. The name she had given me, her gift, hadn't really been her name at all. Even her speech seemed to be changing, her vowels becoming broader, flatter, hinting at an accent I'd never suspected was hiding beneath her own. I remembered quelling my own speech in just the same way, forcing myself to say *the* and not *t'*, to sound out my vowels, turning what was natural into a matter of painstaking thought.

Emily – *Emeline* – rubbed her eyes and rose to her feet. 'I've said too much. It's just that I've been so terribly alone in the secret. Please forgive me, Ivy, and forget what I told you. It is not your burden to carry, and yet it has been such an awful thing to keep quiet. Can you imagine – no one even knowing your name? To live this way – please believe me when I say this is not truly who I am.'

I stood too, and met her eyes. Hers were wide, reddened with tears and yet beautiful. A feeling came over me; a longing to reach out and wipe the tears from her cheek. I didn't care about any of it. What if she had lied? She was innocent and shouldn't have been so judged by everyone around her. She was still the person I'd always known. She was kind and gentle and not like the others. It was a *good* thing they didn't like her. It meant they couldn't take her away from me, not like Daisy, nor like Beatrice; they wouldn't even try.

Why should her past matter? It was *now* that mattered. She hadn't even done anything. She'd been *imposed upon*. She meant there had been a man, I supposed, but what of that? She hadn't wanted him; of course she hadn't. It wasn't as if she'd been in love.

My eyes blurred and for a moment her image separated, no longer one Emily but many, all their faces alike. I saw Mademoiselle Blanc, our teacher; Emélie Sagée, a character in a book; the stranger, Emeline Jones; and Emily – the one I felt I knew best of all, and who she would remain, at least to me. I blinked and they became one again, all the iterations of her, her other lives. I thought of images within a zoetrope spinning faster and faster until they became one moving, breathing, living creature, with only the suggestion of something else in the flickering: a shadow, an after-image – a doppelgänger. But that was an illusion. It was never real.

I gave her a gentle smile. 'Of course I will,' I said. 'Of course I'll forget. It's nothing to me, any of it. I shall never speak of it to anyone.' *Except you*, my mind added.

And I told Emily of my own secrets. I held back nothing, speaking freely at last of the farm and of my sister. I told her who I *was*, and she didn't look horrified or even surprised. If anything she seemed comforted by it, and I was glad. I wanted to soothe away her concerns. I wanted her to be able to stay here always and always.

'Look,' she said. 'Our pictures. That seems so long ago, doesn't it?'

She was right, it did. We removed the sheets and looked at them afresh and found that time had much the same effect as a mirror. Our pictures had been made strange to us, and yet we didn't see their faults. Hers was free and beautiful. Mine was almost lifelike and Emily swept a hand over its flatness as if to reassure herself it was only a painting. The single white rose at its centre was the loveliest and most real thing of all.

I told her that hers spoke to me of meadows and flower-scented breezes. I could almost smell them.

She smiled. 'You may have it, if you wish.'

'Really? Do you mean it?'

She laughed at my eagerness. 'Of course. Come, I'll roll it for you.' She did, forming it into a cylinder, neatening the edges before presenting it to me. 'For listening. And—'

Not telling, I thought. I took the picture and bobbed a curtsey before glancing at my own painting. Should I offer it in return? I suddenly felt shy. I wanted for her to possess it – to *want* it – so very deeply, I couldn't bear to say the words.

'Leave yours just there,' she suggested, as if she knew how I felt. 'You can add to it later, or look at it again next time, to see how you're progressing.'

Next time. I smiled and nodded my gratitude, and she said it would be best if I returned to my room. The idea of being among the other girls left me cold, but she was right, I must go. I said farewell, but before I left, she leaned forward and kissed my cheek. I stepped into the corridor and the door closed behind me and I walked away. I clutched her gift to me as I went, careful not to crush the paper. I could still feel where her lips had touched my skin; it was the same place where Sophia had slapped me, but that was behind me now. I was full of new secrets, new smiles, and entirely, contentedly alone.

24

Emily White's secret was like a warm meal inside me, like comfort, like home. The other girls hadn't spoken to me when I'd returned, refusing even to look in my direction, and I hadn't cared. Emily had confided in *me*. The others refused to accept her and that was its own punishment, for they would never have her friendship; they wouldn't know her as I did. They'd brushed their shining hair and softened their shapely hands, these paragons of the school, and I saw them for what they were: whited sepulchres like in the Bible, smartly painted but full of rot.

I had thought of little else. I'd barely been able to sleep. Now we were gathered in the eyrie, and Sophia, the worst of them all, was opening her pretty lips to sing. Her voice was glorious as it rose over us: *Holy, holy, holy.* My own voice was low and a little hoarse and I scarcely breathed the words.

The teachers were in front of us, the servants behind, all in our rightful places. At least my chair was at the end of a row so that I could look out of the windows if I turned my head. Of course, it would be shocking for any young lady to wish to be distracted from the edification of a sermon. We couldn't afford to ignore moral instruction; we did so at our peril. We weren't permitted to be curious. Besides, the parson was handsome and although the headmistress had bandages over her hands and pain in her movements, her eyes were as sharp as ever.

And what was there to see in the world outside? The rye had long burnt itself out. Alone among the fields it was empty of colour, as if a little piece of night remained long after the sun had risen. The breeze occasionally lifted and turned the charred stems as with a pitchfork, carrying drifts of ash towards us. From time to time they floated past, like spectres we had forgotten to fear. Otherwise the day was perfectly bright, the sky a gift of blue, full of birdsong far more lovely than our caterwauling at Heaven. I wished I was out there somewhere below, riding on Captain's broad back, breathing in the good smell of horse. One day, perhaps I could show Emily how. I'd wager she could learn to ride as quick as anything.

Then I jumped, because she *was* there: a tiny figure, a little like a doll. She stood just beyond the garden, at the gap in the wall, her back turned. She was wearing her cape. She was looking out over the burned field.

I returned my gaze to the dais. Reverend Aubrey glared at my inattention, but I didn't care for him. I looked past him to where I thought Miss White had been standing and saw that she was still there, and she too was gazing back at me, though with softness in her eyes. It didn't warm me, not now. *It's real*, I thought. Of course: I'd seen it in her room after all, a dark shadow, wearing her face.

Suddenly the strength drained from me. I grasped at the chair in front of mine.

Miss White, outside, hadn't moved. She was as motionless as a statue, even as a wreath of ashes drifted over her. It didn't seem to trouble her. She didn't even notice it.

I tried to tell myself again that someone had borrowed her cape. Or they'd draped it over a fence post and a trick of the eye had lent it flesh. Still I stared and stared and she didn't vanish and didn't change into anything else. It was *her*. I'd have known her anywhere. Even with her back turned; even if she refused to look at me.

Still Miss White stood on the dais singing, just as she should be, her expression pious, though her eyes had gone quite blank.

The song reached its end. Miss White moved before anyone else, almost falling into her seat. Was she half in a trance, weakened from creating her double or from sending out her will, casting a spell over my mind? Was I especially suggestible, since I'd made myself her friend and vulnerable to her? But she *was* my friend. We'd told each other everything that mattered to us. She'd touched my hand and kissed my cheek and told me her names, all of them she'd ever had. She would never—

The girls retook their seats and I hastened to do the same as the parson started up again. Now it wasn't so easy to see out of the window. Was she still there? Perhaps she'd come for me. I might turn and she would be sitting next to me, not the Emily I knew but someone who only looked like her. A reflection, wicked where Emily was good; an opposite, made of shadows and bad thoughts, her hair hanging in a damp draggle over her face.

I forced myself to look. There were only the other girls: their lips, cheeks, eyes, their straight backs and folded hands. They might almost have been one girl multiplied, images repeating into the distance. Each was motionless, like a statue; perfect semblances of life.

I half rose, trying to see the doppelgänger once more. She was still outside, but she had moved. She was in the garden, her face hidden beneath her hood as she stooped to pick a flower. The white lily was bright against her cape. How had she moved so quickly? Had she simply appeared elsewhere at a thought, somehow passing through the garden wall?

'There – my God! Do you see?' Sophia's blasphemy cut off the parson's drone, silencing him.

I heard a soft sound in my ears: the *tick . . . tick . . . tick* of a zoetrope beginning to spin. This was no toy in a classroom; it was bigger than that, the namesake of them all. This was the wheel of life, bringing something towards us – or taking something away.

Another cry, inarticulate this time, and the others rose to their feet. I half expected the windows to shatter, the walls to topple. All the images of perfect girlhood separated and scattered. They pushed back their chairs and exclaimed and peered to see who'd cried out. Of course, it was Sophia; it was always Sophia, the centre of the wheel upon which they turned. Now she was unmoving, staring towards me, past me, out of the window.

It was no use telling myself I hadn't seen the doppelgänger. Everyone had.

Madame Dumont called for quiet. She wouldn't have this behaviour, not today, not ever. Her voice was drowned out by the sound of hurrying feet as twenty-six young ladies flocked to the window.

They pushed around and past me, all their pretty manners forgotten. They wanted to see what Sophia saw. Amelia and Frances and Matilda and Grace and all the others moved with her. I couldn't see Lucy; once again Sophia had left her cousin to jostle with the rest. Reverend Aubrey's mouth hung open, a word half formed on his lips, but he never completed it.

The teachers didn't protest. They followed in Sophia's wake. They were nothing but skirts, knees, elbows, shoulders battling for position. Only Emily didn't move; she and the parson remained on the dais. Was she too drained by the presence? Or shocked by their actions? There was no recognition in her eyes as she stared at us – she might have been anywhere, and we anyone. She was an emptiness, a *blank*, and I wanted to rush to her side and shake her until expression returned to her grey eyes; until she saw *me*.

Someone cried out, 'It's gone.'

'The other side, quick!' said Sophia. She rushed around the eyrie's circumference, her hands patting at the window frames as she went, as if it were they that were in motion and she wished to hurry them along. She didn't stop until she was overlooking the front of the folly, and there the others caught up with her, crowding around the window, all pushing to see.

A sharp crack: a dark line appeared on the glass.

I too had caught their fever. Besides, I wanted to see her again. She was *mine*, not theirs. I started pulling the others away, but they were already moving, for the window had broken. The once solid surface was as thin and fragile as an illusion.

I looked through it and there was nothing to see. There was no little caped figure, not standing in the grounds or on the gravel or walking away from us down the lane, and I felt oddly bereft. I turned towards the dais. Emily stood very straight, supported by no one, pinned in place by curious, hateful glances. Even Madame Dumont eyed her with something like fear. Reverend Aubrey opened his mouth, but this was beyond his experience or his powers and no sound emerged; he had nothing to offer us.

Sophia raised her hand. Her palm was seeping blood. It dripped from her, falling to the floor. She had surely done it to herself but she showed it to us as if it were proof of something. Then she pointed. 'There.'

She indicated not the window but a corner of the room near one of the staircases. A picture hung against the curling yellow wallpaper. It was of Fulford; an old painting, badly composed and poorly executed. There was a coat-stand too, rarely used, now holding a single garment: the parson's greatcoat, casting its shadow against the wall.

It was not a shadow. Realisation crept over me, the cold of it blossoming in my chest. There was a shape hidden within that shadow: a figure.

I shook my head. The corner was made darker by the contrast with the windows. My eyes were confused. My mind was too, trying too hard to make sense of what I saw. Little wonder that Sophia had been fooled; it was nothing strange if a shadow seemed to take on the form that was so present to all our minds.

'There!' Sophia said again, and the girls shrank back, gasping in fear.

In the corner, something shifted. A cloud must have passed across the sun, deepening the shadows. I tried to say so but my voice was smothered in my throat.

Madame Dumont stepped forward. She would put an end to this – but she was only trying to get a better look. She too wanted to see what Sophia saw. The other girls gathered around Sophia, now edging forward, now shrinking away, like a murmuration of twittering starlings.

'She's coming! My God—' Sophia made no apology for her words, not even to the parson, who remained motionless on the dais. She retreated and the others moved with her, like one creature. Amelia clamped a hand to her mouth as if she'd seen something terrible. Grace let out a low wail.

'There's nothing,' I tried, but Sophia's words swallowed my own.

'Can't you see her – don't you *see*?'

They *did* see. They cried out in alarm.

Sophia never looked away from the corner. 'There – Amelia, look out!'

Amelia shrieked and stumbled away, trying to get behind the others, as if they would protect her. Of course they didn't; they all tried to do the same, hiding behind everyone else. Only Sophia stood steadfast, her eyes unblinking, focused on something I couldn't see. No: something that *was not there*. It was only shadows. Only a trick of the light.

Only a trick.

'Grace, she's looking at you!' Sophia said.

Grace screamed. She grasped Frances's shoulders, dragging the girl in front of her.

'And you – Tilly!'

Matilda shrank away, her cheeks turning white.

'And you!'

She commanded them. She made them dance. The air felt alive with an electrical charge that might at any moment break loose. My hair prickled with it. There was a smell, I realised: lilies?

Emily, on the dais, fell to her knees. Tendrils of her hair came loose and snaked over her shoulders. No one helped her. No one ordered Sophia to stop this. They did nothing but watch. The parson, however, moved at last. He strode towards Emily, then past her – away from her. She half reached for his arm as he went and he didn't even see her.

With a sick feeling, I realised that everyone would have to believe Sophia now. Otherwise, how could they ever have permitted such behaviour? How could they have been so taken in? How would they explain that to themselves, in the quiet judgement of their rooms?

Sophia held out her hand once more, this time in a gesture that meant *Stop*. 'Don't be afraid,' she said, over her shoulder. 'I won't let her touch any of you.'

How could she protect them from *nothing*? Yet they all watched her as if pleading for her help.

'Get away!' Sophia stepped sharply aside as if to cut off someone's approach and as one, the others caught their breath.

It was happening, I realised. *The most remarkable example . . . happened in this wise.* but *the most remarkable example* wasn't in the book: it was here. It was now. I had thought it impossible for Sophia to duplicate a sighting of the doppelgänger that was witnessed by everyone, and yet she *was* duplicating it. She hadn't needed them to see it with their eyes. She only needed to make them think they did – and she *was*.

Sophia raised her arm. This time she didn't cry out; she no longer seemed aware of anyone else's existence. She only appeared to reach for something – she ran her fingers downwards, just as if she were stroking someone's arm.

'Oh, she is *soft*!' she said. 'My fingers—'

She shook her hand to rid herself of the touch of it, something tainted, something *unnatural*.

'What are you?' she whispered. 'Are you real or spirit? Are you—'

She didn't finish. It was as if her voice had been stolen from her. She moved her lips, but no sound emerged and no one looked away or moved or spoke. They were all of them under her spell.

Sophia reached out again, at once reluctant and fascinated. Slowly, she defined a figure in the air in front of her with her fingertips. She started to shake her head – quicker and quicker, her face crumpling in dismay.

Then her hand shot to her throat. She took a step backwards, and another, as if she had been grabbed by the neck and someone was pushing her. She leaned until the angle was impossible; *unnatural*. She must surely fall, but she didn't fall. One hand remained outstretched, trying to fend off some invisible assailant. The other remained at her throat – clawing, trying to prise someone's hand away.

She opened her mouth and let out a choking sound. Her cheeks reddened. The sound she made was desperate, rough. It was as if she couldn't breathe – as if she were being strangled in front of us.

She managed another stumbling step backwards, then, painfully, another. She had almost reached the window. Her outstretched hand grasped at the air, inelegant, *unpretty*. I heard a dull sound as the back of her head met the glass. It was the pane that had cracked.

Sophia's breath whistled as she gasped for air. She struggled, desperate. There came an aching creak as the web of lines multiplied around her.

Everything seemed to happen terribly slowly. Sophia gave one last gasping choke. A shard fell from the glass; a breeze snaked in. I felt, rather than saw, a figure race past me.

Quicker than anyone, the parson grabbed for Sophia as she teetered. For a moment, she flailed – if she truly had an invisible assailant, they'd let her go. His hand grasped at her sleeve – which stretched and held, and he seized her wrist, pulling her towards him. He gathered her in, wrapping her tightly in his arms – her shoulders, then her waist. He lowered her to the floor. And the glass held, though it wasn't whole any longer; splintered edges flashed silver in the air, and gold, and all colours. Sophia was safe, but still he didn't loosen his grip as she clung to him. She began to sob against his chest. She was helpless and pitiful and beautiful, like a heroine in a fairy tale, and he her gallant rescuer.

Reverend Aubrey pulled his handkerchief from his pocket and presented it to her. She mopped discreetly at her nose, turning her distress into all that was simpering and charming. She shuddered, whispering, 'Horrible – horrible!'

'Whatever happened, my dear?' He spoke those words softly: *my dear*.

She roused herself a little, adopting a brave expression. 'She seized hold of me,' she said. 'It was Mademoiselle Blanc's double – her *shadow* – we've all seen it. It's just like her, in *every* way. She tried to push me out of the window, just like Bea, but it's all right; she's gone now.'

He couldn't reply, but he didn't move away from her either.

'I think it must be a bad spirit, like the ones spoken of in the Bible.' Now Sophia had found the words that would most appeal to him.

He only whispered, 'Shhh . . .' into her lovely hair.

'Did you see her too?' Sophia didn't look up but she spoke louder; and there were voices enough waiting to answer.

'Frightful,' shivered Amelia.

'Did you see her eyes?'

'They burned like flames.'

If Miss White hadn't known what the girls were doing before, she could be under no illusion now. Her gaze went from one of them to the next, helpless as their voices joined in.

'I saw 'er! Eyes flashin' like a devil's!' Sukie said, as forward as she ever was, but no one shushed her; no one told her to mind her place.

Madame Dumont stood and listened to it all, cradling her wounded hands as if her injury had only just happened. She appeared smaller than she had before and a little stooped, her expression uncertain. Was she waiting to see what the parson would say? He was a man after all, and carried the authority of God on his shoulders.

Tell them, I willed him. *Tell them to stop.*

Without removing his arms from Sophia, Reverend Aubrey said, 'I cannot be certain. I saw – *something*. I shall pray for guidance for us all. Now, Sophia, perhaps I can help you to stand.'

My eyes narrowed as he assisted her to her feet. He'd stalked straight past Emily when she'd fallen; now he held and supported Sophia. The girl leaned on him as if she couldn't move without his help and he gazed down into her eyes; her lip trembled at his look.

Emily was so different to Sophia. She too was shaking, I saw the tremor in her hands, but she clasped them more firmly in front of her. Any woman could shed false tears; surely only Emily could now have held hers back.

'Girls, go to your rooms.' Madame Dumont took charge at last. 'Madame Pelletier, please attend to Sophia. No, I thank you, Reverend Aubrey, but we can manage very well.'

Another lie, but it was accepted by all. There was no time to dwell on it, for she had us fall into lines and file from the room. I walked away from the shattered window, chill air stroking the back of my neck as I was banished from the eyrie along with the rest.

25

Later, Sophia returned to us, walking alone, without assistance from parson or teacher or anyone. She didn't need it any longer. She'd had that already, and in front of us all. I waited, not sure I could bear to listen but not wishing either to leave. I had meant to remain among them for Emily's sake, and so I would. Sophia took her time, giving an impressive shudder as she sat. Lucy plumped her pillow and she settled into it.

'I don't think I can talk now, girls,' she said. 'I feel so very weary. That *thing*, when I touched it—'

'What did it do to you?' They all wanted to know.

'*She*.' Sophia smiled weakly. 'What did *she* do to me.' She shivered again and looked around, pausing only a moment when she saw me among them. Did she think she'd convinced me into seeing what she wanted? Or did she know I *hadn't* seen, that there were only the two of us who knew the truth?

'I shouldn't have tried to touch her,' she resumed. 'That only made her angry, I think. I tried to stand in her way – I don't suppose anyone had tried such a thing before.'

They made the appropriate sounds: concern, excitement, admiration.

'What did it – *she* – feel like?' Lucy asked.

Sophia softly reached out to stroke her cousin's cheek. 'Awful,' she declared. 'Not like real flesh at all. There was resistance, strong enough to – to do what she did, but I could sense at a touch that she was – oh – empty. So, so very empty.'

Her dramatic sigh was taken up, multiplied.

'The wound on my hand went numb at once. I was afraid I'd never feel anything again, not properly, but that wasn't the worst of it. I could feel her on some other, higher level, with a sense other than touch. My gift, you know – it was warning me about her.'

I could practically see her mother standing behind her, dewy-eyed with pride. The others leaned in, rapt. They stared at the picture she painted of herself: a medium with powers beyond us all, a way of seeing that was better than our own.

'I could taste it, too.' Her eyes went distant and the others leaned in closer. 'Something *cold*, like metal.' She glanced around as if only now realising we were there. 'I really must rest.'

Yes: keep them hanging on, I thought. The delay would pique their interest, though they'd enjoy this a while longer yet. They'd enjoy it for hours, days; their whole lives. They'd relive it whenever they had a silent hour to fill, feeling again each frisson of excitement, every shiver and gasp. None of us would stop hearing of it; it would follow us beyond these walls. In future years their acquaintances would say, 'Look! There goes one of *those* girls, from the school where Mademoiselle Blanc—' and so it would go on, always and for ever.

Sophia stirred. Even now, she hadn't quite finished. 'It wasn't the look on her face that was so terrifying, you know.'

She paused long enough to be certain that every pair of eyes had turned towards her.

'It was more terrifying because of the lack of one. The sheer indifference on her face as she tried to push me from the window. Even as she tried to murder me in front of you all.'

She pulled down her blood-stained collar, exposing her throat. A line of bruises was forming there, darkening as we watched, like shadows; the shape of fingerprints blossoming on her milky skin.

26

I ran, threading the web of corridors, running my hands along the walls to catch myself when I stumbled. I didn't know where I was going until I emerged by a staircase with a familiar window, one I'd looked out of many times before. The view was of the stables, two chestnut horses nodding over their stalls, matching in almost every respect.

Pretence.

I didn't care about them. It was Sophia I saw before me at every moment: Sophia stroking her neck with a pained expression; Sophia lying languorous on her bed, fluttered around by everybody, heeded; listened to. I hated her. I hated her helpless expression, the one that said she was responsible for none of it.

Pretence. Pretence. Pretence.

I closed my eyes and saw again the events of that morning: a caped figure stooping to pick a lily, a funeral flower, purest white. Sophia, pointing towards a corner where shadows seemed to linger and shift. Sophia stumbling away from someone I couldn't see, pressing up against the cracked glass. And Sophia safe in the haven of the parson's arms, sobbing pretty tears.

I curled my hands into fists and imagined her tender neck beneath my fingers. I imagined placing them against those shadowed bruises and pushing deeper.

Which is, of course, what Sophia had done. She'd held one hand to her own throat while she pretended to ward off her assailant with the other. Just how tightly had she squeezed? I thought I knew. I should have examined her bruises more closely. I should have made her place her own fingers against them to see if they matched. She'd hurt herself before, after all; she'd held her palm to a flame and let it burn.

What happened in the eyrie had to be play-acting and trickery. I knew that better than anyone, for why would the doppelgänger appear to me one moment and in the next, only to Sophia? If it had entered the room, it would have come to *me*. It was connected to Emily, after all, and I knew Emily better than anyone.

Emeline, a voice whispered in the back of my mind – Emeline, a person I didn't know at all, and I banished the thought. I *did* know her. I was her *friend*.

I stared out at the horses, two creatures so alike I couldn't tell which was which. Gadling must have been wielding his paintbrush again, making them match, ensuring everything looked just as it should. I stared for a long moment. Then I turned from the window, knowing at last where I should go.

It wasn't far. I descended the stairs, where the door let onto the yard. I didn't go out, however. I went to the row of capes hanging on their pegs.

Finding the one I sought, I ran my fingers over the fabric. This was the one I'd worn in the fog, when it got so damp. It wasn't damp now but that didn't mean it hadn't been worn; the day had remained fine. There was a lingering trace of smoke in the fibres and nothing more, nothing to say who'd last worn it – or when.

The figure in the walled garden never had fully raised her head. I hadn't seen her face. Everyone was distracted by Sophia's antics – and how couldn't they be? She'd created chaos, just as the figure outside had vanished. She'd guided what they saw and what they *thought* they saw. Had that been deliberate – neatly timed, to allow an accomplice to slip away?

It might not have been a doppelgänger standing outside. The cape was here, within reach of anyone. Someone could have taken it and pulled the hood over their face. They'd done it before, hadn't they? I'd felt so sure it was Emily I'd glimpsed, but how could it have been? I had only been as suggestible as all the rest.

The cape in my hands was heavy. Its thick wool possessed a solidity that was somehow reassuring. I turned the fabric, stroking it as if I could really sense her, like a medium reading an object to learn about its owner. Could this have retained something of the person who'd borrowed it? But it was Emily's shape under my hands, impressed into the unyielding fabric. I felt inside it too, seeking her, running my fingers down the soft lining – and found there the traces of dried, blackened blood.

She took a hold of Captain's cheek-strap and whispered in his ear. Stood there in the rain while he bled. Soaked, she was . . .

Soaked in blood as well as rain, and it still hadn't been washed away. I pictured my old friend, his knees broken, the life pouring out of him. Gadling, his shirt sticking to his skin, that awful look in his eyes. I could almost smell the musk of horse, the rawer taint of blood and fear. But somehow the scent that came to me was sweeter: bergamot and lemon. I buried my face in her cape. It was *her* scent, fresh and clean.

I heard her whisper as if she were at my ear. *You understand, don't you, Ivy?*

I replaced the cape on its hook, leaving that scent hanging in the air behind me, and I knew that I didn't. But perhaps – perhaps I was beginning to.

The walls flew past me as if the corridors were all the same, the school more than ever like a zoetrope that was spinning, spinning, the past presenting itself anew, the seconds flying by quicker and quicker. Lucy was in her room. She had no time to look surprised as I pushed her back, away from the door, and slammed it behind me.

'Where is it?' I grasped at her clothes and something tore but I took no notice, pulling at her skirts, trying to see. For of course she must have been the one to wear the cloak and carry out Sophia's nasty wishes. It must have brushed against her; surely there'd be a trace of what she'd done, chestnut hairs clinging to the fabric? Yet I could find nothing and I stood back, blinded by fury. Had she already brushed them away? Well, she couldn't hide the lie for ever. I sniffed, trying to detect bergamot, or smoke, or the more cloying scent of the lilies she'd picked.

'What are you doing?' She pushed my hands away and I grabbed at her again. For a moment I couldn't see; there was a whirl of movement and I felt thin bones beneath my fingers. I snatched them back as her own hands went to her neck. I stepped away, breathing hard. I hadn't meant to hurt her. I was doing what I needed to do. I had to prove that Emily was innocent. I couldn't let them send her away from me.

Hands grasped my shoulder, pulling me aside. It was Frances; she hugged Lucy close as the girl started to cry. Matilda was with her, as always, and I caught her glare.

'You see, Fran? She's under her *control*—'

I turned and ran. Lucy may have concealed what she'd done, she might hide her guilt behind tears, but that didn't mean she hadn't done it. I knew she *had*. I didn't try to persuade them; they wouldn't listen. They were too far gone in their fantasy and I let out a disbelieving laugh as I rushed away, taking each turn without hesitation before I even knew where I was going.

❧

I found myself kneeling on a thin, faded carpet, in front of an open cupboard. I could barely remember coming here, the intervening time oddly blank, but that was because my thoughts were spinning. I was under no one's control but my own. I couldn't even remember pausing to knock, though I sensed the room at my back and knew that it was empty. Emily might be surprised, even angry if she found me here, but I had to see.

My picture remained on its table. Our flowers wilted in the corner. The air smelled of nothing, but I knew I was close.

Empty, Sophia had said. *So, so very empty.*

But Emily wasn't empty. She had lived a life, more than one life, and here was the proof: the possessions she'd accumulated over the years. There were needle-cases and notebooks and keepsake boxes, bottles of ink and nibs and blotters, but I wasn't looking for those. I sought what lay beneath a little pile of linens, and their scent had reached me already: the sweetness of bergamot and lemon.

Why should that scent have so troubled my mind? Soon I would know, for the letters were here: the ones she'd rushed to retrieve when I spoke of *evidence*. I'd smelled it even then, for her scent had clung to them, these memories of a past she'd wanted to forget. I saw again the way she'd clutched the letters to her, terrified that someone might have seen. I knew I shouldn't pry. This was the most terrible breach of trust, but still I couldn't stop myself.

Do you understand, Ivy? You do, don't you?

I didn't, but I had to.

I'd assumed the letters were from her previous school, but how could they be? Schools didn't dab scent onto their writing paper. They didn't season their words with such remembrance. No: it was women who did that, though not in correspondence with their employer.

I was imposed upon, she'd said.

There had been a man. I couldn't picture it. It had seemed so unlikely; or perhaps I hadn't wanted to think it might be true. I'd imagined a dark shadow of a fellow, too big and too strong; someone, I supposed, a little like Gadling. I'd imagined her mistreated, insulted in some way. Now all I could think of was Daisy, holding out her hand to me and saying, *Swear! We'll never love any man, not as we do each other – because we're sisters. We'll always be closer than anyone . . .*

Why, then, were there letters? Emily had never said, *I wrote to him.* She had not said, *I was in love.* Had *Emeline Jones* been the recipient or the sender? Her scent might have got onto the paper as she read them. He might have written them to her, pleading forgiveness, perhaps even *imposing upon* her further.

I found the top of a page, saw the words *My Dearest, I count the hours until I may be free of this school and in your arms,* and I pressed my eyes closed. I saw again the face that had become so dear to me – but she wouldn't have been Emily then, would she? She was Emeline, someone I scarcely knew at all. I pictured her writing this letter, smiling wistfully as she poured out her longing before dabbing her perfume onto the paper, then touching it to her lips. She had wanted to bring herself nearer when he read the words meant for him.

And then what? Emily had been forced to leave the school, but they were never married. There was no real connection – no *faithfulness*. They had never become one another's family. He'd cast her off, this nameless, faceless being, this man. He must have. If he'd *imposed upon* her, why had he troubled to return her letters? And why would she keep them? No. Emily had wanted him – and he'd rejected her.

Do you understand, Ivy? You do, don't you?

I didn't, and felt I never would. How could I? I was only her pupil, and she my teacher, and she had every right to her secrets. What if she *had* loved him – why should it even matter to me?

Still, it felt as if my heart would break. I could see shards flashing before my eyes: silver, gold, all colours, falling through the air. I had so wanted someone here – just one – to be my own.

I told myself the past was gone. That had been another life. Emily was here now; she'd wanted to leave it all behind her so badly she'd even changed her name. And she had given her true name to me.

I rocked back on my heels. I wouldn't read any more – I didn't want to. I told myself that whatever her life had been, it couldn't matter now. And I felt hands on my shoulders – not rough, accusing hands, but gentle, caressing. I knew without needing to turn that it was her.

She knelt down behind me. She wrapped her arms around me and leaned her head against mine and stroked my hair. She comforted me. We were so close I could feel the ripple of her heartbeat through my skin. It was at once delicate and powerful, sounding in my blood and bone, bringing me to fresh life. She must be able to see what I'd done. The open cupboard was there in front of her, the bundle of letters in my hand. Yet I felt that I was forgiven, and the sweetness of it flowed into me. I closed my eyes and knew, perhaps for the first time, the sweetness of being altogether accepted; of being altogether loved.

27

A short time later I was seated on a hard chair outside Madame Dumont's study, waiting to hear what my fate would be. Voices rose and fell from beyond the blank of the closed door and their tones didn't speak of kindness; they didn't speak of acceptance.

I had no need to make out the words to know what was being said. Nor did Lucy, seated opposite me, though she wouldn't meet my eye, only glaring angrily at my feet. Her hands twitched in her lap. Occasionally, they went to her neck. Her bruises weren't as impressive as Sophia's; there was barely a trace.

Her sleeve, however, was torn from wrist to elbow, and I would have to answer for that. I'd have to answer for all of it, but I had no words to say. What was the use? One look at her teary eyes and they'd declare me irredeemable and send me back to my grandparents. I wondered if they would even have me, now. They'd tried, after all, before throwing up their hands in despair and sending me here. What, then? I'd be returned to the farm, the place I'd so longed for, but to go home in shame — I couldn't bear that. My parents had hoped to make a lady of me, and for them to fail so dismally . . .

Had I really ripped Lucy's clothes? Had I clawed at her neck? *Do you see? She's under her control* . . .

I could say that was true, of course. If I claimed to have been driven by Mademoiselle Blanc's will, forced to do her bidding just like the doppelgänger, they'd have to believe me now. But I never could. Someone here had to care for the truth. And I could still feel her arms around me, holding me close. Remembering, I felt better, clearer. I knew what I had to say.

Inside Madame Dumont's study, Gadling's voice rose higher. He'd been in there when we arrived and I couldn't think why. The pair of us hardly breathed as we tried to listen; we might have been carven statues, chained to the wall.

'Of course it was her,' he said, followed by something quieter. Then, 'He allus knew when she were near. Bard knew.'

Were we back to that? What was it to him anyway — was he really seeking revenge for the loss of his horse? Anyway, it proved nothing. Bard hadn't even liked *me*. I could only hope such nonsense would awaken Madame Dumont to the madness of the rest.

Inside the room, footsteps strode towards us. I crossed my ankles and folded my hands in my lap, ignoring the curl of Lucy's lip. The door opened an inch and a white shirt came to fill it — he'd turned back towards the headmistress. 'I'll tell you summat else,' he said. 'She'll cost us all our place. That farmer's lost his harvest 'cos of her, an' no one's ever proved there were owt wrong with it. She were just after saving her own skin. Made enemies everywhere, an't she? Of the school, an' all.'

I heard no answer, but Madame Dumont must have dismissed his words before he'd even closed the door. He seemed surprised to see us there and his gaze rested for a moment upon me. He walked away shaking his head, as if to dismiss the lot of us as he returned to his stables.

'Lucy.' Madame Dumont's clipped voice lifted the girl to her feet and drew her into the study, leaving me alone in the corridor.

Since no one was there to prevent me pressing my ear to the door it was easier to eavesdrop on Lucy, though less interesting, since I already knew what she would say. And she did. She described the way I'd attacked her, pulling at her clothes as if to tear them off her. She said I had unnatural impulses. She said I was ungovernable. She said I was practically from the gutter and a polluting influence and she shouldn't be expected to be acquainted with me, that her father would consider it an indignity and an imposition, and after that I ceased to listen. I picked at the skin around my nails until Madame Dumont scolded her into silence.

I darted back to my seat as Lucy fled, crying once more, scurrying off to report everything to her cousin. There was no time to sneer. I was summoned inside.

It was odd to be standing in Madame Dumont's room again, and to find it all so quiet. No fire burned in the hearth; there was no billowing smoke. Still a trace of charring hung in the air and I swallowed, remembering the reek of singed flesh. Was that what I was smelling now – her burning skin? Was it ingrained in the petit point cushions, the flowery wallpaper, the Turkish carpet, the air?

I took a deep breath, reminding myself how calm I'd been then, putting out the flames, taking charge. I tried to recover that calmness as I recounted everything. I told her the truth. I explained the girls' silly ideas and how I believed they'd played their trick that very morning, how they'd tried to make a fool of her and Reverend Aubrey and the whole school. I left out the part about Emily White not being our teacher's real name. I didn't tell her of her past. What did that matter? It only mattered who she *was*.

When I voiced my suspicions about Lucy wearing Miss White's cape she listened but said not a word. Her demeanour hadn't changed a whit since I'd entered the room, but how could she deny reason? Mine was surely the only acceptable explanation for any of it.

She took a deep breath. 'And so you tore at her clothes.'

I admitted I had. I said I was sorry for it and that I'd found nothing but that didn't mean there was nothing to be found. If she questioned Lucy again on the matter, I was certain she'd tell her everything. The girl was surely not so far gone in pretence as to withstand that.

'I've heard enough stories.' Madame Dumont stared down at her bandaged hands as if the answer could be found there. 'I have one girl who lost her life and two more injured, or nearly so. Do you wish to blacken their names too, Ivy?'

'But—'

'I do not suppose such girls to be capable of this invention. Sophia has been falsely accused already. What do you imagine her father would say, if I called her honesty into question now? He is of the first respectability. She is surely above reproach.

Lucy would certainly never dream up such a thing, and of course she was present with us this morning – did you think I could so easily mislay one of my girls?'

I hadn't thought of that, though I should have. Madame Dumont always liked us to be in our places, with matching expressions and straight backs and folded hands, never thinking or reasoning for ourselves. Always the same: never *one*. She wanted perfect painted girls, roses that swelled into crimson bloom before new buds took their place.

There had been nothing to shake the composure of the school before Mademoiselle Blanc came here. There was order in the classrooms and quiet in the corridors. There had been no gossip then; there had been no stories. It hardly mattered what Madame Dumont believed. Her reality was composed of decorum and reputation, of keeping things always the same.

And what of Emily? Madame hadn't known her a year. She had no connections, no friends. She was alone in this world, and what was that against all the Sophias and Lucys in it?

Madame Dumont was gathering herself even now, readying herself to say the words that would most easily dismiss me. I wondered what explanation she would give – but she offered none, not to me. She simply said, 'You may go.'

I felt all my reasoned arguments fall away, remnants flying about the room like ashes. I was suddenly cold and wished Emily's arms were around me again, someone to care, with no words necessary, no explanations. I hadn't even needed, then, to turn and look into her eyes. I hadn't needed to see her expression.

I'd already been able to picture it, more clearly than anything: the soft lights in her grey eyes.

Now she would be sent away. I'd never see her again. The first intimation of pain glimmered inside me and I wrapped my arms about my body, gripping tighter. I couldn't reach my sorrow, couldn't touch it, but that didn't mean it wasn't real.

I would be alone.

When I turned to leave, Madame called after me. 'Sophia had a servant send a telegram to Lucy's father, you know. He is aware that his child has been attacked by another pupil and furthermore, that that pupil is not the daughter of a gentleman. I am not certain which news will upset him the most.'

Blood rushed to my face. I would be sent away too, then – and it struck me that Emily and I could somehow help each other, that our fate might lie together. I suddenly couldn't speak, but she added, 'Lucy is very likely to be withdrawn from the school.'

My hope faded. How could it ever have lived? If Lucy left, it was unlikely I'd be expelled too. There would be little purpose in Madame Dumont losing another fee. My grandfather's pride would remain intact, and therefore my parents'. He would continue to help them and I would avoid disgrace. I should be glad, but all I could think of as I was dismissed for a second time was that Emily White would go; and I would be forced to stay.

28

The morning after the decision was made, we crammed into a classroom for prayers and Bible readings, since the eyrie was out of bounds with its cracked window and bad memories. Miss Peel announced there would be a new future for the school. There would be fewer teachers but even greater care taken over our education and wellbeing, everything our parents could wish for. I didn't have to look around to see that Emily was absent. I felt the loss of her. The cold that had crept over me in Madame Dumont's study had remained in my bones; the cold of being only *Ivy* once more.

We were divided into groups. Some were taken for languages and some for singing, and the rest of us, who should have been with Miss White, were told to practise our embroidery under Sophia's supervision.

She led us to a classroom on the first floor, overlooking the front of the school. Yet here was a difficulty, for sewing was normally carried out in the light of the eyrie's tall windows, and our embroidery circles remained stored in its cupboards.

Sophia barely hesitated. Madame Dumont had instructed her to take embroidery and thus tacit permission had been given, even if Madame hadn't actually thought of it. She ordered us to wait while she fetched our work and I despised her more than ever. She was so sure of her position in the world, always certain to be thought well of. She was believed by everybody. She took it as her due, and why not? She'd won. She didn't even seem sorry that her little cousin was leaving, but then, she didn't need Lucy any longer.

We didn't sit meekly in our seats while we waited but gathered at the window in an echo of what had once been, on a different day, in a different life. The London train left Lundby Bridge at 1 p.m. and Miss White would be on it. That was probably meant to be a secret, so of course we all knew. After the train, I didn't know where Emily would go. She'd said she had no one and I thought of her wandering the capital's hard streets in despair until she stood on the parapet of Waterloo Bridge, contemplating the dirty brown waters below.

And I would sit here and make my tiny, useless, perfect stitches, one after the other. I didn't even know what my sampler ought to say. The 'Not' had lined up so very neatly with the 'Thou Shalt', but what came after that? There were so many choices, so many things I shouldn't or couldn't do.

A sound came from outside, a jingling and rattling I knew too well. It wasn't yet time, but Gadling had readied the carriage. Below me, the horses trotted into view. Was it my imagination that Gadling's movements had an air of self-satisfaction about them as he reined them in? He'd given the horse's blaze a fresh coat of paint and the carriage was polished. The day was treacherously fine. White scudding clouds hid and revealed the sun by turns and somewhere a bird sang high and sweet. I couldn't bear any of it.

Emily's trunk was strapped into place. They'd wasted no time in having it brought down; I'd seen it standing in the hall yesterday evening. They must have made her pack as soon as their decision was given, unless she was forced to stand by while servants stuffed her possessions into boxes. I wondered what she was doing now. Was she waiting alone in her room with nothing to do, no one to say goodbye?

I hadn't been a friend to her, not really. All my efforts had gone awry or failed. Now I couldn't even see her. I couldn't finish my painting and present it to her as I'd wished – why had I been such a coward?

The door opened. It was Sophia with her crown of golden hair, her arms laden with gifts for her courtiers. She called us to our seats and distributed the embroidery frames, holding each aloft for us to identify them. We handed them back along the rows of seats and they flowed before me: *The Lord is my shepherd. Bless this house. Let not your heart be troubled.* Then the one I recognised: *Thou shalt not.* What should fill that blank? I still didn't know.

Heads bowed over our coloured silks, turning occasionally, not to follow the path of our flashing needles but glancing towards the carriage. I leaned over too, though I wasn't sewing. All the moments felt like one moment. What was Emily doing now – and now? Why couldn't I be with her?

A distant voice drifted through the thin window: a woman's.

'Ivy, why aren't you working?' Sophia's voice jabbed at me, sharp as a needle.

I scowled like a sulky child. I did the one thing I could think of: I held up my embroidery frame and said, 'This isn't mine.'

'Of course it is. I showed it to you and you claimed it. If it is not, what have you been doing all this time? Kindly continue.'

'It isn't. I made a mistake. I should go and find my own sampler.' I rose to my feet, barely able to stop myself from rushing from the room. I must see Emily. I had to say goodbye. I had to at least obtain her address so that I could write to her. Perhaps one day, I might even see her again.

'You shall not! Sit down.' Sophia threw down her own work, a design of colourful petals, flowers appearing without the help of stems or leaves. 'You are not to enter the eyrie. If you say your work is there, I shall go and fetch it myself.'

After a long moment, I sank into my seat. She rose from hers, came and snatched the embroidery from my hands and stalked from the room.

Outside, footsteps crunched over gravel. More words were spoken; a woman again, though I couldn't make them out. Anyway, I didn't think it was *her* voice. Soon, it would be. Why should she linger?

There was no one to stop me, not now. Sophia would be furious, but I didn't care; I would be a coward no longer. I rose again and without looking back, I left the room.

243

I ran straight to the gallery overlooking the entrance hall, where the stairway wrapped the space in shadow. This was where I'd first seen her – there, stepping onto the parquet, leaving her trail of muddy footprints, her hair hanging loose about her neck. She had looked so young then. She couldn't have known what would happen. For a moment I almost glimpsed her, a shadow moving across the floor; then she was gone.

I clattered down the stairs. She might even now be stepping into the carriage. She would be settling into her seat, thinking no one cared enough to see her off. There would be no one to wave at her as she went.

I thought about who might be out there with her: Madame Dumont, ensuring she really left; perhaps a servant – Sukie, triumph lighting her dull eyes; and Gadling, who hated her. I didn't care for any of them. I only wanted to see Emily: the familiar curve of her cheek, her soft grey eyes. I wanted her to look into mine, to see one face that wasn't full of contempt.

I stumbled out onto the stone steps at the front of the building and met with a startled silence. There was the headmistress, as I'd expected. Miss Peel had left her class to their singing and stood close by. Gadling wore a clean shirt and an eager expression. Of Emily there was no sign and Madame Dumont opened her mouth to remonstrate with me as Bard tossed his head, rattling his harness. The carriage door was open. I rushed past them to see if Emily was inside, but the seats were empty.

It was too soon – as bad as too late. Now they'd send me away before she came down and in the looping corridors of the school, I would miss her. She wouldn't even know that I'd tried.

Madame Dumont commanded me to return to my lesson. Miss Peel muttered. I didn't hear their words as I moved back up the steps. They were of no more consequence than the phrases they'd drummed into me during all the dead days I'd spent here: *Are not umbrellas of great antiquity? Yes, the Greeks, Romans and all Eastern nations used them to keep off the sun . . .*

I turned, searching for Emily, and their faces spun around me. They blurred, pictures in a zoetrope waiting to be brought to life; eager to repeat the motions laid out for them, doing just what they were supposed to do. It was I who was out of place. I couldn't be their carven statue, chained to the wall. It would all come down. It would all shatter—

And something *did* shatter, a sound chiming higher than birdsong, and light flashed where no light should be. Sharp edges cut the air and I tried to make them out, but it was too late; glass pattered to the ground all around me and I could only wonder as something struck the steps at my feet.

It was dark, limp, heavy. It was out of place. It struck the corner of each stone step with a succession of distinct dull sounds, though what I heard was *tick . . . tick . . . tick . . .*

The thing was wearing clothes. It wore clothes and had golden hair and left a trail behind it. I wished the shape would stop moving so that I could make it out and then it did and I wished it would move again, not wanting to see any longer. It lay so very still.

Her face was pale and white. She had no pretty manners, no grace left. Her limbs were splayed, skirts disarrayed, and blood ran from her; blood that glistened in the sunshine.

But they've scrubbed the steps, I thought, and had to swallow the strange, mad laughter that rose to my lips.

She was clutching my embroidery frame. Her elegant fingers still held on tightly, as if it might have saved her. *Thou shalt not*, it said, and then only a blank. The white backing fabric was darkening, turning crimson. It would never be finished now and something floated free inside me, like a bird rising into the air.

There was absolute, perfect silence.

Then came the startled snort of a horse, the scraping of an iron shoe. Miss Peel let out a strangled sound, worse than any scream. Madame Dumont's mouth hung open. They looked as if they'd never move again. They only stared at what had been Sophia—

But I couldn't look at Sophia.

Belatedly, one of the horses took fright. It was Bard; perhaps, as had been claimed so many times, he *knew*. He tossed his head, pulling the rein from Gadling's hand, who leaped instead for the bridle. For a moment he was lifted from his feet but Bard was held back by the other horse, the nameless one: the false twin that had taken Captain's place.

There was broken glass in Gadling's hair. It glittered in the sunshine, though what I thought of was droplets of rain; rain falling on a day that we had so longed to be fine. We had wanted to glimpse who was coming towards us. But rain had come anyway, speckling the windows and the carriage and the ground.

I started to walk, each step grinding broken glass into smaller and smaller pieces. The shards dazzled, almost pretty, like tiny flowers opening their eyes everywhere I looked. I stopped when I reached Sophia, my boots just short of the blood. A picture came to me: a young girl with a rose in her hands, blossoming red, but it didn't stop; it withered and died, its petals turning black, spilling to the ground.

Sophia's eyes were open. There was blood in them. There was blood in her hair, marring its gold. She'd have hated that. Her curls were loose and dishevelled. Her head was the wrong shape. I could see the start of a gash in it, deepest jewelled crimson. I reached out to cover the unsightliness with her hair but she looked too soft, as if she might fold in upon herself like muslin if I touched her. Anyway, I couldn't bring myself to lay my hands on her. I wasn't worthy to do that; I never had been. There were clouds in her eyes, behind the blood: small, high clouds and very white.

They were motionless. The world had stopped spinning; everything was still.

29

Arms pulled at me, trying to drag me away. I shook them off. They seized me again, strong and hard: Gadling's arms. He lifted me into the air and I wondered if blood would get on his shirt and I did laugh this time; I couldn't seem to stop. I realised I was calling her name – not *Emily*, the one I'd sought, but *Sophia*.

Madame Dumont and Miss Peel spoke in high, rapid voices, half hysterical. They made me think of chickens, burbling and clucking. Gadling set me down and I pulled away from him just as someone stepped from the door.

Emily's eyes were downcast. She clutched a carpet bag in her white-gloved hand. Her cheeks were pink as if conscious of people watching her and she lowered her head, concealing her face under her bonnet. She was wearing her cape. She was ready to leave. She saw nothing except the open door of the carriage and she stepped towards it.

Bard was still skittish. Gadling had seized the rein again, but when he saw Emily, he let go. He strode to intercept her, opened his arms and grabbed her as he had me. Ignoring her cry of protest, he held her there, as if he'd apprehended a criminal; as if she'd been trying to escape.

Emily looked around her, blinking against the brightness. She didn't seem to have noticed Sophia. She hadn't even seen me.

'She was up there.' Gadling gestured upwards with his chin. 'When that 'un fell, she looked right out o' that window. Didn't you see her?'

I followed his gaze to the eyrie. Its many panes of glass reflected back the perfect day, all save one. That was dark as a pulled tooth, a few fragments of glass shivering in the frame. It was the window where Sophia had claimed to struggle with Emily White's doppelgänger; the one that had been cracked.

'I saw 'er.' He shook Emily's arm, though she didn't seem to feel it. Her face was a terrible blank. She stared down – she had seen Sophia's body at last, though there was no recognition in her eyes. She might have been in a trance.

'You hated her,' Madame Dumont said to Emily. 'Didn't you? What have you done? She complained of you. She had you dismissed. Was this your revenge? Did you push her? She was a *child*.'

No, I thought, *she was not*. But Sophia was nothing now: not a child, nor an adult. She would never have her fine white dress. She'd never join the dance, never marry, never have a child of her own. The circle was broken; the zoetrope had ceased turning. There was no handsome hero to save her. No one would even want to touch her now, they wouldn't want the taint of her on their hands, and I tried to feel glad of it but I couldn't. She was more alone than I had ever been or could be, not until my own death came to meet me.

Scuffling steps announced Sukie's arrival in the doorway. She saw everything at once and her hand went to her mouth.

'Sukie, don't just stand there,' Madame Dumont said. 'Come and lead the horses back to the stable. Gadling, I need you to stay here.'

Sukie looked horrified. She trailed slowly down the steps, then, when she'd passed Sophia, her steps hurried onward. When she reached the horses she looked dubious, wrinkling her nose before she took hold of the reins, giving them a sharp tug. Gadling glared, but he only said, 'Tell Simons to have one of his lads fetch the constable, quick now.'

'The doctor,' Madame Dumont cut in. 'Send someone for the doctor too. And Reverend Aubrey.'

'The – *constable*?' It was the first time that Emily had spoken. Her words were soft, but we all heard. She suddenly looked very young; younger than any of us, even me, for as I looked at her the years seemed to creep over me, weighing me down.

'Yes, Ma'am, the constable,' Gadling sneered in her face.

Mademoiselle, I thought but didn't say. Not *Ma'am*.

Emily tilted back her head. She saw the shattered glass hanging in the window frame. Her face creased into a frown. Uncertainly, she shook her head. 'But I didn't do anything. Why would I? I didn't push her or anyone. That's outrageous. Of course I didn't hate her.'

I did, I thought. But I couldn't say it, not now that Sophia was dead; no one would. Sophia had gone beyond any of us and everyone would love her more than ever − at least once the sight of her, broken and twisted, *unnatural*, was removed from them. But she'd deserved my hatred. She'd deserved Emily's too, but of course our teacher must deny it now.

Again, Emily shook her head. 'I wasn't even there,' she insisted. 'I was in my room, waiting. No, not just waiting − I can show you. In fact I *must* show you, at once: I can prove everything, if you will only follow me.'

And so we did follow her. We didn't wait for the constable or the doctor or the parson. Gadling took her arm in his grip and she led him and all of us − or was marched − along the corridor towards the teachers' rooms. I went too, trailing along at the back, and no one noticed me or told me to leave. When we reached the room with a blank where a name should be − that would always be a blank, now − Gadling released her. Emily was the one to step forward and let us inside.

'You see,' she said, gesturing, 'I was here all along. I had a little time to wait and I wished to calm my nerves, so I did all I could think of: I was painting.'

The picture on its table was the only thing in the room that gave any sign of its ever having been occupied. Beside it was an empty water glass, though her little box of paints was nowhere to be seen; she would have packed those in her carpet bag before she left. Everyone stood there as if deciding whether to listen to her and I slipped between them, moving closer to the painting. It was just as I had left it, almost finished but not quite; so very nearly like the life. And it was alone, of course, since she had given her own picture to me.

'I painted it this morning,' Emily said. 'You see? I couldn't possibly have done all this and been wandering about after Sophia at the same time. How could I? See for yourself how much detail there is!'

And there was. I recognised it all: each imperfection in the petals, every speckle on every leaf. I recognised each one of them because I had been the one to paint them, under Emily's eye, trying so very hard to please her. I wondered if, now, I had.

In the corner of the room, the subject of the painting remained where it had been. The flowers were wilted; they were dead. I sniffed, detecting the hint of decay. The petals were limp against the glass jug, the leaves inside smeared into slime. At any moment the others would see it too, for all that Emily had taken care to position herself between them and the flowers. They would understand the falsehood. They would know her lie, and knowing it, they would assume they knew the truth.

For an instant, Emily met my eyes. Hers were soft and grey and pleading and so familiar to me.

'Why would you be painting, today of all days?' Madame Dumont was already suspicious.

'Well, my packing was done.' Emily's voice shook. She could hang for this, after all. 'You insisted that it was done yesterday. I had nothing left with which to occupy myself. Painting is my – my solace; it always was. It's the best way I have found to forget myself, for a little while. To – not exist.'

They were almost the same words I'd once said to her. Were they all she could think of now? I wished I could go to her, move to her side and take her hand, but how could I? I hoped she could see my faithfulness anyway, by my look. I knew that Emily would never hurt anyone. If she'd been forced into a small untruth to gainsay a false and terrible accusation, I couldn't blame her; and there was no one else to speak for her.

She had held me close and comforted me, in this very room. She'd leaned her head against mine. She had kissed my cheek. It didn't matter if she'd lied about the letters. Some things were more truthful than words could ever be.

And where else would she have been, this last hour? She must have been sitting here alone. Perhaps she too had been remembering the times we'd spent together. She would have rested her head on her hand, gazing at my picture, hoping for a friend to come and say goodbye to her; and I hadn't come. If I'd only found a way, I might have saved her from this.

I glanced again at the water glass – which was no longer empty. I stared. It *was* empty a second ago, wasn't it? I felt sure of it, and yet as I watched, paint began to spiral through the water. It was as if a brush had just this moment been rinsed after adding some detail to a leaf. I blinked. There *was* a brush, resting in the glass. How hadn't I noticed it before?

Emily gestured towards the glass as if to show them too. Now I wasn't the only one who'd seen: Madame Dumont took it in and pursed her lips.

The flowers in the corner, too, were changing. I could almost see the sap rising through the stems, instilling them with new life as they straightened. The water they stood in slowly clarified as if its greenness was being reabsorbed into the plants. The petals became fresh and new, brightening, resuming their old shapes. The gentle scent of a single white rose reached me and I breathed it in.

Emily White's eyes were so clear, so very dear to me. I could almost feel her arms around me, assuring me it would be all right, as if I were the one in need of comforting. I shifted my hands to touch hers, but of course they were not there.

I heard her voice from across the room, slow and somnolent. 'I picked those flowers this very morning. Look at them – you can see how fresh they are.'

'They might have been picked yesterday,' said Madame Dumont, dubious. She barely glanced at the flowers, as if she didn't want to admit what she must: that their freshness spoke the truth of Emily's words. But she *did* glance at them. She had seen.

'I was here,' I blurted. 'I was in this room yesterday afternoon. Those flowers were not here then.'

It was scarcely a lie. I didn't know how, but *those* flowers had not been in the room, not as they were now; not the same. And I saw something else the others hadn't.

I walked towards the picture – *my* picture. I grabbed it from the table and held it up before them. 'This is still wet,' I said. 'Don't you see?'

I angled the surface, catching the light from the window. This time I didn't need to lie; they could see for themselves. The paper glistened with moisture. As I tilted it, wet paint pooled in the shadows, where it lay deeper, and the tension broke; drips began to run down the image, ruining the edges of the petals, smearing their colours.

'Very well,' Madame Dumont sighed. 'It has been freshly

done, I see, though why you should have been painting at such a time is beyond me.'

'Well, that's that, at least,' said Miss Peel. 'I never did believe it – not here, not at your seminary, Madame. Not *that*.'

Not murder, is what she meant. Not at Miss Dawson's seminary for young ladies, such a fine establishment, and I watched as that thought sank into the headmistress. No: God forbid it could ever be that! She'd never have another pupil. There would be no school, no livelihood, no respectability, no character remaining to her. She would be just like Emily White.

I breathed in the fragrance of wildflowers, so delicate and fresh, as the atmosphere in the room shifted. I felt the danger passing, their accusations turning to dust, their opinions beginning to change.

And my opinion – was that changing too?

I saw it before my eyes as if it were happening again: the glass filling with water, paint spreading through it. Flowers returning to life. *My* picture, dripping and running with fresh paint. How had that happened? How had Emily managed to lie to us all, not just in her words but in what we saw?

She had told her story and it appeared in front of our faces, just as she'd wished it to be. Her words had taken on form, coalescing, becoming real; becoming *true*. Was the world so malleable? Could any strange notion or uncanny thought at any moment become real and solid – because Emily White wished it so? Or was it only that she had sent out her will and seized hold of our minds, making us see whatever she chose for us to see?

She has powers. Who knows what she can do?

I thought of a dark shadow-version of her standing in the

corner of this very room. I thought of her outside, wandering in the fresh air when she also stood in front of us in class. I thought of Sophia grasping at her throat, clawing at someone I couldn't see.

With a start, I realised that Emily was staring at me. Her look was penetrating, as if she knew everything, each thought that passed through my head. I opened my mouth to speak and closed it once more. What could I say? She gave a single nod and my voice retreated further, buried in my throat.

A small voice interrupted all our thoughts. Sukie, forgotten, unnoticed by any of us, had crept back again. 'Please, Ma'am, the constable is here. He's calling for you.'

Here already? I pictured what he must have seen as he rode up: Sophia's body on the steps, blood leaking from her, clouds shining in her eyes. And no one attending her, no one to explain. Worse, she might have been discovered by others: surrounded by a host of hysterical girls, or perhaps the crows had found her, pecking and darting with greedy beaks. Madame Dumont muttered to herself as she pushed past everyone. Authority had arrived and already she had been found wanting. Miss Peel followed. Gadling reached out and grasped Emily's arm once more, but at her look his grip loosened and fell away. She went after the headmistress, Gadling following at her heels. I was left quite alone.

I stared down at the picture in my hands. I knew every inch of it. Now it was ruined, marred with ugly drips. But its work was done; they had all seen it. They were Emily White's witnesses now. But what of the rest?

The flowers were wilting again. In front of my eyes, rot was creeping back into them, darkening their loveliness. Had

Emily moved too far away to sustain the illusion? Was she already too taken up with questions from the constable and the doctor and the parson to maintain it? With that triumvirate of masculine authority to answer, it was hardly likely she could think of anything else.

Then I must do it for her.

There was no time to consider; I could picture the constable scratching his head over these wilted, damp, dead flowers. I took hold of the jug, half expecting it to vanish when I touched it, but there was only smooth glass under my fingers.

I lifted the jug, flowers and all, and left the room.

I hurried down the stairs, expecting at any moment that someone would see me and call me back, but there was no one. The flowers in my hands still smelled of decay. The touch of their petals was like too-soft skin. I longed to be rid of them. I hurried past the row of capes, shouldered open the back door and escaped into the day.

Everything was oddly the same as it had always been, though the sun was burning the last of the clouds away. They trailed in long wisps, like the lacy bridal train Sophia would never wear. Time had passed; it was still passing. I strode across the yard to where a little tumbledown gap in the wall let onto a blackened field. The glass was slippery against my fingers as I stepped over the fallen stones.

This field had once been golden. Now it was ruined, the earth turned to nothing but ash. Would someone find these flowers among it all and wonder how they'd come to be here? But why should they search for them? Madame Dumont had seen the living blooms. No one could doubt her word.

I threw the contents of the jug into the edge of the field, where a few charred stems of grass still thrust outward from the wall. I hurled their makeshift vase after them. All that remained was the stink of foul water, a streak of cloying green on the back of my hand, and the sweet-rotten scent of flowers already lost to sight.

30

The entrance hall was full of shadows stirring and shifting against the walls, with sighs and whispers. It took a moment for my eyes to adjust and make out what they were: girls dressed much as I was, their faces as pale as mine must be. They had come from my embroidery lesson. They must have begun to wonder where Sophia had gone.

Perhaps they had been forbidden from stepping outside, but they'd refused to be banished. Now they hovered in the corners of the gallery like so many ghosts. Had they heard something of what had happened? The windows were thin enough, after all.

I walked beneath them and they watched me go.

The constable, the doctor and the parson had all arrived with haste; they were outside the door. The school was cloistered and separate no longer. Madame Dumont and Miss Peel stood by, as attentive and carefully blank as the servants. The doctor crouched by Sophia. His bag was at the ready, though it remained closed.

He straightened, tilting back his head towards the eyrie.

The parson didn't seem to be looking at anyone — not the teachers, the doctor or Sophia. His gaze was far away, as if searching for a place to escape. Only the constable looked at me. He was older than the rest, grey of hair and whisker. His apple cheeks bespoke a fondness for the inn, his spectacles an equal fondness for reading, but his eyes were as sharp and bright as the buttons on his uniform.

Sukie waited on the topmost step, holding a crisp white sheet, neatly folded. The doctor had finished his peering about; he took the sheet, shaking it out before laying it over Sophia. It billowed and settled, patches of the snowy fabric turning dark. I pictured Sukie scrubbing it against a washboard later, the suds turning pink. That somehow made it all worse and I looked away. I tried to summon my old hatred for Sophia, but it had evaporated into the air; the colour was draining from my memories. We had shared so much, I realised. For all our differences, in the end, we were both alone.

The constable eyed me again, as if demanding a reason for my presence. Madame turned to me too and I blurted, 'I disposed of the flowers.'

Suddenly everyone was looking at me. I was exposed, pinned by their eyes, and I squirmed; I was more used to being invisible. I said, 'They would only have died in there.'

They went on seeing me without seeing me at all. Emily's was the only face I couldn't look into, and I passed over her, making of her nothing but a blur.

'Well, that is regrettable,' the constable said. 'They were evidence of a sort, were they not? I should have liked to see everything myself.' He addressed Madame Dumont, as if I was already dismissed. I didn't complain. I was nothing but a child after all, just a silly schoolchild who'd done something foolish, and a female besides – but we were all of us that. All so fragile and so sadly exposed to death. If he were to test us, we might break. He would have to deal with our crying and wailing. He would have to see our tears.

'But you all saw this for yourselves? The groom seems to *think* he saw her at the window, though the light must have been in his eyes. You're quite certain she was in her room, painting?' He paused. 'There are bruises at the girl's neck.'

The silence stretched out, intolerable, and so I broke it. 'I'm afraid Sophia did that to herself, before this happened. She was acting a part – it all got a little carried away, but everyone saw it. That was in the eyrie too. She had been told not to go back in there. We all were, but she went anyway.'

My embroidery hoop, clutched in Sophia's fingers, still jutted from the edge of the sheet. I closed my eyes; when I opened them the constable was looking at me strangely. I saw him making the decision that my reaction was quite natural, all that could be expected of one of Sophia's friends. And I let him think it, though the sight of her left a taste like ashes on my tongue. I would taste its bitterness for days; years.

The constable tilted his head as the doctor had, taking in the broken window, the shards of glass still flashing back the light. 'And the window was already cracked.'

'It was,' Madame Dumont cut in. 'I told the girls most particularly to stay away from it.'

Her tone somehow reminded me of what had been said about Beatrice. What would they say of Sophia? That she was wayward – disobedient? Equally defective, not in her body but her morals? I could already feel the explanations slotting into place. I even heard the sound it made: *tick . . . tick . . . tick . . .* as the world began to turn again.

'And you say the girl was not unhappy?' The constable said.

'Certainly not.' Madame Dumont dismissed that at once. Wilfulness was one thing, self-destruction quite another. That was a stain Sophia's family would not tolerate.

'A terrible accident, then.' The constable sighed. 'I suppose you will be closing the school?'

Shards might have fallen from the window and pierced Madame Dumont's tongue. She couldn't speak, yet still he waited for a reply. When she managed it, her voice was as sharp as glass, as quick as falling. 'As I said, Sophia was unfortunately out of bounds. She should never have been in that room. The danger had of course been identified and the eyrie forbidden to pupils until the window was mended. They all knew the rule.' Ruefully, she shook her head. 'Such a headstrong girl . . .'

Tick.

'I think we're finished here,' the constable said. 'We should move her inside. You may send word to her family.'

He asked no further questions and no one offered any answers. There had been no mention of doppelgängers or spirits. No one spoke of how Sophia had claimed to fend off an invisible attacker at that very window. No one raised the spectre of visions or hysteria or madness, or the outrageous fancies of respectable young ladies.

With Sophia dead on the ground, perhaps they didn't seem so picturesque. And nobody would relish the prospect of courtrooms or police stations or difficult questions, particularly when they might be shamed by the answers. And so they were silent and did not speak of it, at least not there; not then.

Even Reverend Aubrey saw the wisdom in keeping silence, despite the way he'd leapt to Sophia's aid in the eyrie, or perhaps because of it. He shifted uncomfortably, offering nothing: no words of balm or advice or instruction. Then, surreptitiously, he wiped his eyes. He stared down at the white sheet, ruined now, as a flush spread from his collar up his neck to his sallow cheeks. His eyes shone too brightly as he glanced at the window, tracing the path of her fall through the air.

He was weeping, I realised, and suddenly I wanted to laugh. He was still picturing himself the hero and she the tragic princess, though he hadn't been able to save her after all. Then it came to me: he imagined she really had been in love with him. He thought Sophia had leapt from the window because of him, because they never could have been together. Her father would have thought him beneath her and for all her posturing, Sophia wouldn't have broken with his wishes. She had lacked the courage my mother had possessed, and I drew myself taller. Perhaps I had decent blood in me after all, though not in the way Sophia had meant.

I hid my scorn. I doubted Sophia capable of love. Rather, she had wanted a conquest, someone to admire her and think of her; and now he would. Reverend Aubrey had never really known her – but then, he was a man. It would be natural if he thought this was all about him.

Through it all, Emily stood back, unnoticed by anyone. She didn't see me watching her. She gazed towards the lane, the one that led away from us and towards the world; the one that would take her from us, to the railway station and from there all the way to London. She could leave now. There was nothing to stop her; and there was still the evening train.

31

I returned to my room. No one else was there and I was thankful for that. Perhaps we'd been called into lessons to recite our interminable catechisms. After what had passed, Madame Dumont would want us all watched more closely than ever. Still, no one came looking for me, and I wondered if they hadn't noticed I was missing or if they didn't care. That thought brought spite with it and not a little self-pity.

But all that mattered now was: where was Emily White? What was she thinking at this moment? More importantly, how had she made us see the things we did? And how had she lied so easily, just as if it were natural to her, claiming my picture for her own?

What was she?

She hadn't just lied with her words. She had lied to our senses. Did she really have some mesmeric power over us all, something that Sophia had begun to understand – Sophia, who'd been silenced? *I always tell the truth*, Sophia had said.

And I hadn't believed her, assuming her the greatest liar of any of us – but was she?

The wet paint had run and dripped and ruined my picture. I had smelled the wildflowers, felt their clammy touch on my skin. Or had I only imagined those things too?

Emily must have been aware that I alone knew the truth. How had she been so certain I wouldn't speak out? I could have told them the picture was mine.

But I *had* started to speak, hadn't I? I hadn't intended to give her away but even so, my voice was smothered in my throat. Had she done that to me somehow? If I had tried to tell the truth, would she have done more – choked me with invisible hands?

I heard a soft sound outside the door. I didn't move, thinking it only someone passing by, then realised it had been a knock. It opened and I turned.

Emily walked into my room, a soft smile on her face. She looked down at me. Her grey eyes were gentle, her expression kind. She looked at me as if she knew every thought passing through my mind and had already forgiven me for ever having thought them. She reached out her hand and I half expected it to pass straight through me – she surely couldn't be here, now – but she rested it on my shoulder, lightly, as soft as muslin.

She sat down next to me. 'I came to say goodbye, Ivy.'

I opened my mouth to protest but again, my voice wasn't there. I was a ghost in my own body.

She said, 'I wanted to see you before I left.'

When I spoke there was a taint in my mouth, like rotting petals, like something dying. 'You really are leaving, then.'

She nodded. 'I am still dismissed, even if they no longer imagine me a murderer.' She lifted her hands in front of me and turned them, as if demonstrating that they were clean of blood. 'I wanted to thank you, Ivy. For everything.'

A strange feeling came over me: a rush of blood to my cheeks, warmth blossoming at the centre of me, a crimson bud unfurling. I closed my fingers as if to grasp onto something but they were empty, useless in my lap. 'I didn't do anything.'

'I think we both know that you did. And I am grateful. They would never have understood otherwise.'

I waited, thinking she was about to explain everything: the doppelgänger, the visions, what had happened to Sophia in the eyrie. But she did not.

'I'm sorry that you had to tell a falsehood, Ivy. I wouldn't have had that for worlds. But it was a lie that enabled the truth to be known, in a sense. So it was not such a terrible one, I think.'

A lie that enabled the truth to be known. Yes, that echoed my own thoughts, though the untruth had been hers, not mine. I forced a smile of my own. 'But I didn't lie, not really. I just didn't tell them the picture was mine. I knew – I *knew* you couldn't have done anything wrong, Emily.'

'Ah,' she said, with soft laughter in her voice, 'but you did. You said you were in my room yesterday. You said the flowers were not there.'

'But that part was true. *Those* flowers were not there. They weren't the same then, not at all – not as they were today.'

Confusion spread across her features and she shook her head. 'You were in my room, then, Ivy? Why? And when?'

'You know I was. You came in and found me there. I – was waiting for you. You—' I forced myself to say it, since she made me do so. Was that what she wanted, to hear our affection put into words? 'You put your arms around me. I leaned against you, like *this*. I felt—'

But I didn't say what I felt. I only reached for her, pulling her near, twisting to place my shoulder against hers. In another moment she would put her arms around me. She would lean her head against mine.

Instead she drew away from me, catching her breath. 'Whatever do you mean?'

'You held me close to you. You – comforted me.'

She shook her head. She was frowning again and I didn't like the expression that had come into her eyes. They had hardened – hardened against me.

'But that didn't happen! I never saw you, Ivy. I didn't lay eyes on you after that morning in assembly, not until just now. I never saw you in my room. And what you describe – that would have been entirely improper, don't you see? You are my pupil and I your teacher, not—'

But she never said what came after that *not*. She never said what she might have been to me. She only stood stiffly, smoothing down her skirt. I could still feel her, though – the touch of her lingering like a ghost, just as if she had held me after all. I shook my head in bewilderment, wrapping my own arms about my body. I was cold; cold right through.

'I never saw you,' she insisted, as if I'd pressed her, as if I was no better than another schoolchild, playing a silly game or a nasty trick. As if I'd *imposed upon* her. Then she turned and walked away from me, leaving no gentle looks behind her; not even pausing to say goodbye.

The door closed and Miss Emily White was gone.

32

I stared down at my empty hands.

Do you understand, Ivy? You do, don't you?

But I didn't. I understood nothing at all.

How could Emily have denied seeing me in her room? We had been so very nearly like sisters. It was the closest I'd been to anyone since Daisy was snatched from me and Beatrice turned from me, and Emily had claimed it was nothing. If either of us could deny it, I thought wildly, it was me. I never had looked into her face, not even when I knew, finally, that I must leave her – but I had known it was her. I would have known her anywhere. I had felt her solidity, her warmth when I'd leaned into her, and she had held me in her arms and I'd known that I was home.

Accepted.

Loved.

Yet she had shaken her head. She had walked away just as if she'd never been my friend. I had kept her secrets, supported her lie, played my part. I had helped her and then she'd cast me aside as if I'd never existed.

Unbidden, a memory came: a figure standing in the corner of her room, bedraggled hair hanging over its face as it watched me walk in. What might its expression have been? Had it really been some dark antithesis of her – or something else?

Everything about me grew still.

I never had looked into its face.

I hadn't looked into her face when she held me, either.

Now I pictured that shadow, the doppelgänger, opening the door to her room and walking in, finding me seated on the floor, rummaging through its originator's secrets. I pictured it kneeling behind me, wrapping me in its arms, pulling me close. But it had been *solid.* I'd felt its heartbeat in my flesh. It was *real.*

Or had I only thought it was?

Emily might have been telling the truth. She might never have come into her room. There was only the *other* . . .

And the comfort I'd felt, the warmth – were they only in my mind too?

But if it had come to me, perhaps she'd sent it. The doppelgänger had still been *her.* It must be an unknown and unacknowledged part of her, a secret even to herself, but still it had come to me, wrapping its arms around me, caring for *me,* because she did too – because it was her deepest wish to be with me at that moment, even if she couldn't acknowledge it herself.

I wanted to rush after her, to call her back. To make her see. The two of us might be bound by the strictures built around us, carven statues chained to a wall, but the doppelgänger was different. It wasn't manacled like the rest of us. It was free to go where she wished, to do what she must dream of doing; to enact all the dearest wishes Emily had been forced to suppress because that's what she was supposed to do, what she had to do.

And Emily hadn't even been aware of it. She hadn't been in control of it in any conscious way; it went deeper than that. She didn't understand the powers her own mind possessed. Possibly she didn't even know she'd cast illusions over us all.

She didn't know how extraordinary she was.

The smile faded from my lips.

If the doppelgänger was Emily, and it was free – what else had it done without her knowledge? Was it a harbinger of death – or a bringer of it?

I still didn't know how Beatrice had fallen from a window. I didn't know how Sophia came to fall from the eyrie.

Beatrice had insulted her. She'd joined in with Sophia's mockery. Perhaps she had even seen something of the truth of Emily. And Emily had hated Sophia. She'd caned her and shamed her, but still Sophia had won. She'd had Emily dismissed. Emily had lost her home, her livelihood, her reputation: everything.

What might the doppelgänger have done then?

I pictured Sophia battling her invisible assailant in the eyrie. Could that possibly have been real? I had thought the girls saw nothing but an image planted in their minds by Sophia's words. If the shadow had been there, surely it would have shown itself to me – or had it concealed itself from me somehow, because out of everyone, it most cared what I would think?

And when Sophia went to the eyrie a second time, sent there by my words, to fetch my embroidery, what had she seen then? Did it come to her again, her old enemy – did it take her once more by the throat and push her towards the window?

Gadling thought he'd seen Mademoiselle Blanc in the eyrie, just as Sophia fell. The sun had been in his eyes and he'd disliked Emily and the constable had dismissed his words, but had he been a true witness after all? Both things might have been true. Emily could have been in the eyrie *and* in her room. The real Emily hadn't been painting; that was only a ruse, the thought of a moment. She would have been sitting and waiting – waiting, perhaps, for me. But no one had come. She'd been alone.

And she hadn't been aware of any of it. She couldn't have begun to suspect what those hands, in every way like her own, had done. Emily wasn't wicked. She could never knowingly have committed murder. Not the Emily I knew.

Emeline, I thought. *Not Emily at all.*

I rose to my feet and hurried for the door. Even if I'd never really known who she was, if I hadn't even known her name, I couldn't let her go like this. I had to see her again before she left. If I could look into her eyes once more, I would surely understand everything.

33

The carriage was at the door, the horses caparisoned and ready, as if nothing had changed. They were a perfect pair, everything just as it should be. The broken glass had been brushed from the carriage roof, which gleamed in the fading light. Sophia's body had gone, the steps scrubbed clean again.

Gadling was already in his seat. He grimaced as he flicked his whip – and the carriage began to pull away. The familiar grind of wheels on gravel covered the sound of my feet as I ran down the steps.

The carriage didn't pause, only gathering speed as the pair settled into their paces. I was too late. Emily White was leaving; and the horses didn't seem to mind her presence at all.

This time no one else was there, no headmistress to order me away, no servant to trouble me with curious glances. I tried to peer in through the carriage windows as it turned into the lane and the rumble of wheels quieted. The blinds were drawn. It seemed that Emily hadn't wished for any last sight of what had been her home; she hadn't wanted to wave goodbye.

She was beyond my reach and I stared after her in despair, quite certain I would never see her again.

34

Inside the school, shadows clothed every corner, each one of them like a waiting figure. And figures there must have been, for I heard them; the patter of footsteps around and above me, a host of them passing by, never seen. The other girls must have wanted to watch Emily leave too, for different reasons to mine. Now they would giggle behind their hands. Emily White would be nothing but a name on their lips, a source of gleeful gossip and delicious shudders, repugnant and yet still savoured; still enjoyed.

I didn't want to see any of them and decided not to go in to supper. Instead I went up the stairs, wishing to be alone. It seemed even that would be denied me, however, because when I stopped outside my room I heard voices within, low and cruel. They were waiting for me. They would want to see if I was tarnished by her friendship, to enjoy the sight of me brought low by my acquaintance with her. *Tainted.*

My hand slipped from the cool brass of the door handle and instead I went along the passage to its odd little corner, where there was nothing but a store room and a window. Who would look for me there? I had only ever seen Sophia in this place – Sophia with her matches, setting the flame to her book. I almost felt I could see her now, her hair golden and gleaming, her face glowering and scheming in the burning light. Of course she wasn't there and a deep breath steadied me as I went to the window. I pictured her falling, all the lovely life ahead of her snatched away in a moment; the glitter and the light; a brief stream of bright hair.

There was only the field, quiet and dead and black.

I turned my back on the sun, lowering now and near the horizon, and paused. There was another shadow, standing near the corner of the passage, back the way I'd come. It was deeper and more solid than the rest. Had I been staring at the sun too long? This was like an after-image in reverse, a dark blank marring my vision. I blinked, telling myself it would dissipate, but it did not change.

There was the suggestion of a shoulder somewhere within it. The edge of a cape. I stared. I could not allow myself to blink. The shadow had eyes. It couldn't be; but I stared and stared and it went on looking back at me.

Impossible, I thought, but it grew more solid by the moment – then it stepped towards me.

It was Emily White. The shadow was wearing her face.

I told myself again that she had gone. I could still hear the distant rumble of carriage wheels; she had almost reached the road. They hadn't paused in their journey. Gadling would never have allowed it. She couldn't have alighted and yet she was here, in front of me. Emily White had returned to me, and she was waiting.

Soon, soon she would vanish. I would be forced to blink and then she would be gone because she couldn't really be there. This was only the image of someone I had been thinking of and wishing for and that my mind had, for a moment, supplied. Or she was thinking of me, and unbeknownst to her, she'd sent this part of herself to be with me, travelling through the ether to where she most wished to go. At any moment, the bond between them would break. She would be carried further away from me each moment and any trace of her would vanish. But still the seconds passed by, *tick . . . tick . . . tick . . .* and the unreality remained.

She was wearing her cape. She raised her head a little and I made out the smooth softness of her skin. There was no darkness, not now. No shadows shifted and stirred in her eyes.

I stepped back until the hard wood of the windowsill pressed against my spine. Behind it was only glass; only air.

The doppelgänger took a step towards me. Me – the only one who truly knew who she was, what it all meant; what she'd done. Her eyes were grey and soft and full of secrets. Another step and she was directly in front of me. My legs turned soft as muslin, so weak that at any moment they might spill me to the floor.

My hand went to my neck as she leaned towards me. Her expression changed as she reached out, becoming more *her*, as if all she'd needed was to find me to find herself again. A part of me wanted to pull away but I could not and would not, and she placed her hands on my shoulders, squeezing so that I felt the pressure increase against my spine.

Soft, Sophia had said, but to me she was as real as anything in this world. For a moment her hands rested there and then she drew me in, shifting her hands to my back, holding me close. She placed her cheek against mine.

'Dearest.' I heard the word, a whisper between us. I did not know, then or ever after, which one of us had spoken.

35

For a time, my visit from Emily White brought me comfort. She had sent her double to be with me; she must have longed for me, just as I had so often longed for her. But the feeling faded, as feelings so often do, wilting like a wildflower in a vase. And what took its place was fear; fear that she had only ever come to say goodbye, as we should have said goodbye.

So I went in search of her – to the place where we had spent time together, focused on our painting and yet always conscious of the other, a mirror at our side. I sneaked along the corridor, anxious that her room would be locked; anxious too that it would be open and yet empty, stripped of her so completely I couldn't even imagine her being there. But the door gave under my hand and I slipped inside.

The room wasn't empty. My picture, the one I had painted for her, that had been ruined for her sake, was still there, on its little table. I walked towards it and saw again the flowers we had painted together. It might have been yesterday. She might have just this moment stepped from the room.

I had been so sure it would be gone. I'd never said that she could have it, not in words. But after it had saved her, after what it had done for her, she surely must have known it was hers; it always had been. Yet she'd left it here as if it were nothing. It had served its purpose and was ruined and she'd discarded it as if it were fit only for servants to use to light the fire.

I regarded the flowers again, not in their little glass jug on a plaster stand, but depicted on a sheet of paper. The single white rose was the clearest of them all, lovelier even than the moon pennies. It was fresh and pure and unspoiled, still present in every detail. I could remember painting it so well, this more than any other, and it alone was flawless. Of all the flowers, I hadn't looked for its faults, but had taken such very great care to see its perfection. There before me again was the lovely softness of its petals, white, blank; *Blanc*.

I turned and went to the cupboard and fell to my knees. I yanked open the door and saw only empty shelves, the wood grey and cracked. I ran my hand over them but I could already see that she had left nothing else. She had taken her precious letters with her, then —and she'd left the picture that had meant so much to us both.

I squeezed my eyes closed – and found myself thinking of what it is that artists do. I pictured our hands moving side by side, wielding our paintbrushes, creating something that wasn't there before. Concentrating so hard upon our subject, fashioning our pictures, so that the object could ever be brought before our eyes again, long after it had passed from sight.

So very like the life.

I stood once more and returned to my creation. I could remember every detail, every stroke, the way I'd shaped the petals, coloured the leaves. She had guided me and I had learned – I had grown. I closed my eyes and reached out and stroked its surface as if to prove to myself that it was only a picture, only paint. And my fingers met with resistance.

I didn't look, only reaching for it, tracing its shape. I felt for it – longed for it – delved for it from somewhere beyond the air, beyond the surface of things, and twined myself around it.

When I opened my eyes, I was holding a rose in my hand. It was so fresh, so beautiful. It glowed in the light from the window as I regarded it from every angle – and realised it wasn't quite perfect after all. An odd line marred one of its petals, a line that could never have been found in nature. It was smeared with a running drip of paint.

I could only stare. And at the same time I longed for something – something I would not or could not name, something I could never have back again, not for all the roses in the world.

She had never cared for me, not really. She hadn't come to me one more time to say goodbye. How could she? Emily had been far distant by then, surely too far to project even a shadow-image into my life. She couldn't have directed her doppelgänger to follow me, comfort me, to find me wherever I went. Even as the carriage pulled away she must have been so consumed with what lay ahead of her that she hadn't troubled with what she'd left behind. And Emily had all but told me, the last time I truly saw her, that she hadn't been thinking of me at all.

You are my pupil and I your teacher, not—

Not, she had said. I was *not*. She hadn't finished her sentence, but I knew what came after that *not*: I was *nothing*, not to her, not then, not ever.

She had wanted me to tell her what the other girls did and said. Was that why she had been so kind to me – then, finding me silent, had decided to be more careful? She had lied to me about her letters. Why? Had she thought me so like the rest that she must stop short of admitting a scandal – had she never really seen me at all? And when I'd discovered the truth about her past, when she'd let it slip, had she kissed me and presented me with her own painting to bind me close – because I knew her secret and she needed me to keep it for her?

They were ugly thoughts and I hated myself for thinking them, and yet the truth remained: I never had known what lay behind her calm demeanour. The impressions of her that I'd held so dear were nothing but illusions created by my own mind. I had sought companionship and so that was what I'd found. There had been so many different versions of her, but perhaps in the end, none of them were real. They were only what I wanted to see; everything I had wished her to be to me.

But the rose in my hand was real. Or did I only think it was? I could feel its soft leaves, its petals soft as skin. I held it to my face. The rose was in *my* hand, not hers. And the room was empty. I could sense that Emily White was gone, as absent as if she'd never been there at all. My gaze went to the corner, where I had glimpsed that figure, waiting for me. I'd told myself I'd only seen an arrangement of light and shadow and my mind had tried too hard to make sense of it. I had looked for her and therefore I'd seen her.

I had looked for her and therefore I'd seen her.

I had looked for her while I'd wandered aimlessly outside, wearing her cape. My thoughts were all for her, and when I'd returned I'd found she'd been asking for me too, making enquiries of Beatrice, yet the real Emily had known nothing of it.

I'd looked for her through the window of a classroom, thinking of Emily, the way she had been so at home when she walked in the garden picking flowers. And that was where Lucy had glimpsed her, even though our teacher was inside all along, about to walk into the room.

Even when the doppelgänger was witnessed by Matilda and Frances rather than my own eyes, I had been rushing towards Emily White, at once eager to show her my paintings and reluctant, wishing she was miles away, without a thought for me. And so she had been. She had been split in two, both waiting for me in her rooms and walking away, her back turned, into the fog.

Oh, there might have been imposture too – once set in train, the notion of a doppelgänger must have been irresistible. Did a double really stand at our teacher's side during our music lesson? Had one of the girls pretended to be Mademoiselle Blanc, wearing her cape, wandering about where the rest of us would see her and the teacher at once? Perhaps their trickery had even fed my own suggestibility. I had expected something to happen in our German lesson, just as Sophia made us all think it would – and so it did. Had I responded somehow by *making* it happen? I couldn't be sure; and yet each time the apparition appeared, I had been thinking of her.

But then, I was always thinking of her.

Was it my longing that made the others see what I had so dreamed of? Each appearance had exactly coincided, not with Emily's wishes, but with my own. Was the doppelgänger never Emily's creature, but mine?

I might have summoned it with *my* powers. I had made the others see what I wanted them to see, and I hadn't been aware of any of it.

What then of the things it had done?

I dropped the rose and looked down, turning my fingers in the light. I gazed at my hands as if I could read my actions, my desires, in the lines on my palms – hands that a fortune teller couldn't bear to touch.

I thought of Sophia. She had held out her own hand like this, to show us the wound she'd said the teacher inflicted. Had she really held it to an open flame? She'd claimed it was burned by Emily's powers, but it was me who'd wanted her hand to pain her. I had decided her punishment wasn't harsh enough and willed it to be worse.

I had wanted her book to burn. I didn't like the stories it told or the way Sophia put it to use, casting aspersions on Emily. I would have thrown it on the fire myself – in a way, had I done so? Wishing for its destruction, had I made it burst into flames, not caring if Madame Dumont was hurt too?

But those weren't the worst things. I knew they weren't. I closed my eyes and thought of Beatrice. I saw again the way she had confided in me, the way she'd told me her father hated her, couldn't bear to look at her. She had missed her mother too, although she hadn't been permitted to grieve her loss, and I'd understood that.

I'd lost my dear sister, the companion of my life, and there had been no one to share how I felt. Beatrice had whispered to me that she was alone, just as I was, and I had comforted her. I'd held her close and felt perfect understanding pass between us.

She was crying and crying, and you – what were you doing, Ivy? You'd wrapped yourself so tightly around her we couldn't get her free. You were smothering her. Choking her.

But Bea hadn't been crying then, had she? She had been comforted. She'd given a soft smile and rested her face against mine. And I reached for the memory, seeing it afresh, as if it was before me again: a moment of absolute quiet, one I hadn't *wished* to see, had refused to see.

Bea had pulled away from me, just a little. My hair had come loose from its pins and strands of it were sticking to her damp cheek. Her face was empty, as if she only half remembered where she was. Or was it that I'd been saying something to her – something about love? She tried to push my hand away, but there was something wrong: my hair was caught between her lips. It was in her mouth. She wasn't choking, not then, but I had suddenly feared she might and I'd grasped for those strands, too hasty, too clumsy, pulling at hair and clothes alike.

She had pushed at me then – tried to push me away. But I had to stop her from choking, had to explain to her; I couldn't let her cast me off. I reached and twined and wrapped and clung—

And I felt hands on my shoulders. I saw Sophia's face as she stood over us, shocked and angry. The others were with her and I heard their exclamations. They were half horrified, half thrilled, and they started pulling at Bea too, as if to rescue her, taking her from me, leaving only an empty space behind. It was then that Bea began to cry again, as if she was glad to be rescued; as if I really had been smothering her.

Words rang in my ears, the words I'd tried to wind around her, to draw her back to me. *Forgive me. Be my own . . .*

I shook my head to rid myself of the memory. I hadn't meant it; I hadn't intended to say those things. Was it the prospect of having someone close again, almost of having a sister again, that had so overwhelmed me? For in that moment she *had* been like a sister – yet still Bea had fled to the others, happy to be the centre of their attention, the focus of their delighted horror. And I had hated Beatrice then. I'd loved her and I'd hated her and I closed my eyes and knew I hated and loved her still.

And Beatrice was *dead*.

Had I created the doppelgänger, the image of Emily, the teacher Bea had mocked – the one she'd so disliked – and sent it to her? Did I make it creep up behind her while she recovered from her faint, make it seize hold of her and push her from the window?

If I had, it must have been a small step from her to Sophia.

Sophia hadn't wanted to go to the eyrie again, but I had sent her there. I had thought my claim that the embroidery wasn't mine a momentary impulse, but was it more than that? Had a part of me known, deep down, what would happen?

The bruises at her neck might have been her own creation – but were they? And did I watch her through eyes that looked like Emily White's as she searched for my embroidery – for my *Thou shalt not*? Did I step quietly after her as she moved nearer the broken window? And did I set the doppelgänger's hands to her throat, just as if they were my own, or did I only make her believe they were there – using her own fear against her? She had practically set it all in motion herself, after all, except that the 'gift' of summoning was never really hers but mine. Her own wild notions had made her vulnerable to me.

And I had hated Sophia – more than anyone. I had hated her for the way she looked at me, for her poise, her grace, her beauty. I had hated her for being all the things she was supposed to be, that everyone wanted her to be, and hated her because she wanted to be those things. Or was it only that I knew I could never be like her?

I must have seen her terror. Did I feel pity, or had I remained cold, hiding behind someone else's face? All I had been aware of at that moment was the thought of Emily leaving me. I had been so very desperate to find a way of making her stay. In a way, I almost had.

I'd cursed myself for seeing the others' tricks and never managing to stop them, for doing nothing. And yet I had done everything, hadn't I? *Thou shalt not.* Was there anything I wouldn't do? That space would always remain a blank now. And yet I hadn't *known*. I hadn't consciously chosen to kill her, hadn't even known that I'd done it. I had been a stranger to myself.

I had always been two things. I could sew neat little stitches and I could face down a charging ram. I could paint lovely flowers and pull a wet slippery lamb from its mother. I could stand in the eyrie and fold my hands demurely and sing *Holy, holy, holy*, and I could glean every last stalk of corn and gather all the apples without bruising a one. I was at once one of Madame Dumont's exemplary young ladies and a ragamuffin with muck on my boots. I was from a grand townhouse full of gleaming mahogany and a hoyden running wild along country lanes. I had always been two, where one should have been.

But wasn't everyone? We all present different masks to different people. Even Sophia had been different in the eyes of her own mother and father. We all have our various lives, the ones others see and the ones they don't, and no one truly knows who we are – not even ourselves.

I had even lied to myself afterwards. I'd lied to everyone, though not in the way I had thought. I'd followed Madame Dumont and Miss Peel and Gadling and Emily up the stairs to our teacher's room. Water had appeared in an abandoned glass and I had been astonished. Life had returned to a bunch of wilted wildflowers and moisture spread across my painting. I had done all of it, even ruining the gift I'd so failed to give my teacher, allowing the wet paint to run, smearing the truth. That was never Emily. All she had done was tell a desperate lie and hope no one would look too closely. And perhaps they wouldn't have – but I did. I saw how her lie would fail because the flowers were dead, the water glass empty, the painting long since dry, and I had mended all of those things.

What must she have thought? She had probably been so relieved that the flowers appeared fresh she'd persuaded herself they never had been so very wilted. Perhaps she thought I'd carried out some baser trick and thrown water over my own painting, forgetting that the glass had been empty. I saw her again in my mind's eye, remembered her confusion when I said, *Those flowers were not there*. But she'd been equally puzzled about my claim to be in her room – that was her first concern – and I hadn't thought any more of it.

I had seen everything and nothing at all.

I thought that Emily White had sent her doppelgänger to my side, consciously or unconsciously, because she so desired to be my friend – to be my sister. What a fool I'd been. I had thought everything was her; that she'd reached out and touched all our minds, making us see what she wanted us to see, shaping our thoughts and actions just as if her hands had wrapped about our own – like a plant that probed and clung and twined, a plant that strangled, that *choked*. A plant like ivy.

It was always me.

And what of the way she had held me, in that very room – holding me close, so comforting, so dear? She had pulled me to her as if to say that of course she understood, she knew me and it was all right, she would always be my friend; no one could ever be closer than the two of us. No one could snatch her away from me. But even that wasn't her. I had only ever been alone: Ivy. I.

I had been wrapped in nothing but myself.

Empty, Sophia had said. *So, so very empty.*

And I knew that I was.

Yet the door softly opened at my back and closed once more. There came the sound of footsteps moving towards me. I didn't look around. I didn't turn. I felt a presence, though, just behind me. I could sense the beating of its heart.

She moved closer and wrapped her arms around me, drawing me close, and I let her. I breathed in as the scent of bergamot and lemon drifted across the room.

36

LONDON 1922

I step away from the mirror. I no longer wish to see my white hair and lined face, my eyes staring out from such a changed visage. I do not want to see someone who only appears to be a fine lady when all the tell-tale signs are there: my cheeks age-spotted from too much sun, my fingers arthritic from years of work. My hands are wrinkled and dry now, the knuckles a little too prominent, unable to hold a paintbrush and wield it with the delicacy required. Yet they betray no sign of what they have done.

I raise my eyes once more to the mirror. Emily White was correct: if one learns to look in just the right way, one can see all one's faults. I see them now. Indeed, I can see nothing else, and have not done so for many years. That is not the only reason I had most of the mirrors in the house removed, why I reduced the tri-fold at my dressing table into a single necessary glass. I cannot bear to see more than one of me – my reflection doubled, trebled, multiplied again and again, until I am nothing but doppelgängers: many, where one should be.

I could never capture a true reflection of those times, I realise; I could never convey the full reality to anyone else. In putting myself into words, and Sophia and Beatrice and Emily – especially Emily – I would only make more images, never entirely themselves. Their story would evolve with each teller, with each reader. Each would see the things they imagined, what they most wanted to see. The people I had known would be nothing but doppelgängers, repeated over and over and yet never entirely the same.

I close my eyes and they resolve once more into their own familiar faces. They are ranged about me, images in a zoetrope; it is only Emily who remains unclear, as if I had never really known her at all.

Perhaps it is strange that the person I see most clearly now is Sophia. I remember the way she fell through the air: the way she shone, the glitter and the light, the lovely arc she made. She will always be beautiful now.

We had a memorial for her at the school, as we had for Beatrice. The parson wept as he gave his eulogy. He wiped tears from his eyes as he thought of the lovely girl who had thrown herself from a window for the love of him. His gaze was drawn over and over to the mended glass and I'd wondered if he would ever truly love again. After all, Sophia would remain more desirable than any wife could ever be. Her looks would never fade. She died long before any decline into airless afternoons and cold silences could begin. Her foibles and failings would never irritate him, her stories never bore him. In some strange way, I had made her the thing she always dreamed of being: perfect.

She is what I am not, for I will never be that, of course.

And yet Emily White did not abandon me. I knew it couldn't be her, but that didn't mean she wasn't there. Emily had gone, as had Emeline Jones and Mademoiselle Blanc and Emélie Sagée, but she stayed with me still. I had created a world for us, after all: a world for the two of us alone. And I couldn't abandon her. Ivy always did mean faithfulness.

Faithfulness – not truth.

Whenever I needed her or wanted her, or simply missed her, she came to me. She was my perfect rose, my lily – my gentle shepherd, but not beautiful for a single day: she was always the same, always perfect. We had found acceptance; we had found love, and all of the shadows had gone from her. She came to me in my darkest hours, when no one was near. She came to me in the empty, dull days with little to lighten them, no kindly glances. She came when I was alone, when I despaired of finding a single soul in the world in whom I could confide, who would understand the way I felt, who I *was*.

No one else at the school ever saw Emily White's doppelgänger again. I was careful of that. I never allowed myself to long for her or think of her too deeply when they were near. I became adept at conjuring her at will, or hiding her – I was good at hiding things, after all. Wasn't everyone? I thought of the parson, in love with a Sophia that lived only in his imagination. Of girls leaning over a gallery, peering at a young woman with a good heart and seeing something shabby in her place. All those parts of us that others can't or won't accept – we are each of us turning into shadows all the time.

There were moments when she seemed more real than I was – yet I didn't know if she had any physical presence, or if I only thought she had. She was at once a part of me and a reflection of me, and yet she was something else too, both better and worse. She was all the words I dare not say, the thoughts I dare not think. She was all the things I would or wouldn't do and I still hadn't found the boundary of them.

When she touched my hand, I believed I felt it. That was enough.

And was she, as Sophia once suggested, evil? Was she everything in myself that I'd denied and pushed beneath – my worst, most secret desires? If she were those things, my wickedness and my bad thoughts and ill deeds, all of the *Thou shalt nots* I could imagine, then evil had always seemed perfectly ordinary to me. I wasn't even conscious of her actions, but committed them without contemplation or thought or hesitation. Were they all the more monstrous for that? Perhaps. Perhaps.

Yet I still couldn't bring myself to reject her. I couldn't turn her away; I could never choose to be simply *I*.

The world would have condemned me utterly, of course. But I had decided not to care for the world's opinion long ago.

I never did follow my charted course. I didn't accept the chains that would bind me to the wall. I didn't become a wife or a mother, though I had my chance, and if that choice were before me again I would again refuse it. My heart never could fit the narrow mould that was designed for it. It couldn't be squeezed any tighter. I was considered a hopeless spinster by the age of thirty and am considered an old maid now, and such a creature has only ever attracted the world's scorn. If children were to throw dirt at my windows or shout insults through my letterbox and run away, no one would stop them; why should they? I rejected the protection of a man long ago and am therefore unworthy of protection. I spurned Society and have in turn been spurned, and I would not change it for the world.

When my grandfather brought me home, not because of any troubles at the school but because his little flower was in bloom, he did what I had so long expected. He had me put on a fine gown and invited a business acquaintance to a lavish dinner. The fellow was not the worst of them, nor the eldest, I'll give my grandfather that, though he was approaching fifty and had florid, fish-like lips that quivered when I walked in. He approved what he saw, asked his question and I refused. I told them what I had in mind as an alternative, and there put an end to living in my grandparents' house.

For my grandfather, it was a slight against his judgement and a blow to his position. For my grandmother, it was simpler: I had earned her contempt. 'It is extraordinarily low,' she said, 'for any woman to profit from her labour.' She looked at me as if I had turned into a frog or a toad, or possibly had been one all along and was only wearing some clever disguise.

But my dearest shored me up. I drew strength from her presence. She was there when I wept and doubted myself, when they told me I must leave. When I walked from the door she was waiting for me at the end of the path and I felt stronger once I had taken her arm; equal to anything.

And I had something else: a new catechism to replace the ones I had been taught or had recited as a child.

I can pull a wet slippery lamb from its mother.

I can face down a charging ram.

I can paint a flower so real I can pluck it from the page.

I can create the semblance of life.

I can create my own life.

I can make it so that I am never alone. I never need be alone again.

And I realised it was true. For I was an artist: and it was Emily White who had shown me that, in all her different ways. I could be what she had made of me – in a way, I suppose we had each of us created the other.

And so I painted flowers, just as she had taught me, depicting them in every lifelike detail. When I applied to publishers I was quickly given commissions for various plant studies – realistic images to be printed alongside descriptions of their petals, parts, leaves, fruit, distribution, preferred habitat and care. Horticulture was still in vogue and my style a perfect fit for their catalogues and guides. I found myself a botanical illustrator, and a good one, highly regarded for my meticulous detail.

In such a manner I paid my own way, and it did not feel *extraordinarily low* to me. I never had wanted to marry, not the likes of Reverend Aubrey or Gadling or my grandfather's acquaintances or any of them. Oh, I met other men, over the years – even some I danced with, even some who, in another life, I might have bedded in the straw – but I never met a man I wanted to belong to. I wanted something else: something almost shameful to name, a life the society I lived in could not encompass. I wanted my freedom.

Not long after I began my work, I was asked to provide illustrations for Mr Berenger's book on the botany of South

America. Many would have refused; they'd have called it scandalous. I couldn't paint specimens as they were sent to me but must travel as part of the expedition, discovering new places and new flowers as he did, describing them with my brush as he wrote of them with his pen. I sat in his offices and tried not to smile when he warned me, quite openly and honestly and before I agreed to anything, that if I really wished to go, I would have to be prepared to ride a horse.

I signed the arrangement, doing the best I could to conceal my delight. And a new vista opened before me: all the narrow corridors and high walls, the dainty little steps and meekly bowed heads falling away, to be replaced by a wide blue horizon. It was another life, a different life, and at last, I felt I could breathe.

It was unconventional to be sure, but what did I care for convention? It had never cared much for me.

There was only one thing left to do, and that was to say goodbye to my parents.

37

It would be false to say I didn't feel some trepidation. I hadn't seen my father and mother in so very long and time changes everything; certainly I was no longer the same girl that had left them. And while I was determined to feel no shame in the life I had chosen, I knew how the world would paint me.

Still I refused to lie, for the time for pretence was past. In anticipation of the longer journey that lay ahead, I hired a horse for my visit, a big gleaming chestnut. The ostler was a gruff fellow who bade me choose from 'this 'un' or 'that 'un', and I was too busy scowling at his impertinent gaze to ask their names. I decided to call the horse Captain, but he proved too skittish for that. He snorted and stamped at my approach and when I tried to stroke him, to place my face against his nose, he wouldn't have it. He backed away, the whites of his eyes gleaming, and I wondered what it was that horses did or didn't know. Had he sensed something about me – something *unnatural*? In the end, I called him Bard.

I had told myself that my mode of arrival was in preparation for my greater journey, though I can't deny there was a touch of mischief in it. I arrived at the old farmhouse sitting astride, just as I once had on Mags, as if the years had rolled back and I was at the beginning again. Skirts such as those I'd worn at the seminary wouldn't do for that, of course, so here was another little trespass against propriety: I had adopted the wearing of bloomers, and my over-skirt only covered them as far as the knee. Yet as I approached, I was no longer certain they signalled my freedom. I almost felt as if I were a little girl again, returning along the lane after some mischief, wearing the shorter skirts and pantalettes of a child.

Along the lanes, wildflowers bloomed. Moon pennies were in season and they opened their brightly shining eyes everywhere I looked. *Daisy.* I slipped from Bard's saddle and let him lip at the hedgerow while I picked a bunch of them. They would be a fitting tribute; I never had visited my sister's grave. She wouldn't have wanted hothouse blooms that wilted the moment they were removed from their protective glass. She would have been happy running free, poking into the hedgerow to find birds' nests, tugging the seed heads from long grasses and tossing them into the air. I could almost see her running ahead of me, trailing laughter over her shoulder.

I mounted once more and followed in her wake, peering to see the farmhouse and my namesake, ivy, clambering over its walls; but I saw with dismay that there was none. The glossy green had all been cut away, leaving only shadows of itself behind: dark streaks on the stone in the pattern of climbing, twining stems, ghosts of what had been.

I blinked back the tears that came at the sight. They had done it for the good of the stonework, I supposed; it didn't mean anything. And there at last were my parents, and I forgot everything else.

My mother was at the door, still wearing her apron, shielding her eyes to see who had come to visit on such a fine horse. My father was walking towards me from the three-acre field, along with Archie and Tom, no doubt equally curious. Laughter bubbled in my throat. I couldn't wait for them to realise it was me. I couldn't wait to see their dear, familiar, surprised faces. I jumped down from Bard, who skittered sideways as I landed, and ran towards them. Restraint was forgotten. Decorum was behind me; ladylike long abandoned. I stood in front of them and grinned.

My father frowned at my attire. Mama looked quizzical. Tom looked me up and down as if he didn't quite know who or what I was. Archie sneered at the horse – a handsome animal, admittedly, but ridden by a woman, and such a woman as he'd never seen. I wasn't suitable. I wasn't *acceptable*, not even for the farm. Not even for my family, who after all had been at pains to send me away, to learn better manners than they possessed. I suddenly felt sick. I should have listened to Madame Dumont. I should have attended to my lessons, dressed myself after a French fashion plate, presented them my calling card. Then they might have held out their arms and smiled to see me coming back to them; but that wouldn't have been me at all.

No one spoke. Everyone awaited my father's judgement. His verdict was the one that counted.

He gave a little nod. And my mother stepped forward and stared into my face and patted my cheek. Then everyone was talking and exclaiming, and I was crying, and everything was just as it had been. We gabbled our news – and Papa said he must go, because they had managed to buy a new field and the stones must be cleared or they'd never plough or plant or reap. He stood back and looked at my clothes and shook his head a little – and decided it wasn't any use. He wished me well and kissed me before returning to the land, Archie and Tom trailing behind him.

Then I was alone with my mother in the kitchen, breathing in the scent of baking bread and rosemary and tracing old scars on the deal table with my fingertips. I always had preferred sitting in here to the old back parlour, no matter how cosy. This was where the life of the house was, after all. This was where I had sat so many times to beat eggs or shell peas or knead dough. My mother's instructions had been stern, her looks sharp, but then, I had so often wriggled or daydreamed or whispered behind my hand with Daisy. We hadn't been as close as some, I supposed – not like Beatrice with her mother – but she was still my Mama. Had she ever imagined, back then, sending me away from her? It pained my heart to think I'd spent so long in that starched, sombre school, so far away. How could she have thought I would ever belong there?

She poured tea for us and we sat smiling at each other, yet scarcely knowing what to say. How to begin? So much had happened since I'd last seen her. I felt like a stranger, not even certain what I'd become in her absence, and I wondered if she could see it there beneath the skin of me: if she knew what it was I'd done. But she could never have suspected the strangeness or the secrets. I could hardly believe in them either, not there; not then.

The moon pennies were on the table, looking at me with their bright little eyes, and I wished for Daisy so suddenly and viscerally I caught my breath.

'What is it?' Mama said, tilting her head.

'I brought these for *her*, Mama,' I said. 'I'd like to visit her grave. It's time I did. Perhaps we could go together.'

She went very still. And something happened to her eyes – they became wary, guarded. Was it so very hard for her to see me here, without my sister? One, where two should be – perhaps it would have been easier not to see me at all. But Daisy *was* here. She was in every memory, haunting each corner. She had never left, not like me. She had made no new memories to displace the old; the dead never could be cast out. I expected any moment to hear the echo of her voice from the next room, to glimpse her face peeking over my mother's shoulder.

'Not this.' She rubbed at her eyes as if I had wearied her with my request rather than making a reasonable suggestion, a *natural* suggestion.

'What do you mean, Mama? I have to see her – to say goodbye. She is my sister.' *Was*, I had meant to say. *Was* my sister. But what of that?

She frowned and pushed herself up from the table, standing with her back to me. I could still see her face, reflected in the old foxed mirror on the farthest wall, though her eyes were in shadow. She didn't lift her gaze. 'I told him I never should have written it.'

'Who, Mama? What do you mean?' I frowned, but suddenly I knew what she meant: her letter. The one she had sent to me at my grandfather's house, the one that told me my sister was dead.

What was she saying – that she shouldn't have *told* me? But she couldn't have kept it a secret, not for long. Of course I would have found out. I'd have *felt* it. Still my heart beat too hard and too fast, as if something would happen; as if any moment my sister would appear.

Mama whirled to face me, her eyes narrowed, not in sorrow but in anger. 'You have to stop this, Ivy. It is madness. Stop this pretence.'

'What do you mean?' I could only repeat the words. It felt as if the earth had shifted under me, or that everything was spinning, the whole world off-kilter again, nothing solid; nothing true.

'You never had a sister called Daisy. There – is that clear, Ivy? Do I really have to say this to you? Can we have an end to it, after all this time?'

I was silent. How could she say that about her own daughter? What could have happened – had they cast her off? Perhaps they had, putting her out of the house, striking her name from the family Bible, and never a word to me. She was the naughty one, after all. She was always the one dreaming up mischief, leading me into trouble, teaching me to indulge every wild whim or secret wish that came to me. And yet I looked for her, peering into the corners, out of the window, towards the doorway into the next room.

When my mother spoke again it was slowly, as if to an invalid. 'She didn't exist, Ivy. Oh, you pretended often enough – all the time! Daisy this and Daisy that – Lord knows, you almost had me thinking I even saw her once or twice. Almost that I could hear two voices giggling in your room, not just yours.

'I should never have indulged you in it. All those times you pretended to talk to her – it was enough to drive anyone mad. And I put up with it – I tried to smile, for heaven's sake! I tried to tell myself it was natural, charming even, to have a little pretend companion.'

Such a funny, secret child you are, Ivy . . .

She had said that to me, so many times. And her eyes had been hard – as hard as they were now. I would run to her and throw my arms around her skirts, but she never stroked my hair or kissed me. She had never looked at me as she looked at Archie and Tom, so full of pride – so full of love, no matter how much I wished and wished for it.

'I shouldn't have allowed it for a second,' she went on. 'Your brothers thought you were a lunatic, did you know that? We all did. Why else do you think I agreed to send you away and not one of them? You were all the help I had about the house. Your grandfather might have taken one of the boys, *would* have done, if you hadn't needed shaking out of it. Archie could have got his Greek and Latin. He would have been set, but you were getting worse and worse – we thought if you went away, it would make you better. Now look at you!'

I stared at her. The world was no longer spinning; it had dropped away. There was nothing to moor me to the ground and I was floating, floating.

'It didn't make you better at all, did it? It wasn't any use. You kept on writing to your Daisy, saying how much you missed her and longed to see her again, asking when she would follow you. So I did the only thing I could think of. I wrote and told you she was dead. It seemed the only way to rid you of your delusion.'

Delusion. Defective. Deficient.

It couldn't be true. I couldn't have been so wrong about

everything. It was my mother's words that were madness and I waited for her to smile and burst into laughter at her prank. I had known Daisy all my life. She had always been at my side; there never was anything else. She had been with me every day, my little shadow, just as – as Emily was now, there for me, ready to fill any lack . . .

But my sister wasn't like that. I would have *known*.

'Always Daisy,' she went on. Now she'd begun, she didn't seem able to stop. 'Daisy this and Daisy that, Daisy dreaming up schemes, thinking up mischief, Daisy leading you everywhere. Daisy deciding what to do; Daisy's *fault*. You always blamed everything on her, when it was always *you*. There was only ever you. I should never have let it go on, Ivy, but you're grown now, and my foolishness no longer excuses your own.'

My mother was crying, not tears of joy at our meeting, but at the sight of me, there, in her kitchen.

'It frightened me. It frightened me to see you talking into the air just as if someone really was with you. As if your sister really had—'

She crumpled then, collapsing in on herself, her face turning creased and red and ugly. 'As if your sister really had come back.'

I was frozen. Frozen with the horror of her words, and with the knowledge that came over me; the sense of recognition. Because the feeling creeping into my bones was at once strange and terrible and yet altogether familiar. I had felt this way before.

'We always said we wouldn't tell you.' She raised her head and her eyes were full of the light from the window, reflected in her tears. 'You'd shut it out. We always thought you'd forgotten her, until Daisy came along. But what can I do now? I have to tell the *truth*.

'You only had to watch her, Ivy. I know you were small, too small perhaps, but other girls did such things. Only *watch* her.'

I couldn't look into her face any longer. I was cold right through, as cold as if I would never be warm again, never feel again, never speak or move or live again. And yet I did move, as if I were an automaton and had no choice – like a painted figure spun into motion.

I turned to the door that led to the parlour, the parlour I never had liked to go into, despite its cosiness. A room I had closed the door against a long time ago and tried never to look inside again. I'd never even allowed myself to think of it.

Now I pushed it open and went inside.

It was all so familiar and so strange. I recognised it all: the sagging, faded chairs, the cupboards, the nest of tables. And the other thing, the thing I expected to see, was there too. It wasn't in the room – it had long since been cast out – but I saw it anyway: a carved wooden crib, a pattern of star-shaped flowers entwined with leaves around its edge. For a moment I even saw the baby nestled within it, lying there quite peacefully; quite still.

I looked down at my hands. I was twisting them together so hard, the knuckles were white. I had prayed so hard for her, I remembered. I had prayed for God to send me a sister, someone who wouldn't always be too busy in the fields or about the house, who wasn't too old to play with me. Someone who'd be my own.

And this had come. A sister, but not the kind I'd meant; not the kind I'd wanted. *Flora.* The name was a ghost of a whisper on my lips. Not a sister, just a mewling little thing that lay there and cried and needed watching and changing and washing, yet another list of tasks to carry out.

I hadn't wanted to watch her. There were better things to do. A cat had given birth to kittens in the barn, using an old barrel for its den. There were six of them, wriggling, squeaking, smoke-grey balls of soft fluff. I planned to take Flora's silver rattle, a relic of the days before my mother quarrelled with her fancy relatives, and use it to reflect spots of sunlight to entrance the kittens. I would enchant them with its jingling, make them stare up at me with their blue-grey eyes. I wouldn't leave Flora quite alone, though. I'd never do that; anyway, I didn't want her to wake and miss me and cry. No: I left my doll in my place, so that she would have someone to be with her, to comfort her if she woke. She wouldn't notice the difference – would she?

I had treasured that doll. My father carved it for me from a bit of wood. He had taken such care over it, and I'd loved that. I'd even loved it when he'd snip-snipped a long lock of my hair, that wild hair with red lights in it, and stuck it to its head.

I had thought the cat would let me play with her brood, but she didn't. She swiped red lines across my hand with her claws and I screwed up my face and sobbed, and when I'd finished sobbing I went in search of comfort.

I found my mother in the parlour. She was on the floor. She was kneeling, her apron thrown up over her face. My father was there too, his expression stricken as he paced up and down, though he didn't seem to see me. Tom did, though. He didn't blink, just stared as if he didn't quite recognise me. Archie was crying. I had never seen Archie cry. He didn't look so very much older than me after all and it made me forget to wonder why no one soothed me, why nobody stroked my cat-scratched hand.

Flora was in the crib. She was lying quite peacefully, perfectly still. Her face was blue. She was different; a shadow-child. There was something wrong with her lips. I leaned in to see better. There was hair spilling from them, hanging down, wrapped about her. I teased her lips open – her skin was soft, but cool – and I saw that her mouth was full of hair. It had come off the doll, but it wasn't my doll's hair, it never had been; it was mine.

And I had turned to see the way my mother looked at me. The way they all did, their eyes all the same. And I remembered the sense of being separate, alone, that crept across me, prickling my skin as it wrapped itself around me, into me, twining about my bones, into my heart, until there was nothing else left and that was all there was. Until I was nothing but Ivy. *I*.

I blinked and the baby dissolved before my eyes. The cradle too was gone. There was only a patch of sunlight from the window blurring the pattern of the faded carpet.

I knew my mother was behind me. I no longer wanted to see her face – I didn't want to look at her and see that expression in her eyes, the one that was always there, that had haunted all the days of my childhood. The one that made me long for someone to be with me, to hold me, to tell me that it was all right: that I was altogether accepted; altogether loved.

I never did what I had gone home to do. I never said goodbye to my mother. I rushed past her, grabbing the moon pennies I had picked for my poor dead sister, and ran from the house.

A short time later, I stood in the quiet shade of a great yew tree that spread its limbs over the graveyard. I had tethered the horse that wasn't Bard to the lychgate and left him there, cropping the grass. I found myself searching the inscriptions on the stones, though not for Flora – that was too much to encompass. I couldn't let her in, couldn't think of her, not then; even her name was strange to me. It was Daisy I sought, just as if my whole childhood hadn't been false, along with so much else in my life. It had seemed so real. Not only real but so dear to me and it felt as if my heart would break to let go of it – of *her*.

But wherever Daisy had gone, she wasn't there. I still held onto her moon pennies, though they were crushed by my grip, wilting from the heat of my hands. They were real flowers, after all – real flowers for a painted sister.

But she had always been real enough for me.

Gently, I placed the moon pennies in the grass by the old and crumbling wall. They shone brightly amid the green. I stayed there a long time and let the memories come. Hiding in the old shed when we were supposed to be gleaning the last of the crop. Darning our brothers' socks badly on purpose, making them lumpy so they'd get blisters. Stuffing our mouths with blackberries until our tongues and pinafores and fingers were bloody with juice. And that final trick: pushing me onto Mags's broad back, my skirts filthy, and sending me off to meet my grandparents.

My mother's words returned to me. *You always blamed everything on her – when it was always you.*

I shook the thought away. How could I have imagined her? Daisy had always made me more than I was. And it came to me then – if I really had created her somehow, why couldn't I do so again?

I closed my eyes and pictured her face. Her hair was redder

than mine, her smile freer, her laugh less guarded. Had I really taken everything I wanted in this world and turned it into a sister? I had so craved her love, even if I didn't deserve it. I had needed her forgiveness. And what then – had I used her to make my wild longings happen, to make it all right to want them – everything that was forbidden to me?

Thou shalt not.

What was it that I would or would not do?

I envisaged her walking towards me. Grinning, skipping over the grass until she stood a little behind and to the side of me. Was she shy of me now that I'd grown and she had not? For no matter how I tried, I couldn't imagine her any older than when I'd last seen her.

Was that a breath? I spun around. The sward was empty. There were only the silent graves, no longer with many names carved into them, but one, echoed over and over: *Daisy.*

I couldn't believe in her, I realised, not any longer. My mother had killed her with her letter just as surely as if Daisy really had died. There were only little flowers opening amid the grass – not moon pennies but true daisies, tiny and perfect and fragile and everywhere.

I walked to the edge of the graveyard. Over the wall, I could see across miles of fields. Some were dotted with sheep or cattle; some bore the fresh green of new crops; none, now, were golden. They faded into a haze in the distance. And I realised with a start that I wasn't alone after all. Someone was standing a short distance away, their back turned, their face hidden. It was a woman. She wore a wide bonnet that was just a little out of fashion and a grey travelling cape, and she too gazed out across the fields, towards a land that was miles and miles and an ocean away.

38

I too gaze into the distance now, beyond the unfamiliar elderly face in the mirror, with its fiercely pinned-down hair. Behind me, the door softly opens. I hear footsteps approaching, so easy, so free. They cease when they reach my side. Fingers entwine with my own and I hold on to them as tears well at my eyes. Our hands are all I can see, her fingers merging with mine as my vision blurs, until they are one. Hands that never had known what they were doing – had they?

I know that my dearest is not Emily White, though she looks so very like her. Her hair remains fair; her eyes are just as soft and grey as hers were. After she was driven away in the carriage, I had thought her a shadow – a shadow, not of Emily, but of me.

Empty, Sophia once said. She would say so now. She would say I'm as hollow as a doll, unable to attract a friend or keep one; that I'm so very lonely I had to invent a companion to be with me. That I am nothing but a child with an imaginary friend.

And I thought that she had spoken the truth.

I had never considered mine to be a ghost story. For a long time, I had scarcely considered the story to be mine at all. It was Emily White's; it was simply another of the lives that belonged to her. I was only her pupil after all, as confused as anyone by the talk of doppelgängers and opposites and reflections and shadows, of madness, but not of ghosts; not for long, not really. Lucy had grasped it at once, of course, though she had misunderstood its nature and anyway, no one had believed her. *A ghost*, she had said. *It's a ghost, a ghost.*

But perhaps my sister never had left. And perhaps, somehow, we had found each other again. Perhaps it was never Sophia who had the ability to *bring the spirits*, but me. I had so longed for her – yet my true sister was with me all along. She had been there all through my childhood, wearing the face I painted for her, following the steps I set out for her, answering to the name I gave her: Daisy. I'd turned her into the sister I had wanted. But it was Flora who had come to be with me, ever at my side – like a doll placed in a crib. She had given substance to all of my dreams, all of my imaginings, and helped me to seize hold of them.

She had stayed as long as she was able, as long as I could believe in her. And then she'd come to me instead in the only way she could find, in the guise of Emily, whom I'd also longed for – in whom I thought I might have found another sister. I never had known what Flora would look like as she grew, after all. She only had me to give her shape, and so I had; I'd lent her features and form and hands and I had guided them and shown her what to do. Hadn't I even thought of her that way – a shadow, wearing

Emily's face? And she was. She had looked to me for everything and I'd set her in motion, spinning, spinning . . .

I had given her what she needed: a chance to live. And she had given me what I'd always wanted more than anything else: a sister.

I remember the way her hair had hung across her eyes. The darkness that had obscured her face, almost as if there were another presence half hidden beneath it. A shadow-sister.

Of course, I never could have married. Aside from my longing for freedom, how could I ever have ousted her? What would have happened to her then? My sister and I had always sworn to love each other above any man. And after my visit to my old home – one I have not repeated – I could never risk the chance of having a child.

But still, I am Ivy. I always did need someone to twine around.

And so my dearest has stayed with me. She comes in at my will and goes out at my will. She holds me when I long to be held and is silent when I wish to be silent, all without my having to say a word. Her presence is nearest and strongest when I need her the most; when I am most alone. Sometimes she is there when I don't even know that I need her, but I *do* need her; I always have.

And I have spent my life painting all the flora of the world. It has been my deepest joy and my greatest punishment. For I would think of her while I painted: Flora, my little sister in her crib, waiting for me to return to her. Wrapping herself so tightly in my hair.

Now I hold her hand in mine and lead her to the picture that hangs on the wall. This one is unlike the others that adorn my rooms, so carefully and meticulously detailed. This is fresher: it depicts a simple glass jug of flowers, plucked by Emily's hand. The blooms are wild and lovely and beautiful, a single pure white rose among the rest, and we stand side by side in front of it. It is the picture painted by Emily White – by Emeline Jones – by Emélie Blanc. It's the one she gave to me before she left my life for ever.

My dearest and I do not paint together, though she looks so very like Emily White. Her hands are shaped like Emily's and I suppose I could guide them, be her teacher, but I have always feared that her work would lack the joy of the original; that it would lack the *life*. I would not want to look upon her brushstrokes and know her to be nothing more than a carven statue, beautiful and perfect and chained to a wall.

I sometimes wonder what happened to the real Emily White. Perhaps she found another school that would take her in and there found better fortune. Perhaps she married and had children of her own. Perhaps she assumed another name and lived a whole other life, one that was separate from mine and oblivious to it. Or perhaps she starved after all and is dead, and all that remains of her is here with me.

I never did try to find out the truth. For me, in a way, she too lives on, and will continue to do so for as long as I breathe. And no one is frightened by that. No one is scandalised or even gives her a moment's thought. There are no more strange stories of ghosts or goblins or doppelgängers whispered behind closed doors. The two of us have risen above the judgement of Society at last and no one will trouble us; for in the eyes of my neighbours, I live always and ever alone.

THE END

❧ ❧ ACKNOWLEDGEMENTS ❧ ❧

A lot of people deserve a lot of thanks for their help in seeing *The Other Lives of Miss Emily White* into the world. First of all, my fabulous editor, Daniel Carpenter, for the helpful and erudite suggestions that made this a better book. In fact the whole of Team Titan deserve medals for sheer awesomeness and boundless enthusiasm, with special shouts for Sarah Mather, Lydia Gittins, typesetter Charlie Mann and copy-editor Steve Gove. Natasha MacKenzie, you continue to astound me with your cover designs; I am in awe of your talent. And thanks to my agent, Oli Munson, for setting this book on course for publication in the first place.

Going back rather further, my gratitude goes to all of the participants in the Folklore Thursday hashtag on Twitter, where I first saw the snippet about Emélie Sagée that set me dreaming up this story. Sometimes, social media is more than a time suck.

I have read a huge number of books on the Victorians for previous novels, not to mention a lot of actual Victorian novels! I am indebted to all of their authors, historians and researchers all over again, but to avoid repeating myself I will just send out special appreciation for Ruth Goodman, who doesn't stop at telling about Victorian life but experiments in living it as well.

For information about some of the catechisms used with schoolchildren, *The Victorian Woman* by Duncan Crow, Stein & Day, 1972, was especially helpful. As was the source of the accounts of a rather odd teacher surrounded by odder stories read out by Sophia in this book: *Footfalls on the Boundary of Another World* by Robert Dale Owen, J.B. Lippincott, Philadelphia, 1860.

It perhaps comes as no surprise, since so much of it is about being alone, that *Emily* is in the main my lockdown novel. As such, I'd like to send thanks to my book-loving and writing friends on Facebook and Twitter for helping to keep me sane during the writing of it. Also to Priya Sharma, Mark Greenwood, and Cate and Simon Bestwick for the slightly less than sane Zoom quizzes. To Gary Fry, Gary McMahon and Mark West for the giggles. To Heather and Gary Foley and Karen and Craig Knighton for the catch-up calls. To Marie O'Regan and Paul Kane for persisting in the organisation of ChillerCon through trials, tribulations and cancellations, not to mention an actual ceiling falling in, to finally get the genre crowd back together again.

Closer to home, thank you to my dogs, Dex and Vesper, for making me laugh and dragging me into (and across) the great outdoors. To my better half, Fergus Beadle, for reminding me about all that is good in life. To my parents Ann and Trevor

Littlewood, for the love and support and well, everything. And of course, a huge thank you to everyone who worked so hard and gave so much of themselves during a difficult time to move the world back towards an even keel. You are true heroes.

Last but by no means least, thanks go to you, the reader – always.

ABOUT THE AUTHOR

A. J. Elwood is the author of *The Cottingley Cuckoo*, also from Titan Books. She studied literature and history, which she was told would never have any direct relevance to her life, but following what you love can lead to some unexpected places . . .

Elwood lives in a three-hundred-year old house where floorboards creak, doors open of their own accord and rooms spontaneously transform into libraries. She enjoys travel, particularly to cold places; she dreams of living above the Arctic Circle with mysterious lights and the silence of the snow. For now, her beloved Dalmatians wouldn't let her. She's happy to remain in Yorkshire with her partner Fergus, a collection of books on weird history, a mysteriously multiplying number of fountain pens and increasingly inky fingers. She also writes as Alison Littlewood. @Ali__L

For more fantastic fiction, author events,
exclusive excerpts, competitions, limited editions and more

VISIT OUR WEBSITE
titanbooks.com

LIKE US ON FACEBOOK
facebook.com/titanbooks

FOLLOW US ON TWITTER AND INSTAGRAM
@TitanBooks

EMAIL US
readerfeedback@titanemail.com